# DARACH

*Immortal Highlander Clan MacRoss Book 2*

## HAZEL HUNTER

# HH ONLINE

Hazel loves hearing from readers!
You can contact her at the links below.

Website: hazelhunter.com

Newsletter: HazelHunter.com/news

I send newsletters with details on new releases, special offers, and other bits of news related to my writing. You can sign up here!

## Chapter One

The moment she was inside and alone, Charlotte Walsh pulled off her too-thin black jacket and grabbed the duvet from the hotel room bed. Housekeeping must have just changed the linens, as the fabric seemed stiff and smelled of detergent. She didn't care. During the ride back from the funeral she had grown so cold her hands and feet had gone numb. She looked around, desperate for a place to sit and huddle. Aside from two wooden chairs by a tiny table, a shallow windowsill, and a low dresser under the wall mirror, only the bed offered a perch. She hadn't slept more than an hour or two for weeks.

*If I lay down I will never get up again.*

Sitting on top of the dresser, Charlotte leaned her head against the mirror. Her muscles ached with stiffness; all through the service she had sat rigid and unmoving, her gaze fixed on the flower-draped, smiling portrait of Zoey Vincent. Every word delivered by the minister had sounded soft and consoling, but that had been his job. He'd been there to provide spiritual reassurance for the family and friends Zoey had left behind in life. According to him the young artist had been a kind, generous person who had contributed so much to the community through her extraordinary talent. She had moved on to a better place now, the minister had promised, but she would not be forgotten.

*That's such a load of crap,* Zoey would have said. *I hated my family, drank my way through art school, wasted what little talent I had painting tedious tourist scapes, and slept around too much. I even got myself brutally murdered—only that was your fault, wasn't it, Blondie?*

Condensation from Charlotte's breath formed on the mirror in a misty swatch of white that widened and shrank. She knew the voice in her head didn't belong to her dead friend but her conscience, which had been tormenting her ever since finding Zoey's body. She could do nothing but endure, and hope in time it would stop. For now she just needed to rest and collect herself; in a minute she would get up and turn off the air conditioning. In the glass she saw the reflection of tiny words printed in white on the front of her black T-shirt.

*Stop staring at my boobs, pervert.*

The shirt belonged to Zoey; Charlotte had pulled it on this morning thinking it was solid black. No wonder everyone had given her those weird looks; she'd worn a joke T-shirt to her friend's funeral. For the past three days she'd been functioning on autopilot, doing whatever was required of her but remaining emotionally disconnected. She'd been like this ever since coming back from her studio and seeing what was left of her friend on the kitchen floor.

*I let you move in with me and look what happened.* Zoey, sassy and plump and filled with endless energy, grinned at Charlotte from her memories. *He was waiting for you when I walked into the house. You know I was alone with him for hours, right? That too-chatty cop mentioned that I didn't die right away, remember?*

"Stop." That came out of her like an apology, not a warning. "Please."

*I have nothing better to do now, Blondie. Want to know what it's like to be tortured? Not as much fun as sleeping around, I can tell you that. What are the odds that they'll ever find the rest of me? I wonder what the funeral etiquette is for that kind of thing.*

Charlotte pushed off the comforter and staggered into the bathroom, falling to her knees in front of the toilet and ripping off the paper sanitized band before she threw up. Doing that until her stomach emptied finally silenced the phantom voice in her head, but it left her throat raw and her legs unsteady. She hauled herself up to rinse out her mouth and brush her teeth, and splashed her face with cold water before looking at herself in the sink mirror.

Even dripping wet, the tall brown-eyed blonde in the glass appeared remote and unaffected, no doubt the only benefit of inheriting her chic mother's cold, elegant genes.

*Why are you upset?* Leona Walsh would ask her if they had still been speaking. *Better her than you.*

As Charlotte took off the T-shirt and replaced it with a white sweater, she didn't look at herself again. Being blonde, well-built and almost six feet tall had made her unable to escape unwanted attention all her adult life; having her mother's regally beautiful face had been bitter icing on an unpalatable cake. Throughout Charlotte's childhood, Leona had been like an iceberg, silent and invulnerable, ready to smash and sink anyone and anything that tried to collide with her. She never attacked, but whenever Charlotte didn't do as she wanted, Leona would smile and say something devastating.

*Why should you make me happy? You never have before now.*

*You're as careless and ridiculous as your father.*

*Someday when you're in the sewer you'll wish you had listened to me.*

A Parisian fashion buyer who traveled the world, Leona had reluctantly married Peter Walsh after becoming pregnant from, what had been for her, a week-long fling. Twelve unhappy years later, Leona decided that she couldn't squander the rest of her youth mothering her shy, awkward daughter. Once resolved, she had found herself another, richer man, filed for divorce, and promptly returned to France. Before she'd left, Leona had told Charlotte all of the sordid details of her conception, and blamed her for her lack of success as well as the marriage and divorce.

*That is how you ruined my life, by being born. If I hadn't wasted all these years on you and your pathetic father I would have my own label now.*

Peter Walsh had tried to make up for the damage her mother had done to Charlotte, but he'd genuinely loved Leona, and couldn't get over her dumping him. He kept making excuses for her mother when he knew she hadn't loved either of them, and then drank himself unconscious every night after Charlotte went to bed. She'd only found out about his alcohol abuse a few years ago, when Peter had died suddenly. The autopsy revealed the terrible damage his secret drinking had done to his heart and liver.

Dutifully calling Leona once a year on her birthday had been the only contact Charlotte could maintain with her mother. After losing her dad she couldn't bear even that one stiff, unfriendly conversation, and had stopped making the calls. Leona had never bothered to find out why.

*Here I am, throwing a pity party for myself on the day of Zoey's funeral, while I'm wearing her T-shirt. I'm worse than Mom ever was.*

A knock on the room door made Charlotte dry her face and compose herself as she walked out and looked through the peephole. The armed plainclothes officer standing outside had a take-out food bag, and looked bored. He'd been the one sitting behind her through the service; his partner had sat beside her. They had promised not to let her out of their sight until they caught Zoey's killer. She took in a deep breath before she unlocked the door and opened it.

"Some lunch for you, Ms. Walsh." Arranging his expression in a semblance of sympathy, he held out the usual bag and a can of soda.

"Thank you." Charlotte took the food and

glanced down the hall. "How long do I have to stay here?"

"Headquarters finally has the safe house, and we'll move you there tomorrow." As he spoke he tilted his head back to meet her gaze, but the corners of his mouth dropped. Like most men shorter than her, the officer resented having to look up at a woman. "Detective Logan will be coming by later to brief you on what happens from here. We've disconnected the room phone, and I have to ask for your cell."

She handed it to him. "I really don't have anyone to call."

"It would be best if you only talk to us." He pocketed her phone and stepped out.

Charlotte closed and locked the door before she let out a breath. At least the authorities finally seemed ready to take her seriously, but she hadn't been the one to persuade them. Whoever had been stalking her had made it clear he would do anything he had to in order to get to her, and that included killing two patrolmen assigned to watch her. Poor Zoey, who had gone home on her lunch hour to get something she'd forgotten, had surprised the killer as he was searching the place.

*You don't look anything alike,* Zoey's older sister had said, sobbing into a crumpled tissue while they'd waited to give statements at the police station. *Why would he kill her instead of you?*

Charlotte set aside the food the officer had given her, and picked up the comforter, absently folding it before placing it on the end of the bed. She went to shut off the air conditioning unit, which Housekeeping had left on full blast, and pulled back the curtains. Downtown Toronto on a Sunday afternoon still looked busy, and the warmer temperature brought by summer had everyone wearing shorts. They milled below like colorful ants around the skyscrapers as they walked through the pedestrian markets and waited in lines at patio restaurants.

The first wave of the season, tourists and weekend visitors would crowd into the city for the next two months. Would anyone warn them that a serial killer targeting young women had been on the loose?

*Your stalker, you mean*, Zoey's ghost chimed in.

The police still didn't believe the man who had been shadowing Charlotte was the serial killer responsible for six other murders in Moss Park before he'd killed the patrolmen and her friend; they didn't see any similarities between the crimes. Stalkers, she had been told, fixated on one target and if obsessed enough would kill to get to them; serial killers had specific desires and would kill only victims who could satisfy them. They believed the man terrorizing her to be an overly-obsessed fan who had copycatted the Moss Park Butcher, the serial killer hunting prostitutes and drug addicts in one of the worst neighborhoods in Toronto.

Charlotte would have agreed, except for one thing: the stalker had told her over the phone that he was the Moss Park Butcher.

*You've seen the news, haven't you, precious? They won't mention that I drowned those six girls after I had my fun; they're keeping that a secret.* He'd uttered his high-pitched laugh before he'd asked, *What do you think of my art?*

Charlotte opened the can of soda and sipped from it, grimacing at the too-sweet taste but making herself drink. If she passed out from dehydration she'd end up in the hospital, and the killer would have no problem getting at her in there. He'd simply dress up in scrubs and a mask and walk right into her room. Like a ghost this man haunted her, seeing everything she did and knowing every move she would make even before she did. She knew now that he wouldn't stop until he finished this ghastly game of cat-and-mouse, which really left only one question.

*Why me?*

As a freelance artist Charlotte had been under contract as an illustrator to three different publishers over the last five years. Creating the artwork for the covers and stories of children's books had provided her with steady work since she'd graduated college, and she liked what she did. When she wanted to do something for herself she would paint original watercolors on the side, which a few small local galleries sometimes showed in multi-artist exhibits during festival weekends.

Her art allowed her to make a modest living and stay out of debt. After her father died she'd received his life insurance, which had been enough for her to pay off her car and lease a small professional studio. No one would call her rich, however, so it couldn't be money.

As for relationships, Charlotte could count on one hand all the men she'd dated since moving to Toronto from the suburbs. Being very tall eliminated her as a prospect for most guys anyway. The few who had matched or topped her height seemed comfortable with her, but they had all been busy professionals. None had been especially upset when she had called it quits with them. Jack, the realtor whom she'd dated last year, had even assured her that she was great-looking arm candy but a schoolgirl in bed.

*You should try to be a little more adventurous, babe,* he had told her when he'd taken out a pair of handcuffs one night, and she'd stopped undressing. *It's not like you're twelve, and who knows? You might even like it.*

*What's wrong with treating me like a lady?* she had countered.

*A lady?* Jack had laughed out loud. *What do you think you are, royalty or something?*

Because of his penchant for bondage, Charlotte had worried that Jack had been the one stalking her, but after she had mentioned him as a possible suspect the police had investigated and cleared him of any involvement. All that lingered from that relationship now was a weary resentment for having wasted her time on such a jerk. Of course she knew her attitudes to be slightly old-fashioned, but she didn't regard mutual respect as an unreasonable expectation.

In reality she would have loved to find a guy like those she drew in her fairytale illustrations. Her ideal didn't have to be a prince or a knight like the characters she painted, but he would be strong, fair and kind. A gallant soul who still believed in chivalry and courtesy as well as romance would be perfect for her. He would be the sort of man unafraid to be as affectionate as he was passionate. That kind of guy wouldn't need handcuffs to make sex exciting.

Her dream man would never let anything bad happen to her, either.

For someone like that Charlotte imagined she

could finally toss aside her inhibitions and reveal her own wildly romantic heart, but she knew she'd never find him. These days men seemed to be all about themselves, cheap thrills, and how they could personally profit from a relationship. Even after they'd broken up, Jack had still texted her to crow about making an important sale, ask if she wanted to hook up, or suggest his services if she ever wanted to put her condo on the market.

Another knock on the door brought Charlotte back to reality, and once she checked she let Detective Logan into the room.

"Sorry I couldn't go to the funeral with you, Ms. Walsh." A round-shouldered, beefy man with kind eyes, he smelled of recently-applied aftershave. "I'd like to talk to you about your living arrangements. We've secured a safe house for you, but...well, let me show it to you first."

Charlotte sat down at the little table, where the detective showed her the image on his phone. The dingy one-room apartment had water-stained walls, dingy carpeting pocked by holes and tears, and a sagging, mildew-stained window shaker. An army of cockroaches likely occupied every nook and cranny; just looking at it she could almost smell the sour dampness.

"You want me to stay in a place like this?" she asked, just to be sure.

"I'm afraid with our budget it's the best we can do right now," Logan admitted. "It might be better for you to make your own arrangements. Do you have any family in the states or overseas, maybe?"

"My grandparents are in a long-term care home. I have some cousins in the UK, but I don't know them very well." She hesitated before she added, "My mother remarried and moved to Paris."

"Could you stay with her for a while?" he asked, looking hopeful. "It really would be best for you to put some distance between you and Canada."

That was when Charlotte knew he was keeping something from her. "Why do you want me to leave the country?"

Logan grimaced. "I can't get into the details of the case, Ms. Walsh."

He had a decent poker face, but the flash of anger in his eyes told Charlotte the situation had gone from horrible to worse.

"It's the Moss Park Butcher, right? You connected him to Zoey and the two officers who were murdered." That wasn't all, either; she saw the way his mouth tightened when she mentioned the killer. "You know something else about him."

The detective looked defeated now. "We won't know until the coroner reviews all of the autopsy reports, but it appears that you're right, and the two cases are related. We've also found some similarities to unsolved murders in Nova Scotia, Vancouver and Montreal."

Charlotte's scalp prickled with cold sweat as her dread deepened. "How many others did he kill?"

"As I said, we won't know for a while, Ms. Walsh. However, if we can connect him to these cold cases, ah." He ducked his head. "It'll be over a hundred."

In that moment she knew she would die if she stayed here. *Nothing will ever stop him.*

"I'll go to France." If Leona refused to take her in, Charlotte thought, she would live on her savings until she could arrange to work remotely from there. "I brought my passport with me. When can I leave?"

Logan met her gaze. "We'll take you to the airport as soon as you reserve a flight."

CHARLOTTE PACKED WHAT LITTLE SHE'D BROUGHT in her overnight case before pulling on her long black coat. She changed her black trousers for a pair of comfortable jeans, but as she hadn't packed extra shoes she had to wear the uncomfortable stilettos she'd put on for the funeral. As soon as she got to the airport she could buy a pair of runners for the long trip.

As she braided her hair she considered what she would say to her mother once she reached Paris. She'd already decided against calling in advance; Leona would be more receptive to a surprise visit than a desperate telephone plea for sanctuary. She wouldn't tell her about the stalker or the murders, either. She'd simply say that she wanted to reconnect and spend some time together after so many years of estrangement.

*Mom won't fall for that. She'll know the minute you show up on her doorstep that you're in trouble.*

Charlotte collected her messenger bag on the way out of the room, slinging it over her head and across her body; thankfully she'd packed it with her traveling art supplies before leaving the condo. She could buy whatever else she needed for work once she was in Paris.

She stepped out into the hallway, but didn't see the two cops or Logan. "They must be waiting downstairs in the lobby."

Charlotte decided against the elevators and went to the stairwell door and opened it, stepping out onto the landing and immediately slipping and falling onto her butt in a dark, wet pool. As pain jolted through her hip a rank, coppery smell made her choke. Beside her one of the cops stared at the ceiling with a befuddled, frozen look; blood from the deep gash around his neck glistened in the light from the overhead dome. Charlotte's hand shook as she reached out to touch his wrist, but she found no pulse.

*This is how I'm going to die tonight.*

"There you are," a low, amused voice said from above her. "Did you think they would keep me away from you, my precious?"

Everything inside Charlotte froze as she looked up at the hooded figure leaning over the railing. She let go of her case as she scrambled to her feet and ran down the stairs, her heart hammering in her chest as shrill laughter and light footsteps followed her. She reached into her pocket for her phone, only to remember she had given it to the cop. As she stumbled on the steps she saw handprints in blood on the railings, and then the limp body of the other cop sprawled on the second floor landing. She stopped, hoping he was only injured, but when she turned him onto his back she saw his throat had been slashed as well.

"I only want one thing from you, Charlotte," the killer said as he leisurely walked down the stairs. "Stop running away from me, or more people will die." He chuckled. "Well, that's not exactly true. After all this time I really can't stop myself. If you give me what I want, perhaps I will not hunt as often, and fewer people will die."

She made it to the first floor landing, and darted through the door, only to find herself outside at the back of the hotel. A long alley stood between her and the front of the building, but a man was slowly trudging toward her. She ran to him, gasping with relief when she saw it was Detective Logan.

"He's here, the stalker," she said as she ran up to him, and then abruptly stopped as she saw the knife sticking out of his chest. "Oh, no, no."

"Leave me." Logan grabbed her arm and pushed her behind him before he dropped to his knees. "Go."

Charlotte dragged him behind a stack of wooden crates, and then looked over as the hooded figure came out of the stairwell door. She couldn't pull the knife out of Logan's chest; she knew he would bleed to death if she did. If she ran the killer would attack her from behind, and probably cut her throat.

"Do you have a gun?" she whispered, crouching over him. She didn't know how to shoot, but maybe the threat of one would hold off the killer.

Logan shook his head. "He took it." As he spoke some blood dribbled from his mouth. "Ms. Walsh, you have to run."

"I'm not going to leave you." Charlotte closed her eyes to recall her memory of the alley way. Thanks to a strange quirk of her brain she could remember images perfectly after seeing them only once. A high wall closed off the end of the alley by the stairs; the only way out was toward the front of the building. If she stayed in the shadows–

"Are you still trying to hide from me?" A hand took hold of the messenger bag strap and used it to yank her up. "You should know you can't do that, my precious." A vicious tug on her braid jerked her head back. "A hunter always knows where to find his prey." He dragged her away from the crates, flinging her into the brick on the other side of the alley.

Charlotte managed to get her hands up before she slammed into the wall, but her head snapped forward and something sharp stabbed into her forehead. Pain exploded inside her skull as warm, wet blood streaked down her face. Her vision grayed, but she staggered around, facing the hooded killer. For a moment it looked as if there were two of him.

"Why are you doing this to me?" she demanded, bracing her shoulders against the wall and wiping the blood dripping into her eye. "I don't know you. I've never done anything to you."

He pulled off his gloves and slapped her, and a hot streak of pain sliced across her cheek. Breath made acrid by booze blasted in her face as he leaned closer.

"You know why, Charlotte. You painted that

lovely portrait of Prince Ross's cursed sword in the hands of that hideous chieftain. I looked, but I couldn't find it in your house or at that sassy little slut's place." His fingers trailed through the blood on her cheek before he grabbed her jaw. "What have you done with the sain?"

The unwashed smell of his body made Charlotte almost gag. She glanced down at his hand, and the strange, streaked mark on the back of it. "I don't know what you mean. What's a sain?"

"I've read the facking book." The killer's voice changed, taking on a distinct Scottish accent now. "'Tis what I most desire, for 'twill take me back so I may save them. I must save them from the master's treachery. Tell me where you've hidden the sain, and I shall permit you live."

She had known he was insane; what he demanded simply confirmed that. "I haven't hidden anything. I don't have what you want."

"Must you force me hurt you so much, my precious?" He punched her in the stomach so hard she collapsed at his feet, and then he kicked her over onto her side. "Where did you hide the facking thing?" He kept kicking her, driving her back into a heap of garbage bags. "Tell me."

Every slam of his boot into her body sent new explosions of pain through Charlotte. By the time the pile of bags fell on top of her she couldn't breathe or move. Now she knew what her fate would be: being beaten to death. She thought of Zoey, who had been bright and vibrant and like the sister she'd never had. The police officers who had died protecting her. Detective Logan, telling her to run away and leave him to die. Anger surged inside her, pushing through the agony and fear, and filling her with blinding rage.

*Get up. Hit him back. Get up and make him pay before you die.*

Charlotte stretched out her hand to brace herself, and touched something like a heavy bar of metal under the bags. She worked her hand along it to one end, which slid like smooth glass against her palm, and then pushed her fingers inside a gap to take a better hold of it. An image of her mutilated body appeared in her mind, sprawled beside Detective Logan, whose throat had been cut. She looked exactly the way Zoey had when she'd found her dead. She was seeing herself after being murdered by the killer, all over something she didn't understand.

*I shallnae let you die here, child,* a deep voice heavy with sorrow said. *Now you must go back and save my lads.*

She pushed herself up as a wonderful, gentle warmth curled around her hand, and spread up her arm to pour into her chest and belly. The pounding pain of her head wound and battered body dwindled away; the glowing heat seemed to erase the agony gripping her torso. As she opened her eyes she saw the killer, turned away from her and looking back over his shoulder. Her hair began to float in the air between them.

All the lights in the alley abruptly went out, and Charlotte tumbled over and over, as if she were falling through some endless black tunnel.

*It's over,* she thought, immersed in a terrible relief. *He can't follow me now. I'm dead.*

## Chapter Two

Walking through the long stone passages at Dun Lasair made Chieftain Darach MacRoss long for an hour in the bathing spring to soak away the troubles of the day. The squabbles between the men had grown more frequent since the enchanted Fire sword had again vanished from its crystal case in the great hall. That sudden disappearance meant that the MacRoss Clan once again faced an unknown danger that would soon destroy them all.

The blade had been enchanted by their founder, Fae Prince Ross, who had given up his life to bespell the sword to protect the clan in such dire times. Although only the second time the sword had vanished, Darach suspected the saining blade would soon reappear with someone from another place and time, just as it had some months previous by bringing Emery Parker from the twenty-first century to them. He also knew that as soon as the sword came back he should toss the cursed facking thing into the forge's furnace and melt it down.

Only the knowledge that the clan's fate depended on whoever the blade brought back to the MacRoss stayed his hand.

As soon as Darach had finished his duties he returned to his chamber in the garrison to retrieve some clean clothes. There he encountered Master Sage Duine hovering nervously in the passage. The kindly man's usually neat robes appeared stained and wrinkled, and his short fringe of brown hair almost stood on end. He stood twisting his plump hands together as if he meant to pry off his own fingers.

Darach knew the sage to be perpetually anxious and fearful, especially with all the troubles looming over the clan these last months, but he had never seen him in such a harried state.

"Fair evening, Master Duine." Out of habit he turned his face slightly to avert the birthing mark that covered his left eye, which made even those who had known him all their lives uncomfortable to see. "What brings you so late to the garrison?"

"Forgive me, Chieftain." The stout, round-faced

sage bowed quickly. "I would speak to you on an urgent matter, if you've a moment to spare?"

Once inside his chamber Darach poured a mug of perry for the man, who paced about nervously in front of the hearth. Since Emery had come to them she often caused conflict, but he'd thought everyone at Dun Lasair had grown accustomed to her endless curiosity and unseemly modern notions.

"I hope all 'tis well with the enclave," he said, and saw the sage jump a little.

"Aye, Chieftain." Duine took in a slow, deep breath before he said, "'Tis the threat to us and the MacRoss that troubles me. Since the Fire sword vanished on the night of the laird's wedding, I've no' ken a moment's peace. 'Tis been near two moons since the blade disappeared, and with each new day that passes..." He pressed a hand to his brow. "I cannae eat nor sleep as I should."

"Sit, please." When the sage sank down into the chair by the hearth Darach put the mug in his shaking hands. "Drink. 'Twill settle you."

Duine took a sip and made an effort to compose himself before he said, "I went to the laird to discuss the matter, as I ken he's aware of the danger. Our lord kindly listened, but told me he's decided to wait and see what 'twill happen."

"'Tis why we chose Luthias as our laird." Personally he didn't agree, but he had long ago learned to trust his eldest brother's decisions as well as abide by them. "He shallnae act unless there's good reason."

"I dinnae mean to speak ill of him," the sage said quickly. "He's a good man, and a wise one. He but trusts too much in the word of the enemy, and I fear 'twill lead to our ruin."

"Before he died saving our lord and lady, the Carack laird first broke the truce between the clans by posing as a woodcutter and sneaking about our lands," Darach reminded him. "Struan Carack wouldnae accept Luthias's account of how Callum died if he didnae believe his clan at fault for that, or truly suspected we murdered his brother. He wrote as much in the scroll he sent the day after the fire. 'Tis no strife between the clans now."

"Aye, so the laird said as well." The sage quickly drank down the perry and set aside the mug. "Only now rumors spread through the villages and the crofts of what 'twasnae said. Many among the Carack, they've sworn blood vengeance for the death of their laird. They mean to war with the MacRoss, and soon. The Fire sword, 'twouldnae have vanished if that threat to the clan 'twasnae real."

"Before succeeding Callum as laird, Struan served as the Carack's war master," Darach chided. "He'll no' attack us without sound reason."

"Struan Carack refused to permit his clan name him laird." Duine sighed. "He insisted he remain their war master until such time as the threat to *his* clan ends. They yet regard the MacRoss as their enemies, and even now likely prepare for battle."

This was something he hadn't yet heard. "Who told you such?"

"Tavish Carack. After Callum's funeral he heard Struan's refusal as the clan gathered to make him their laird." The sage dragged his fingers through his mussed hair. "He told me as much a week past, when I crossed paths with him in town."

Now the sage's renewed terror made sense to Darach.

"That poor lad Tavish, he's never been right since the mine collapse that crushed him," he told the sage. "We all well ken his penchant for spreading tales that rarely prove true. Someone should make him carry a truth charm."

"Then why should he advise me take my brother sages and leave Dun Lasair before the new moon?" Duine countered.

Darach sighed. "No doubt to cause more trouble, Master."

"I reckon 'twas more a true warning, else he wouldnae mention the time left to flee," the sage said. "I repeated what he said to our lord, that he might prepare. Yet still he does naught."

"'Twould seem Tavish wishes to make mischief by scaring away our enclave. He might then go to Struan and claim 'twas his doing so he might seem more important to the Carack, and improve his own position in the clan." Darach put his hand on the sage's shoulder. "You cannae put your trust in rumors and gossip. Rely on the clan to protect you and the other sages, Master."

"I rely on you, Chieftain." The sage rose to his feet. "I ken you may only speak truth, but 'tisnae an act of betrayal to ready the garrison for the battles that shall surely come. I'm a man of peace, no' war, and yet even I ken if the MacRoss stand ever ready to defend the stronghold at a moment's notice, then a Carack attack shallnae surprise you." As Darach started to speak he held up a hand. "I ken you cannae go against our lord. Only think on what I've said. Imagine the lives you shall save. 'Tis all I ask."

He bowed and hurried out of the chamber.

ONCE THE SAGE DEPARTED DARACH WALKED FROM the garrison hall to his favorite bathing spring, where he stripped off his tartan and boots before he dove into the still water. Like all the MacRoss his body stayed warmer than ordinary men, thanks to the blood he shared with Prince Ross. Even the coldest water could not entirely dispel his heat. Wearing the damp clothes after leaving the warm spring allowed him to cool himself as they dried.

He would soak for an hour and relish the quiet before he returned to the garrison, where no doubt two or three clansmen would converge on him to urge they take action against the Carack. The master sage's warning had not been the first to be brought to him. Nor could he expect it to be the last.

Darach knew the discord between the two clans would never entirely end.

The conflict stretched back to ancient times, when the clans' founders, Prince Ross and Prince Kaer, had dwelled in Elphyne. The magical Fae kingdom, inhabited by immortals possessing great powers, had been a paradise, but not a place of peace. According to the old legends, Ross, whose elemental power over fire had always put him at odds with Kaer's power over ice, had fallen in love with the Fae king's daughter—as had Kaer.

It should have ended with the princess's choice of husband, only she had refused them both, and instead vowed never to wed.

The eternal stalemate and their elemental rivalry

had swelled into hatred that led to a war. During their final battle Ross and Kaer had summoned their elemental powers to destroy each other, only to inadvertently kill the Fae princess when she tried to stop them. The grief-stricken king had stripped both princes of their powers, and exiled them to the mortal realm, where he commanded they spend eternity.

Being shunned by their own kind and cast out of Elphyne had not ended the feud between the exiled princes. They spent the next thousand years building their strongholds in the highlands, taking mortal females as wives, siring half-Fae sons and gathering loyal vassals who would serve them for generations. Their sons, who became the MacRoss and Carack clans, had carried on their fathers' conflict by clashing again and again. Despite countless battles neither side could prevail over the other. After their last skirmish the clans had reluctantly struck a truce to end the killing, and permit the clans to continue on without the threat of death forever looming over their heads.

Only when fire and ice stayed apart could they thrive.

Those centuries of peace had allowed the MacRoss to become one of the most well-connected and prosperous clans in the highlands, thanks to the allies they had made of other neighboring clans, and the quality horses and livestock they bred on their lands. The Carack had also risen in importance and power, thanks to their rich mines, which allowed them to amass fabulous wealth as they crafted gold, silver and jewels into baubles for the nobles and royalty.

Darach would never trust the Carack, but he suspected the rival clan wished to avoid a war as much as the MacRoss did. Only someone had tried to start one by murdering the Carack laird's lover on MacRoss land, and making it appear as if she had ended her life after being used and betrayed by Luthias. The killer had also tried to set fire to a barn to kill the lairds of both clans as well as Emery Parker, whom the Fire sword had brought back from the future to save the MacRoss.

In the end Laird Callum Carack had defied centuries of hatred between the clans and saved Luthias and Emery before dying in the fire.

As he floated on his back and watched the stars appear in the night sky, Darach wondered if for once Duine's fears were justified, and he should begin preparing for a war. The centuries since the time of the two princes had weighed heavily on the two clans, and too many lives had been lost during the old skirmishes to ever allow any forgiveness between them.

It seemed inevitable that something would march the MacRoss and Carack back to the battlefield.

When that day came, Darach would lead his men to war, and too many to their deaths. That he accepted as his duty to the clan, but he hated it.

Something dark appeared above him, blocking out the sky as it grew larger. He lunged out of the way a heartbeat before a body fell into the water right where he had been. A tremendous splash from the impact doused him.

As Darach touched bottom and wiped the water from his eyes, a pale-haired woman surfaced. She thrashed around, completely panicked. Though her back was to him, in her hand he saw that she held the Fire sword as if ready to skewer someone.

*Take the blade from her before she hurts herself.*

He swam back, reaching around her for the weapon, but she turned suddenly and held the tip under his chin.

"Get away from me," she said, her strangely-accented voice ringing out with certainty. "Or I'll kill you."

Watery crimson streaks ran down from a gash along her hairline, and another, shallower cut sliced across her cheek. The moonlight silvered her wet fair hair, and made the blood that spattered it look almost black. She had huge eyes, so dark and wide she appeared on the verge of screaming. He could smell the Fae magic that had brought her with the sword, and saw tiny glimmers of red and gold enchantment still dancing on her pale, wet skin.

"I shallnae touch you." Darach pulled back his hands slowly, aware that the slightest movement could provoke her to keep her threat.

Traveling through time with the Fire sword had not injured Emery, the first person the sain had brought back from the future to save the MacRoss Clan. Darach guessed this woman had been assailed when she found the blade, and would not yet realize she had been transported through time. Like any wounded creature she would fight for her life, so he needed to calm and reassure her that she had escaped whatever danger she had escaped.

"Dinnae be afraid," he said, keeping the tone of his voice low and gentle. "You've come to a safe place."

"You stay over there," she warned him, and then looked around them. "What is this? How did you do this to me? Where is he?"

"I didnae bring you here." Telling her what had, Darach decided, would keep. He gestured around them. "Look, and you'll see 'tis only us."

"What are you talking about? He was standing right in front of me five seconds ago." She lowered the blade. "There aren't any trees around the hotel." Her gaze shifted to him. "Who are you? Where am I?"

Telling her she had landed in fourteenth century Scotland probably would get him skewered, he thought. His own weakness made the situation even worse, for he could not lie to her, so he would have to choose his words very carefully.

"My name, 'tis Darach MacRoss. You've come to a spring outside Dun Lasair, my home." He held out his hands. "Your attacker, he's gone, and I'm unarmed. Would you lower the blade now?"

"Blade?" Blinking, she glanced down at the Fire sword. "I thought it was just a piece of metal. I found it under some garbage bags in the alley." She turned it over, her expression changing from fury to confusion as she studied it. "This is what he meant. What he wanted. It's just like the book."

"That sword belongs to my clan," he told her as he tried to think of what more to say that would reassure her. He didn't even know how to address her. "Can you tell me your name?"

"Charlotte Walsh." When she next looked at him her eyes widened. "Did he do that to your face?"

Darach silently cursed himself for a fool as he turned his head away from her. The huge patch of red flesh that covered one quarter of his face completely engulfed his eye, and made him appear monstrous. He'd never forgotten to hide it from a stranger before now.

"'Tisnae a wound, but a birthing mark," he said as he put some space between them once more. "I ken 'tis a gruesome sight, but you neednae look at me."

"Wait." She surged forward, grabbing his hand and pulling him to her, and then looking over his arm. "No tattoos." She shook her head. "You can't be him."

Her reaction bewildered him. "Who did you reckon me, Mistress Walsh?"

"No one, it's nothing." Charlotte rubbed her eyes before she looked around them again. "You called this place something. Dun Lasair. I've never heard of it. Where is it? How did I get here?"

"'Tis much to explain." The cool softness of her hands on his skin tingled with the magic still clinging to her, and he had to resist a sudden, strong urge to wrap his arms around her. "We should get you dry and tend to your wounds first, Charlotte, and then we shall talk of what's happened to you. Mayhap you should give me the sword."

"No." She tightened her grip on the hilt. "He could come back, and it's all I have to defend myself."

"You've more now, my lady," he assured her. "You've me."

Charlotte hesitated, and then let out a shuddering breath as she handed the blade to him.

The moment Darach touched the Fire sword a wave of Fae magic burst over him, and sank into his flesh. He tossed the blade onto the bank and then turned back to her. She pressed her hand briefly over the wound on her brow, and then stared at the blood on her fingers.

"How bad is my head?" she asked, sounding tired.

Tucking one arm around her waist, he looked closely at the gash. It no longer bled, but looked raw and painful.

"'Twill need bandaging." He nodded toward the edge of the spring. "We must see to all your wounds. Come out with me now."

She nodded, but still held onto him when they reached the mossy rocks that encircled the spring. As he helped her out of the water, she stared at his tunic and trews before stepping back and regarding the rest of him.

"I don't understand." Her gaze shifted as she took in the trees and the trail. "Is this your property?"

Darach had never seen a woman as tall as he was, so it took him another moment to compose himself enough to reply. "The land belongs to my family. I came to the spring for a bathe."

"I thought I knew every place downtown." She

regarded him and glanced at the sword in his hand. "I'm sorry if I scared you."

"Dinnae fret. You've endured enough tonight." Darach leaned over to pick up his tartan. He held it up with one hand, turning to her. When she stepped closer he draped it around her trembling body. He tucked the Fire sword into his belt and stepped into his boots. "Can you walk?"

"I think so," she murmured, her head turning as she looked for something. "I'm staying at a hotel, but there are no buildings here. Is this Glendon? How could I end up across town so fast?"

"All shall be made clear soon, I promise you." He wanted to pick her up and carry her to the stronghold, especially when he saw the dagger-heeled shoes she wore. At the same time he sensed any sudden move might make her bolt from him. "We're close to my home; 'tis but a short walk from here. Take my arm if you need."

Charlotte didn't touch him as she walked with him along the trail from the spring toward the stronghold. Instead she tucked her arms around her middle and kept staring at everything they passed. She stopped only when she saw the first curtain wall, and then stared at the four towers.

"Is that... That's a castle," she said, her voice barely more than a whisper.

"Aye. The stronghold belongs to my clan, the MacRoss." Not for the first time he wished he could lie. "'Tis called Dun Lasair."

"This isn't Glendon. There's nothing like this in Toronto." She gave him a wild-eyed look. "You tell me where I am, right now."

It broke his heart to hear the terror in her voice again. "You've come to Scotland, lass."

"No. *No*." She shuffled back, caught her heel on a root and abruptly collapsed on the ground. Covering her face with trembling hands, she hunched over and uttered a low wail.

"Charlotte." He hurried over to her.

"I can't do this. I can't." She shook her head as he crouched down beside her. "I can't go crazy now on top of everything else."

"You're sane." Darach put one hand on her back to steady her. "My lady, look at me. I swear to you, all you see, 'tis real. I'm real."

"I saw how I would die. Maybe I did." She clutched his arm, tears streaming down her face. "You'd tell me if I'm dead, wouldn't you? If this is what's after life? If he chopped me up in that alley like Zoey?"

Darach didn't know who or what Zoey was, but the tremors now racking her had grown so violent they made her teeth chatter. "You yet live, lass, I swear to you. You escaped him. You're safe now. He cannae come after you."

She gripped his shoulder, and tucked her face against his neck. "Please, could you hold me for just a minute?"

Few women ever cared to come this close to Darach, much less cuddle against him as Charlotte did. Carefully he put his arms around her and rubbed her back with his hands, hoping that taking such a liberty would give her some comfort. He pressed his cheek atop her head, silently marveling at how good it was to hold her as if she belonged to him.

At last she sighed, and her breath whispered against his skin like a caress. "I'm sorry, Mister MacRoss."

"'Tis Darach," he murmured against her pale hair. "And you neednae beg my pardon."

She lifted her head. "Darach, I don't think I can walk anymore."

"If I may carry you, then?" When she nodded he tucked an arm under her knees and lifted her, settling her against his chest before he walked quickly to the back gates.

The guards on duty stared at him as if their eyes might pop out of their heads before they raised the portcullis.

"Summon the laird to my chamber at once,"

Darach told them before he strode across the walkway to the second wall's arch, and then across the lists and into the garrison hall, where the first of the night patrols stood arming themselves, and gaped at the sight of Charlotte in his arms.

"You found the Fire sword, Chieftain?" Mathe, his lead patroller, asked as he lumbered over to him, glancing to where it was hung from his belt. Although it was near summer he wore a heavy fur cloak against the cold night wind. "Och, who should hurt such a beauty? 'Twas a Carack?"

"No, lad. She brought back the sword to us. Take a patrol to my bathing spring, and look for anything amiss." Darach went around him and started up the stairs.

Charlotte looked up at him, her pale lashes fluttering for a moment. "You're a chieftain?"

"Aye, 'tis my rank." He wondered if she knew anything about Scotland or his time. "I'm second to the laird."

"Oh." She glanced over his shoulder. "That man looked like a bear."

"Mathe cannae tolerate cold, so he dons furs atop his tartan." He realized she must be taking in everything she saw, and yet didn't seem afraid. "Forgive me. 'Tis much you dinnae ken."

"That's an understatement." She rested her cheek

against his shoulder and closed her eyes. "I'm so tired."

Inside his chamber he carried her to the hearth, placing her on her feet before adding wood to the flames. Her garments, which resembled what Emery Parker had worn when she had come to the clan, still dripped water onto the floor. He reached for her coat first, easing her arms out of it before kneeling to remove her shoes. Carrying the coat to the rack where he hung his own clothes when wet, he draped it and placed her shoes close to the coals where they would dry without burning. When he turned around he saw Charlotte pulling her sodden sweater over her head.

Darach immediately looked away. "I shall find something dry for you to wear, my lady."

"I'd appreciate that, thank you." She began to unfasten the light blue trews she wore.

Fetching his softest tunic from his trunk, a linen to dry herself, and a warm blanket to wrap around her, Darach came back to the hearth. By then all she still wore was a near-transparent shift that had been cut off at her waist, a band beneath it over her breasts, and a tiny pair of drawers that barely covered her sex. Even her startling height hadn't prepared him for the shock of seeing such long, elegant limbs and full curves; the very shape of her made his mouth go dry.

Without any embarrassment Charlotte glanced down, turning this way and that as she lifted the hem of the shift to press one hand against her sides.

"He kept kicking me after I fell in the alley. I thought my ribs were broken, but I think I'm okay. I've simply got some bad bruises." She met his gaze. "I don't think I have to go to the hospital tonight."

Now he realized mottled dark splotches, not shadows, covered both sides of her torso, attesting to the savagery of the attack she had endured. Outrage roiled inside him as he imagined the sort of spineless fack who would do such to a helpless woman already on the ground. At the same time he wanted to touch her so much he had to put more space between them before he made an arse of himself.

"I'd find the bastart responsible if I could," he told her. "Aye, and make him wish he'd never been born."

"You don't want to go anywhere near that maniac, Chieftain." She met his gaze, her own filled with fear again. "He killed the policemen who were guarding me, and my best friend, and six other women in Moss Park. It's possible he murdered over a hundred more people in other provinces." Her chin wobbled for a moment. "I don't think anyone can stop him."

"He shallnae touch you again, lass." Without thinking he took a step toward her as she moved to him, and then she was in his arms, as naturally as if they'd been embracing for years. The fiery desire became a fierce protectiveness; anyone who wished to harm her would have to first go through him. "You've my word on that."

Charlotte nodded, her cheek rubbing against his chest before she stepped back, clearly befuddled. "I don't know why I did that. I'm sorry. I'm such a mess."

"You've survived a wretched ordeal." He couldn't help admiring her tall, willowy body for another moment before he realized he was staring at her again. Quickly he placed the tunic and tartan into her hands before he turned his back on her. "I shall leave you to dress."

"Please, don't go." She touched his arm. "I think you should change out of your wet clothes, too. I won't watch you."

Her directness swamped him with embarrassment. "I meant no disrespect, looking upon you before thus. You're so unusual and lovely I couldnae help… 'Twillnae happen again, my lady."

"If that's disrespectful, then we're even," she said as she rubbed her arms and legs with the linen. "I did it first at the spring. You're a very attractive man."

Darach wondered if the attack she had suffered had affected her mind as well as her body. She behaved as no woman who had ever looked upon him had, openly gazing at his face and touching him, as if she couldn't see his ugliness. When her senses fully returned no doubt she would see him clearly; for now he would enjoy being treated like any other man.

He went to change his clothes, keeping his back to her. Once he had dressed he went to his wash basin, filling it with clean water and retrieving some clean linen before he returned to her. She had released her hair from the braid, and rubbed the long damp length of it with the linen. In the firelight he could see it was very thick but fine, and hung down to her elbows like long tassels of white-gold silk. Seeing such pretty hair framing her blood-streaked face made his gut knot. Any of the MacRoss would fight for the honor of protecting such a rare beauty.

Only a madman could have wished to beat her to death.

"If you'll sit, I shall bathe your face, and clean the wounds," Darach said.

Charlotte went over to the bed rather than the chair by the hearth, and pulled her hair back from her face as she perched on the edge.

Gently washing her brow, eyelid and cheek made endless sledges of rage hammer through him. The bruise darkening around the cut on her cheek made it plain that she had been struck there by the man's fist, and his ring had sliced through her fragile skin. The coward who had attacked her must have counted on her being too afraid to fight back. He almost wished Charlotte had impaled the worthless fack with the Fire sword before coming to his time, but at least she had survived.

Once he had cleaned the cuts, however, he could see they were not as grievous as he'd first assumed. Within a few days he reckoned she would heal.

"Will I need stitches?" she asked.

"No, but we'll keep close watch over your wounds. I've some salve I use to keep mine from festering. 'Twill burn a wee bit, but quicken the healing, and prevent scars from forming." When she nodded he fetched the pot and dabbed it on her cuts, wincing with her as he did. "For the night I should bandage your brow, for that may bleed again as you turn in your sleep."

As he was winding a strip of linen around her head Charlotte never looked away from his face. "You're afraid to tell me where I am, and how I got here, aren't you?"

"'Tisnae so much fear as my wish to spare you more anguish," Darach admitted.

"I'm better now, and I'd rather know the truth."

She blew out a breath. "You said I'm in Scotland. You weren't joking about that, were you? I'm really not in Canada anymore?"

"Aye, lass. You've come to the highlands in the north of Scotland." He heard a knock on the door, and Charlotte went rigid. "'Tis only Luthias. He's my eldest brother, and the laird of our clan. You heard me ask the men to summon him."

As he stood she grabbed his hand so tightly her nails scored his skin.

"How do you know that's him?" she said, looking aghast. "It could be the killer. He could have followed me here. He's been stalking me for weeks."

"Only you came to us, lass. I swear that bastart couldnae pursue you here without the sword." He clasped her hand between his palms. "Trust what I say, Charlotte. I cannae lie to you."

She closed her eyes for a moment, and then released him. "All right."

Darach went to open the door, and quickly murmured to the laird, "She dropped into my bathing spring with the Fire sword in hand. She's been attacked and beaten by some savage fack in her time just before it brought her to us, and she's yet terrified. I've told her only that she's in Scotland. Ask her leave before you approach her."

Luthias nodded, and stayed where he was as he

looked past Darach at Charlotte. "My lady, I'm Luthias, laird of the MacRoss Clan. Might I come in and speak with you about what's happened?"

"Yes." She watched him approach, the wariness back in her eyes as she studied his face. She started to stand up, but then subsided. "I'm sorry, I'm still a little unsteady." She held out her slender hand. "My name is Charlotte Walsh."

"'Tis a pleasure to meet you, Mistress Walsh," the laird said as he shook hands with her. "I ken 'tis greatly confusing to you. I regret our sain adding to your misfortunes by bringing you to us."

Her expression grew remote. "How could you know anything about what's happened to me?"

"'Tis because you came to Dun Lasair with the Fire sword of the MacRoss Clan," Luthias said, pulling up a stool to sit facing her. "The blade, 'tis a sain of great power—a kind of protector—and 'twas enchanted by the first MacRoss laird, a Fae prince named Ross. When terrible danger threatens our clan, he bespelled the sain to move through time to find one who may save us, and bring them here. 'Twould seem that's you, my lady."

"Are you saying that your magic sword abducted me?" she asked tonelessly. "And then it flew me across the ocean to drop me in a spring in Scotland, just so that I could save your clan?"

"Aye." Luthias grimaced. "Such must sound outlandish to you, but 'tis truth."

Darach expected Charlotte to react with disbelief, laughter or even become angry with the laird. Instead she sat quietly and gazed at both of them as if waiting for them to admit it was all a jest.

"We shall talk more on the morrow," Darach said finally. "'Tis too much for the lady now. She needs rest."

"I just want to understand, Chieftain. I was attacked by a killer in Canada, and then I fell into the water here in what you tell me is Scotland. It took only a few seconds, and I remained conscious the entire time. Since none of that has a plausible explanation, a magic sword actually does make sense." Charlotte shook her head as if she had no faith in her own words. "The problem is the police won't believe any of this. Two, maybe three of their men were murdered while guarding me. They're going to want some answers when I go to the hospital in the morning. Can you come with me, and bring the sword to show them how it works?"

Darach exchanged a look with Luthias, and against his better judgement nodded.

"We've no police nor hospitals here, Mistress Walsh. What happened to you, 'tis how my wife came to us from the twenty-first century," Luthias said.

"That 'twas the same time in which you lived as well?"

She went very still. "Are you telling me that it's not the twenty-first century here?"

"Aye. The Fire sword brought you back seven hundred years, my lady," Darach told her gently. "Our time now, 'tis the fourteenth century."

For a long moment Charlotte didn't move, blink or take a breath. What little color that had returned to her face abruptly drained away. A choking sound came from her as she stood up and then sat back down again, and pressed a shaking hand over her mouth.

"She'll boak," Luthias predicted, rising and heading for the wash basin.

"Wait, my lord." Darach saw the tears brimming on her lashes, but the sound she made was more like a laugh. He sat down beside her, taking her hand in his. "Charlotte?"

"If you're telling me the truth, then I'm safe now. He really can't touch me here." She straightened her shoulders and looked at Luthias. "Your enchanted sword didn't abduct me, Laird. It saved my life. Just before I fell in the spring I saw how I would die. The maniac who was beating me would have cut me to pieces before he drowned me."

"Then 'twas a sain for you as well, Mistress

Walsh." The laird gave her a reassuring smile. "'Tis good to ken."

Charlotte wiped her eyes quickly. "I don't understand why it chose me. What could I possibly do to save your clan?"

"That I cannae tell you," Luthias admitted. "We've only had such happen once before, with my wife Emery. She's a forensic anthropologist. Do you some special work like hers in your time?"

"I'm an artist. Mostly I illustrate children's books." Her gaze strayed to the Fire sword where Darach had set it against the wall. "I think the killer who attacked me wanted to find that blade. He called it a sain, too, and mentioned a chieftain." She rose and went over to study the blade, even running her finger tips over the flame-shaped hilt. "There's something else you should know, and it may be related to the reason your sword brought me here. I'm still not sure if I believe it, however, and I can't explain it."

"We shallnae question whatever you tell us, lass," Darach assured her.

"I drew this blade in a book I illustrated a few years ago. The story was about a knight using it to defend a garden of flowers against frost demons. The blade had gold markings like yours, and the hilt was also shaped like flames. Flower tattoos covered the knight's skin, and he had a huge red rose inked over one of his eyes." She glanced over her shoulder at him. "He looked almost exactly like you, Chieftain. When I first saw you, I thought I was hallucinating my own artwork."

Luthias's brows drew together. "How could you ken what the Fire sword and Darach looked like, my lady?"

"That's the part I can't explain because it wasn't my story," she said. "The manuscript I worked from was written by a historian named Seona Kerrich. I based my illustrations on her descriptions of the knight and the sword."

"I'm in a book." Darach didn't know whether to be pleased or dismayed.

"'Tis yet another mystery we cannae solve now," the laird said. "I wish I could send you back, my lady, but you must stay here until your purpose is served. Once you do, the Fire sword 'twill grant you a wish. You may use that to return to your time."

"I don't need a wish," she said, her voice tight. "I'm never going back."

## Chapter Three

Struan Carack brought a lantern to the counting table he had moved to the back corner of the great hall at Dun Deigh. There he sat down and took out the three scrolls delivered to him from the clan's overseers. He could hear muted voices coming from the garrison, where the clansmen not on patrol or guard duty gathered each night to drink. Occasionally a brawl broke out, but since the death of the laird most of the Carack had wallowed in too much whiskey and even more resentment.

They blamed him, not for Callum's death, but for refusing to attack the MacRoss, their ancient rivals. This despite knowing his brother had given his life to rescue Luthias MacRoss and Emery Parker, the woman from the future who had saved them all from a needless clan war.

Struan spread out the scrolls and studied the figures inked on the parchment. Two listed the amount of gold and silver ore that had been brought up from the mines over the last month, and the third listed the gems and crystals found in the old shafts he had reopened for digging. Using silver jettons to mark the amounts on the scored lines of the table, he figured how much the jewels and precious metals would fetch once worked into baubles, and then combined the totals. They would add even more wealth to the Carack's burgeoning coffers, and assure they could keep their position as the wealthiest clan in the highlands.

*If the MacRoss dinnae go back on their promise of peace and attack us. If I can control my brothers and somehow quench their thirst for vengeance. If we may expose the bastart behind all these schemes, and learn why he wants war between the clans.*

"For one who wished no' be named laird, you spend much time tending to our wealth, my lord," a slurred voice said from the shadows. "'Tis well you cannae keep a wench in your bed, else she be tempted to filch the coin you're ever counting."

Struan smelled the sourness of sweat mixed with whiskey, and now understood why Callum so often avoided the hall after the evening meal. Thanks to his own weakness he would spend every day of the next two months below ground. Until the end of summer he would have to deal with the occasional fool intruding on his work.

"I've no time for wenches or you, Fyn." He rolled up the parchments and collected the jettons. "Why skulk you about the keepe when you should be skinning those boars delivered today? They shallnae peel off their own hides and trot into the kitchens."

"The boars shallnae run anywhere now, Brother," the hunter said as he stepped into the light of the lantern. One of the shortest men in the clan, his narrow face, close-set eyes and protruding front teeth made him resemble a water vole. "I'm curious, my lord. Why choose you remain war master? Ever you've wished from boyhood to be laird. Callum even named you his successor, although only the Gods ken why you've no' named yours."

Being reminded of the old rift between him and his dead brother didn't annoy Struan as much as the manner in which Fyn avidly watched his face. Fortunately he had long experience at keeping his countenance.

"I shall choose a new war master before I take my place on the dais as laird," he told the hunter. "Until that day, I shall serve as I've done since our sire died."

"The clan needs a clever warrior unafraid of death and killing," Fyn countered, drinking from a jug as he staggered over to the table. "One who shall keep the facking MacRoss from crossing our boundaries to slit our throats as we sleep." He leaned close, bathing Struan in the sour fumes of his breath. "Dinnae you see one truly worthy to do such?"

"I ken several of our brothers who should serve us well in time of war or peace," Struan said, and took a moment to look directly into the hunter's beady dark eyes. "Only rest assured, Fyn. Never shall I name you the next war master."

Something like hurt flickered over the hunter's face. "Aye, only soon shall you regret that vow."

Fyn stalked away, his hand colliding with the lantern and knocking it over onto the floor. The oil it spilled on the stone ignited, and the flames flaring under the table forced Struan to rise and move away.

"Permit me, my lord." Master Sage Reothadh appeared, his robes fluttering around his tall, gaunt form as he seized a bucket of sand near the hearth and used it to extinguish the small fire. "Such accidents become frequent of late."

"An accident." He glanced at the arch through which Fyn had departed. "I wonder."

"I reckon the hunter yearns to work out of doors again." The sage picked up the lantern and placed it in the sand bucket. "Mayhap 'tis time to permit the clan to return to their duties."

Struan thought of Callum's burned body being lowered into the grave he'd dug with his own hands. "'Tis proper we mourn the laird as we did my sire, for a full month. I cannae make the moon wane nor wax faster."

"Forgive me, my lord. I dinnae question your right to grieve proper." The sage retrieved a small spade and broom and began sweeping up the blackened sand. "I hadnae a chance to speak with you this morn about the dreamstone you bid me inspect. 'Tis naught missing from the enclave's storerooms."

Before he had died Callum had specifically asked him about the crystal, which he had intended to give to the sages to create a sleeping elixir. His brother had never explained any of his reasons for wanting the potion, or why he had thought any of the dreamstone would go missing.

"The two young sages who came to me squabbling over that crystal," Struan said, "did they speak with Callum before he left to play woodcutter on MacRoss land?"

"I cannae tell you," Reothadh admitted. "'Tis unlikely those brothers would both set on creating the same elixir unless asked by the former laird."

From what the two young sages had said, Callum

had meant to put a great many to slumber, perhaps by adding such an elixir to a well or cistern.

"Find out what they ken of my brother's plans." He glanced down as the sage held out a glass orb illuminated from within by the blue light of a Fae charm. "Why give me such?"

"You carry a torch when you roam the woods after dark." The lines around his eyes deepened. "Coldfire, 'twillnae blister your hands."

He hated being reminded of his weakness, but the sage meant the offering as a kindness. "My thanks."

Struan instructed his personal guards to remain at the gate before he walked into the forest surrounding his stronghold. Even with summer upon the highlands the nights remained cool, and gave him some relief. During the day he spent much of his time in the dungeons, where he had set up a chamber for himself to work while avoiding the hot rays of the sun. Like his father he could never tolerate any heat without his flesh blistering and then burning. All his life Struan had been forced to eat tepid food, bathe in the chilliest loch, and avoid hearths and bonfires. His mind kept going back to the accident with the lantern—if that was what it had truly been.

*Did Fyn wish only to frighten me, or truly burn me alive?*

Ever since being ordered to remain at the keep

for the official month of mourning, the hunter had behaved like a caged wild animal, pacing for hours, drinking too much and taking pleasure in tormenting the servants. More than once Struan had wondered if Fyn might be going mad at last, for since boyhood he had been strange, and at times seemed to teeter on the very edge of sanity. Only Callum had been able to keep the hunter under control, for the hunter had both feared and worshipped him. Seeing Luthias MacRoss bringing the Carack laird's burned body back to Dun Deigh had likely been too much for Fyn's simple mind to grasp.

A small shadow flitted across the trail, and Struan held up the orb as he peered into the darkness. Unlike Callum he could see in the dark, but only as well as most men. "Who walks there?"

A short, thin figure stepped out from behind a broad oak. "'Tis but Revna, *Maister*."

He walked up and reached out so the orb illuminated her face, and painted the rest of her in a soft blue glow. The girl had light-colored hair hanging loose around a small face and big, waifish pale eyes. She looked so young that at first he thought her no more than ten or twelve years, but her mouth had a womanly fullness, as did the small breasts under her stained apron. He'd never before seen such a wench at the stronghold, and glanced down at the shabby gown.

"Revna? 'Tis your name?" Struan asked.

"Aye. Och, no." She seemed to realize at last whom she was staring at, and quickly ducked her head and curtseyed. "Forgive me, my lord. I thought you—I didnae see that 'twas you. I'm Revna, the new kitchen maid."

Struan knew his appearance regularly frightened the younger vassals. With his silver-blond hair, pale hide and unearthly features he looked almost identical to the old portraits of Prince Kaer hanging in the keep. He even had the same eyes, so dark a brown they looked black. On occasion when he walked the passages at night even the guards would flinch, mistaking him as the first laird's ghost.

"You came to work at the stronghold today, then." As she nodded he saw her bare toes peeking out from under the hem of her skirts. "You shouldnae be in the woods alone at night. 'Tis dangerous for a wench."

"Forgive me, my lord. I'll go back now." She bobbed again, and started toward the stronghold.

Struan caught her arm to stop her, and the coolness of her flesh made his palm tingle. Touching others always proved unpleasant for him, as too-long physical contact with another's body could blister his hands, but he experienced none of that from her. She had either grown very chilled, or like most bairns did not have enough flesh on her bones to generate great heat.

*She's no' a bairn.*

"When came you to Dun Deigh?" he asked, releasing her.

"Sevenday past," Revna said. "My da run off in the night, and I've no more kin. The village *maister* asked the steward give me work so I shouldnae starve. My lord," she added quickly, as if she'd forgotten how to properly address him.

The steward should have first consulted him before offering the wench a position, but Struan suspected Callum would have taken her on. He well knew his brother's soft spot for small wenches, although he'd never shared it. For him, bedding a female always proved an unpleasant experience for the wench and provided nothing but release for him. Of late he opted for his own hand over women.

Still, he didn't care for how thin the maiden looked, as if she'd already gone hungry for weeks. "Your age?"

"I'm twenty, my lord." Revna dragged the edge of her teeth over her bottom lip. "I ken I look younger, but 'tis truth." She shivered.

"You're chilled." He didn't wear a tartan, or he would have wrapped it around her, and then he realized how foolishly he was behaving. "Go in and warm yourself by the fire."

"Aye, my lord." Revna touched her arm where he had grabbed her and hurried away.

Struan pocketed the orb and followed her, and once he saw her enter the gates changed direction and went to find the night steward.

The older man dismissed the laundress he was speaking with, and bowed. "How may I serve, my lord?"

"Tell the village cobbler to make a pair of boots for the new kitchen maid, and any of the other vassals who have come to work for the clan of late." He handed him the coin to pay for the work. "I tire of seeing my servants resembling beggars."

"Your pardon, my lord, but I should tell you what I've just heard." The steward glanced in the direction the laundress had hurried. "Two of our maids, they're gone. A trapper, too, just a week past, according to the village tanner."

Struan frowned. "What reason gave they for leaving Dun Deigh?"

"They didnae say to anyone, my lord." The older man made a helpless gesture. "The maids went out walking yesterday and never returned."

Nearly all of the vassals who served the Carack were born into their service, as their families had served the clans for generations. Since they were well-paid no one left Dun Deigh unless they were too ill to work or dead. Now three had left without notice.

Struan recalled what the kitchen maid had said. *My da run off in the night, and I've no more kin.* The trapper had been her father. It angered him to think of the wench having to work to keep from starving, but such often proved the lot of the poorest villagers.

"They likely went home. Go to the village on the morrow and ask why they left our service." He saw the way the steward grimaced. "What?"

"The laundress did so today, my lord, hoping to persuade them return. 'Twould seem they've truly run off, my lord. They're no' in the village, and their families, they ken naught of where they went." He sighed. "Mayhap the wenches travel together to the city. 'Tis said there's easy work there, and you ken how foolish the young think."

Had they run away? Everyone had believed Athdara Martin had done the same to be with her secret lover, and yet had turned up murdered.

"What of the trapper?" Struan asked. "Did he the same?"

The steward shook his head. "The tanner claimed he left home one morning and never returned.

Mayhap he came to harm while checking his snares. Should I alert the patrols to keep watch for him?"

"Aye, and bring the laundress and tanner to me on the morrow," Struan told the steward. "I want to hear what more they ken."

EMERY PARKER PACED UP AND DOWN THE PASSAGE in the garrison corridor, swatting at her dark brown hair when tendrils of it escaped her untidy bun. She wished she had an excuse to barge into Darach's chamber so she could find out what was going on, but that would probably only further startle the new arrival. From what the garrison guards had told her husband, Darach had carried in the pale-haired woman, who had been wounded. Had it happened during the jump back to the past, or had she been in trouble in the future? Not knowing an answer was Emery's least favorite thing.

"This is taking forever," she complained as she stopped and glared at the door.

"You need acquire some patience," Taveon MacRoss said as he leaned against a wall and watched her. The tallest man in the clan, the war master's gleaming black hair framed a clever face so pale it looked as if he'd been carved from snowy marble.

That and his ability to remain unruffled in any crisis had earned him the reputation of having ice for blood. "'Twill only seem longer if you fret thus."

"I'm not fretting. I never fret," she told him, swatting the air between them. "I just have a lot of nervous energy. Stop giving me the black stare of disapproval."

"Aye, my lady." He grinned as she glowered at him, as she did every time he called her that. "'Tis your own fault for wishing to stay with my brother for eternity, and then wedding him after the Fire sword granted your wish. Forever shall you be our Lady MacRoss."

"I may be married to your lord, but I'm still an American, and we don't do titles. So for the rest of eternity call me Emery, or I'm going to kick you where it hurts boys every time you Lady me." She let out a frustrated breath as she leaned against the opposite wall and folded her arms. "Do you think Struan taking over the Carack Clan is the reason the Fire sword brought this woman back to us?"

His brows arched, giving him a slightly devilish look. "You wish to blame the sain disappearing on Callum's successor?"

"Well, who else?" she countered. "He worked as the Carack's war master, and the vassal grapevine says that he was Callum's only full-blood brother, too.

Geez, probably all the guy thinks about now is attacking us."

Taveon sighed. "Aye, as raiding Dun Deigh and killing Carack, 'tis all ever I ponder. You ken naught of war mastering."

"I stopped a clan war, didn't I?" she reminded him. "So what's Struan's deal? From the five minutes I spent with him he seemed polite, even if he wouldn't listen to me. He was nothing like Callum, though."

"Never should anyone call Struan a hot head like his brother," he told her. "He didnae kill the laird when he rode alone to Dun Deigh to bring Callum's body back to his clan. He even bowed to Luthias and thanked him in front of the other Carack. 'Tisnae him that worries me."

"A-ha. So you *are* worried. I knew it wasn't just me." Emery wagged her finger at him. "We both know that the sword wouldn't have disappeared unless the threat to the clan went to DEFCON 1 again. Now it brings back this woman in the middle of the night. There has to be something triggering the enchantment, and the saving part might not take weeks the way it did with me. We might need her to do her thing like tomorrow morning, right?"

"I cannae tell you," the war master admitted. "'Tis only happened twice now."

"Okay." She leaned back against the wall and

folded her arms. "Then who do you suspect is the threat this time? If it's not Struan, then could it be the bone cobbler. He has to be the one who murdered Athdara Martin, and tried to burn me and Luthias along with Callum."

"We've seen naught more of that crazed fack or his filthy works," Taveon said, "and we yet dinnae ken who killed the Carack laird's lover."

Emery made a face at him, but she knew he was right. Someone had tortured Athdara before drowning her to make it look as if she'd killed herself, and then attempted to frame Luthias with a suicide scroll claiming he had used and abandoned her to starve. Emery had examined the dead woman's body and proved she had been murdered, stopping a war between the clans. When she had convinced both lairds to meet her at the place where she believed Athdara had been killed, however, they had been ambushed. The Carack laird had saved her and Luthias, only to die in the fire she was sure the bone cobbler had set.

"This is giving me a headache," Emery complained. "I just want the killing to stop. Enough people have died."

The war master made a soft sound. "You yet blame yourself for Callum."

"I don't want to, but it was my fault." She eyed

him. "He would never have gone there to talk to Luthias on his own. I nagged him into doing it because I wanted them to make nice. Then those two refused to let me search the barn by myself. If I'd just made them stay outside while I looked for evidence—"

"Then you'd be dead, and Callum, for my brother would have blamed him for your death, and cut him to pieces," the war master assured her. "And Luthias wouldnae stop with one dead laird. He'd have gone to war to end the rest of the Carack, and killed the rest of us seeking to do thus."

"You know what? That totally ended my guilt trip. Thank you." As Darach's chamber door opened Emery hurried over to her husband. "Is she okay? What's her name? Where did she come from? Is she a scientist like me?"

Luthias closed the door. "She's wounded, but no' badly. Her name, 'tis Charlotte Walsh. She came from Toronto in the twenty-first century, and she paints."

Emery blinked. "She what?"

"She paints picture books for bairns." He gave Taveon a wry look. "I cannae fathom how such a lady should save the clan, but at least she doesnae wish to return."

"A kid's book artist from Canada. This is like trying to solve crossword puzzles without any clues."

Emery tapped a finger against her lips. "How did she get hurt? Did she cut herself with the sword?"

"She's been hounded and attacked by a vicious brute in her time," Luthias said. "He nearly killed her before she came back with the blade." He hesitated before he added, "Mistress Walsh told me she saw her own death before the sword took her."

"Just like I did before it dropped me here." Emery didn't like to think about the vision she'd had just before the Fire sword had saved her by bringing her to the MacRoss; she'd seen herself on the floor of her museum's storage room with a broken neck. "I need to talk to her."

"No' tonight, my love. She's yet terrified, so we need to treat her gently and give her some time to calm." Her husband regarded the war master. "When shall the healer return from Skye?"

"We expect Mairi and her family back before the new moon." Taveon frowned. "If the lady needs tending I may summon Duine."

"Probably not a good idea," Emery put in. "The master had been so upset since the blade vanished again that Cook has been keeping a pot of calming brew simmering just for him all day."

"Darach shall look after Mistress Walsh for now." The laird held out his hand. "Come, wife. 'Tis late, so you may speak with the lady on the morrow at the morning meal."

CHARLOTTE SURREPTITIOUSLY WATCHED DARACH as he rubbed the Fire sword with a cloth before hanging it on some wall hooks next to a row of other long blades. He didn't like the sain, she thought, judging by his expression as he handled it. She imagined she would have looked the same if someone had handed her a live grenade. But once he turned his back toward her she could look at him openly without making him self-conscious, which he seemed to be because of the large birthmark on his face. The fact that he looked almost exactly like the Rose Knight she had drawn for Seona Kerrich's book should have seemed eerie. Instead it made her relax, as if she already knew and trusted him.

*He won't let anyone hurt me again.*

If Luthias MacRoss had told her the truth, and Charlotte had somehow landed in Scotland during the Middle Ages, then Darach and the other men she had seen were true highland warriors. For men of this time they all appeared young, handsome, strong and very clean. Like the laird, the chieftain had a well-developed physique, with wide shoulders, narrow hips and long legs, but his upper body development seemed far more pronounced. The long, heavy muscles of his arms suggested he not only handled a sword easily but on a daily basis as well. Charlotte's Rose Knight had been a little less muscular, and covered in tattoos, but otherwise they could have been twins, physically speaking.

Looking at him made her wish for her sketching kit, for once she'd stopped paying attention to the birthmark she could see how handsome the chieftain was.

Darach appeared as dark as she was pale, with deeply tanned skin and long hair the color of burnished bronze. His unmarked eye was a beautiful shade of caramel brown, and framed by dark lashes. His left eye looked lighter, almost golden, but it might have been the contrast with his birthmark. The mottling of his skin didn't distract her from the masculine beauty of his features, which had perfect symmetry. That Fate had covered so much of his face with the port-wine stain seemed almost cruel, for without it he would have been the most striking man she'd ever seen.

*Why does it matter?* Charlotte had always thought perfection cold and inanimate, much like her own mother. *I like him better with his flaws.*

"Do I frighten you, my lady?" Darach asked without turning around.

"No." He knew she'd been watching him, but then with his birthmark he must often get stared at by others. She wondered if he even realized just how attractive he was. When she'd painted his fictitious counterpart, she'd made him her ideal, with all the masculine attributes she admired. Darach embodied all of them. "Don't you believe me?"

"I dinnae question your word, but I ken my ugly face." He put away the polishing cloth and walked over to the fireplace to add some wood to the flames. "If you wish I'll find a maid to stay with you."

"Please don't do that." Afraid he would go, Charlotte rose and hurried over to him. "I won't be any trouble." She reached out for him before she realized what she was doing, and dropped her hands. She really needed to stop touching him. "You're the only person I know here." *And trust*, she added silently.

"'Twasnae my intent to oust you from my chamber," he said. "You may stay here as long as you wish. We've many rooms in the garrison where I may sleep."

"Could you sleep with me?" She shouldn't have said it like that, but the thought of being left alone made her panicky again. "I mean, could you sleep in this room tonight, too? I'd be a lot safer with you close by." When he didn't say anything she added, ""I know there's only one bed, but I can sleep on the floor. I don't mind at all."

"I'll stay, and you'll have the bed." He looked all over her face. "You've but to say, and I'll do as you need. Dinnae weep, lass."

Only then did Charlotte become aware of the wetness on her cheeks.

"I'm sorry." She turned away, embarrassed by her lack of self-control. "I don't know why I keep crying. I'm never like this."

"You've survived a terrible thing, and found yourself in a land and time no' your own. I expect if I'd faced the same, I'd be wailing all the night." He went to the hearth, and turned her coat on the rack where he'd hung it to dry. "You're braver than most men I ken."

If only he knew how cowardly she'd been ever since the killer had begun stalking her. "You promised you wouldn't lie to me, remember?"

"'Tisnae that I wouldnae lie to you," he said. "I've a weakness that shallnae permit me do so. I may speak only truth."

What an odd thing to believe, Charlotte thought. "Is it something like the magic sword, then?"

Instead of answering her Darach took a pair of

knitted socks from the chest where he kept his clothes and brought them over to her.

"My hose, they're too big, but they'll keep your toes warm for the night," he told her. "I'll see to proper boots for you on the morrow."

"If you're really unable to lie, then you would have to say nothing or change the subject to avoid telling the truth," she said. "Like you did just now."

He went down on one knee in front of her, looking exactly like one of her paintings from the fairytale book.

"I guess there's more going on here than you want me to know. You don't have to do that," she added as he put one of the socks on her foot.

"I ken." Darach didn't look up at her. "I wish to. You've lovely feet."

He touched her almost reverently with his big hands, and the rasp of the calluses on his fingers and palms against her ankles and arches made Charlotte's toes curl. It had been almost a year since her last, disastrous date with Jack, but she'd never experienced such sensations with him even during sex.

All Darach had to do was touch her and her whole body wanted more.

With all the fear and death she had dealt with it should have seemed bizarre to experience such powerful desire for a man she didn't know. Perhaps the arousal was some kind of hysterical reaction to what she'd been through, but she didn't care. She'd always considered herself slightly frigid when it came to men; the chieftain had her sweating just by putting socks on her bare feet.

He didn't seem to be affected by her, judging by how calm he was. She'd been all over him tonight, in fact, and all he'd done was apologize for looking at her body.

*At least he likes my feet.*

"I won't ask any more questions." Charlotte gripped the coverlet to keep from nudging his chin so he'd stop hiding his face. "But if you want me to help your clan, eventually you'll have to tell me everything. Even the things you wish you could lie about to me."

Darach looked up at her. "'Tis more than you should bear, my lady."

"Oh, I don't know. Other than crying every five minutes I'm pretty strong, I think." She thought of Zoey. "When I found my friend after the stalker tortured and killed her, I knew he would do the same thing to me. I even saw how I would die just before I came here. Only I didn't die that way. I heard a man's voice in my head. It sounded Scottish, like yours."

He frowned. "What said the man?"

She got up and walked toward the hearth, trying to remember. "He said he wouldn't let me die there, and that in return I needed to save his sons. Or maybe I was just hallucinating. It's still hard to know what's real."

"Dinnae dwell on such, Charlotte." Darach brought a tartan over and wrapped it around her, chafing her arms with his hands. "The killer who hurt you, he'll no' be born for centuries."

"That's why I can't return to my time." She leaned against him. "You won't make me wish to go back there, will you? After I do whatever I was brought here for?"

"Never shall I force you do anything." The chieftain guided her over to the hearth. There he sat down in the big chair and pulled her onto his lap, cuddling her like a child as he arranged the tartan over her shivering limbs. "You may stay at Dun Lasair as long as you wish."

Being treated like a frightened little girl was undignified, and she should have gotten up. Being close to him, however, was the only thing that kept her from having another meltdown.

"I'm scared, but I've never been this angry," Charlotte admitted. "I don't understand it. I've always been a calm person."

"Anger, 'tis brought on by the worst fear for some, I reckon," Darach said. "As a young lad, thunder and lightning terrified me. One night I spent too long training, and the watch locked me outside the keepe. A storm soon came, and I crouched by the door, sure I'd be struck and killed. I couldnae stop shaking, but no' just from fear. 'Twas as if the guards, they'd betrayed me. I wished to find them and beat them bloody."

Charlotte realized he hadn't shown a single indication of fear since she'd landed in that spring; not even when she'd held the sword at his neck. "Did you spend the whole night like that?"

"If no' for my brother Kendric, aye, I would've." He stared into the flames. "When I didnae return to the garrison he came looking for me. He dragged me inside and stayed with me until the storm passed."

"You're lucky." The warmth of his big body finally made her trembling stop. "I don't have any siblings, so I've always had to face things alone. I just wish I knew why your sword chose me. I have painted you and the sword, but how can my art save your clan?"

"Dinnae fret on such." He looked down at her. "When the blade brought back our Lady Emery, we couldnae fathom how she might help us. She's but a wee thing, and a scholar only just finished her schooling. Yet she used her training and skill to show what killed another lady. That truth stopped a clan war."

"I would like to meet her." Drowsy now, she tried to push herself upright, and then smiled as Darach rose and carried her over to his bed. "You don't have to keep doing this. I can definitely walk now."

"Indulge me, my lady." He put her down and drew the linens over her. "Now you need sleep. We'll talk more on the morrow."

Charlotte reached for his hand, and curled her fingers over his. "Wait." As he frowned she shifted over, making room for him. "Stay with me. Just for a little while."

# Chapter Four

Charlotte watched as Darach stretched out beside her and tucked his arm under her head. Cuddling up to him and resting her hand against his chest might have seemed brazen, but she'd already stripped in front of the man. She also really didn't care about what was and wasn't acceptable behavior in the fourteenth century. He hadn't shown any sign of being embarrassed or unwilling, and right now she needed someone close to her.

*No, it's him. I need him.*

She'd apologize for her behavior in the morning, she thought, when her sanity finally returned. For now she closed her eyes as she breathed in the heated male scent of him. He smelled clean and woodsy, as if they were still in the forest spring, and that made her remember what he looked like dressed in his soaking wet clothes.

*Is that why I'm being so clingy? Because I'm physically attracted to him?*

She had never asked a man to sleep with her, or stayed the night with a man after making love. Although she'd tried to work up some enthusiasm, sex had always underwhelmed her, so much so that she'd left as soon as possible afterward. Maybe that was why no one had given her such a sense of being warm and safe as this man did; she'd never given anyone a chance to.

*No, it's him. I never met him.*

"You've a husband in your time?" he asked, startling her a little.

"I've never been married." That question made her draw back. "I never thought to ask. Do you have a wife?"

"Who should want me, lass?" As Darach said that he turned his face a little more to hide most of the birthmark over his eye.

"Don't do that." Charlotte touched the raised patch of red skin slanting beneath his eye with her fingertips. "You're not ugly, you know. You're simply different."

"If my face pleases you, then I shallnae complain." He smiled, and his marked eye caught a flicker of light and flashed red-gold. "My thanks for your kind words."

Although she should have told him she wasn't being kind, Charlotte became distracted by his mouth. Like the rest of his face it had flawless contours, and her fingers itched to trace the sensual fullness of his lips. No, if she were being honest with herself, she wanted to kiss him, this stranger she had met only a few hours ago.

Pushing aside the inappropriate urge, she asked, "People with visible birthmarks deal with a lot of trouble in this time, don't they?"

"In some places, aye," he admitted. "The superstitious see such marks as curses on the *màthair* or the bairn. Some zealots call them witchmark, and claim they prove someone evil by nature."

"That's so ridiculous." She shook her head. "It's just an unusual coloration of your skin. It doesn't mean anything."

"All MacRoss have such birthing marks," Darach told her. "Ameron, one of the guards, has one much the same on his neck. Luthias's, 'tis twice the size of mine, but stretches across the top of his back."

"Families sometimes share physical traits like that." Charlotte showed him the two moles on her left wrist. "My father had these in the exact same place."

He rubbed his thumb over the marks. "I'd trade you mine for these, but I wouldnae mar such a lovely face as yours."

"I wish you could see yourself the way I do." She recalled the dozen paintings she'd made of the Rose Knight, and how blissfully absorbed she'd been while creating them. Perhaps that was why Darach made her experience that same consuming, dreamy fascination. "You do look almost exactly like my illustrations from that book. Seeing you like this, it's as if my own art has come alive."

"You must tell me more of the book on the morrow." He tugged the blanket up over her. "Now you should rest, my lady."

Darach rose from the bed and went back to the hearth, where he sat down and watched the flames. The last thing Charlotte wanted to do was sleep, but her body ached with exhaustion. She closed her eyes and gradually drifted off into a light doze. All the fear and anger left her as she remembered the first time she had sketched the Rose Knight. It had been the day she'd signed the contract to illustrate Seona Kerrich's book.

Charlotte caught sight of herself in the mirrored walls as she walked into her publisher's building. She had worn black and white, as she always did for work, and twisted her hair into a sleek, gleaming chignon to add a little sophistication. Zoey had always dressed in wild colors and hair styles, claiming artists needed to be as colorful as their work. Charlotte strived for the opposite impression, as the publishers she worked for expected a professional appearance.

As she stood waiting in front of the elevator she caught a glimpse of Zoey running down the hall, pursued by a man wearing black sweats and a hoodie. The two figures then vanished into thin air.

*Zoey wasn't there that day. This is a dream.*

As soon as Charlotte stepped into the elevator time jumped to the moment when she stepped out of it again, and walked down to her publisher's office. There a secretary escorted her into a little conference room, where her editor and the author were having tea.

"It's a pleasure to meet you, Ms. Kerrich," Charlotte said, shaking her hand after the editor introduced them. "I attended some of your lectures about indigenous people when I was at U of T."

"Then you're probably wondering why I'm publishing a children's series," Seona Kerrich said, smiling as they sat down. "I don't have any kids of my own, but I'm godmother to my best friend's daughter. She's six years old, and loves fairy tales."

With her black hair, big blue eyes, red lips and fair skin the author looked a little like Snow White,

Charlotte thought as she accepted the manuscript from Seona and skimmed through it. On each page the historian had clipped notes about the particular illustrations she wanted.

"A fierce knight protecting flowers from frost demons." She smiled a little as she read the description of the main character. "He sounds very exotic."

"According to legend, he was," the author said. "I've based all the characters on actual members of two ancient Scottish highland clans. My ancestors happened to work for one of them."

As they discussed the project Charlotte took out her tablet and began sketching with her electronic stylus. Since Seona had mentioned the Middle Ages as the story's time period she drew a tall, broad-shouldered man and dressed him in medieval-style garments, and then began detailing the figure.

"I don't know the name of the chieftain on whom I modeled the character, but accounts by an alchemist associated with his clan mention his face being damaged here," Seona told her, and moved her hand over her left eye and brow. "I think he may have been disfigured by burn scars, or perhaps smallpox. Can you turn that detail into something less frightening for my young readers?"

"You could just make him handsome," the editor put in. "It's not like it has to be strictly accurate."

"You have flowers in the story, and kids love color," Charlotte said, and sketched a blooming rose over the knight's cheek before showing the historian her tablet. "What about something like this?"

"Can you draw that over his eye?" Seona watched as she modified the sketch. "Yes, perfect. In fact, let's tattoo flowers all over him. I'll change the story to better suit the character."

Charlotte looked down as a drop of red plopped onto the tablet screen. "Ms. Kerrich, you're bleeding."

"We all will." A scarlet dribble seeped down from Seona's full lips as they curved, and three bloody symbols appeared on her brow. Her face shifted into that of Zoey's as it had been when Charlotte had found her body. "That's why he's going to hunt you like an animal, Blondie. Because he doesn't want you to see. He has to stop you, or you'll see everything."

The tablet shattered in Charlotte's hands, and then someone was rubbing her arms, and she opened her eyes to see Darach. She was also standing right in front of the windows with the coverlet wrapped around her, and he had his hands on her arms as if he'd turned her around to face him. Her knees wobbled for a moment, and her heart pounded in her chest as if she'd just run a mile as fast as she could.

"Didnae you hear me call your name?" he asked.

"I'm sorry. I...I had a bad dream." Still slightly disoriented, she brushed the hair back from her face. That was when she saw sunlight on her skin, and realized it lit up the whole room. "It's morning already. It seems like I just went to sleep a few minutes ago."

"Dinnae trouble yourself over such." Darach guided her over to the hearth, and nodded at the rack. "Your clothes, they've dried. I'll leave you to dress, and then take you to the great hall. 'Tis where we'll share the morning meal with the laird and his lady."

Charlotte didn't want him to go, but knew she had to stop being so clingy. "That would be nice, thank you."

After he left she put the coverlet back on the bed and took off the tunic he'd given her. The bruises on her torso looked worse this morning, and her cheek had grown a little more swollen, but her forehead didn't hurt as much. She wished she had a mirror, but since she was in the Middle Ages that was likely out of the question.

*No hair brush, make-up or toothpaste or toothbrush, either.*

Charlotte poured a handful of water from the jug into her hand, and used that to rinse out her mouth. Once she had dressed in her own clothes she unwound the bandage from her head, and touched the gash, which seemed as if it had scabbed over already. She combed her hair with her fingers before she loosely braided it, and bound the end with the hair tie she'd tucked in her pocket last night.

No doubt the laird would want to talk to her again, but Charlotte wanted to speak with his wife, who had gone through this before and came from her time.

*Why would a magic sword rescue an artist? I can't do anything but paint.*

What Seona had said in the dream came back to her in that moment, as if she were answering her from across time.

*He has to stop you, or you'll see everything.*

Since Callum's death Struan had not altered his daily habits to accommodate the duties of a laird; instead he ignored all but the most important and set them to suit himself. The necessary tasks of listening to the daily reports from his patrol captains and steward he accomplished by sharing his morning meal with them in the laird's chamber. It also served to keep the men and his vassals slightly uneasy, which he preferred.

After the captains finished their food and reports

they left, but the steward lingered, looking as if he needed to ask for a beating.

"What is it?" Struan prompted him.

"I summoned the laundress and tanner to question them, my lord, and they now wait in the hall." The steward grimaced. "'Tis only that I cannae put faith in what they've claimed, and I wouldnae waste your time listening to such drivel."

"I shall determine the value of their words," he told the man. "Bring them in."

The steward left and returned with a middle-aged pair who appeared familiar to Struan. The thin, red-handed laundress he recognized as the daughter of one of the clan's weavers, as she had her sire's bulging eyes and hooked, narrow-bridged nose. The tanner from the village, obviously dressed in his best garments, had a deeply flushed face and twin sweat rings under his arms. He looked like a slightly insane brawler who had been redressed to attend a wedding or funeral.

"You first," he said, pointing to the tanner. "What ken you of the trapper who disappeared?"

"Trapper Dugal and me, we come up together as village lads, my lord." The man rolled back his shoulders and puffed out his chest, which strained at the laces of his fine tunic. "Aye, and we've shared a dram of whiskey at week's end for the last twenty year.

When he didnae come to the tavern last week after promising to share a jug, I reckoned him gone for good."

Struan wondered if the tanner had indulged in whiskey before coming to Dun Deigh. "That tells me naught."

"'Tis but I ken Dugal, he wouldnae go willing." The tanner made a helpless gesture in the general direction of the village. "Ever he's been guarding his daughter Revna since his wife left. Never should he leave the lass to starve or worse, for he worships the wee thing. If he ran, he'd take her with him."

Struan nodded, hiding his satisfaction at being correct about the new kitchen maid's sire being the trapper. "Perhaps he met a lady who didnae wish to raise the daughter of another."

"Never, my lord. Dugal yet loved Revna's mam. Never would he glance at another lady." The tanner moved a few steps closer, dropping his voice a little as he said, "He told me on the half-moon that he'd been paid handsome for some work, only 'twas used for something bad. Hanging bad, my lord."

"Och, what could he do but fashion traps and snares?" the steward said, giving him a stern look. "Dinnae spin lies."

"I speak as I cut hide, sure and true," the tanner insisted. "Dugal vowed he didnae ken what he did, 'twould be used for evil. I pressed him for details, but he wouldnae say more. He vowed if he told anyone he'd be killed. And then no' a week after he vanished." He sniffed. "I reckon him dead by the hand of the *maister* who paid him to do such work."

"'Tis all you ken?' Struan asked, and when the man nodded he regarded the steward. "Pay him three day's wages, and feed him before he returns to the village." He waited until the two men left before he regarded the tired-looking laundress. "What shall you tell me of the two maids gone missing?"

She curtseyed again. "I went to their families to ask after them, my lord. They've no' seen either maid since they left the castle. The lassies, they didnae take their leave of their parents, nor pack their belongings. 'Tis as if they'd walked away with but the clothes they wore, and naught else. Their kin reckon they met a rich tinker and run off with him."

He watched her mouth tighten. "You believe differently."

"Gildie, she's five months gone with child, and set to wed the lad who sired her bairn next week," the laundress said. "Brida just bought new boots and a fine new bodice, only to leave them behind and go in her work gown and shoes. When they left 'twas to collect wild berries up on the slopes. I asked every guard on duty that day, and they all vowed the maids never returned."

"You believe they were taken?" he asked.

"Aye, my lord. 'Twould be naught for the MacRoss to grab the lassies if they strayed too near the boundary." Dislike made the woman's skin draw up around her beaky nose. "No matter what those bastarts claim, 'tis proof they killed Mistress Martin."

It seemed his men were not the only ones who blamed the rival clan for everything that went wrong. "How do you reckon thus?"

"Gildie and Brida looked up to Mistress Martin," the laundress said. "Ever they tag-tailed after her, so they ken all about her and Laird Callum. Mayhap Mistress Martin told them of her dallying with the MacRoss laird, too."

"Did they ever speak of such to you?" Struan asked.

"No, but ever they whispered and schemed, the pair." She hesitated before she said, "When Mistress Martin run off with his gold I reckon she paid them help her flee. 'Twould be how Gildie sudden had the coin to offer as dowry and pay for a wedding, and Brida her fine things."

He knew gossip likely fueled the woman's suspicions—hence his steward putting no weight to her claims—and yet it oddly fit with what the tanner had told him.

"'Tis something more you should ken, my lord," the laundress said. "That trapper's wench, Revna, she's like a witless bairn. She doesnae ken to wear slippers and shifts, nor to cover her hair proper. If she keeps flitting about the men so brazen she'll soon end on her back." As if afraid she'd said too much, she quickly bobbed and hurried out.

As Struan mulled over everything his vassals had said, the steward returned and gave him a wary bow.

"You ken why I reckoned their claims unworthy of your time, my lord," the man said. "How should such simple folk become entangled in secret schemes? 'Tis nonsense."

"Aye." Even as he agreed, Struan wondered if the disappearances were something else altogether: murders to silence unwitting accomplices in Athdara and Callum's deaths. "Summon my patrol captains."

CHARLOTTE FOUND DARACH WAITING OUTSIDE IN the passage when she emerged. As she walked up to him it occurred to her that they were exactly the same height, something she hadn't realized last night. If she wanted to kiss him, she'd simply have to take a few steps and lean into him. She'd never thought that way about any man.

*Why is it every time I look at him I want him?*

"I'm sorry that I kept you waiting," she said, swallowing against the dryness in her throat. Why was she behaving like an anxious teenager?

"'Twas worth the wait. You're just as fetching dry as you were drenched," he said, and then grimaced. "Forgive me. The laird's wife says we shouldnae admire a female's appearance, for 'tis benevolent sexism, or some such."

"I won't tell her," Charlotte assured him.

From his chamber he led her through a labyrinth of halls and into an enormous room where dozens of men sat on benches at long tables. So much food had been crammed onto the tables she wondered if even a clan could consume it all. The hearths in this place appeared to be three times the size of the one in Darach's room, and burned with so much heat it came through her coat as she passed one of them. On the wall above one hung a case made from what appeared to be iridescent glass, inside which were hooks like those on which the chieftain had hung the Fire sword in his room.

As soon as the clansmen saw her they stopped eating and talking to stare, which made her only too conscious of her height again. When Darach looked around and scowled at them they went back to their meals while stealing glances at her and murmuring to each other. The maids she saw were all petite to average height. It seemed as if she'd be towering over other women wherever she went in the fourteenth century.

"Pay them no heed," Darach murmured to her. "'Tisnae often they see a woman willing stand so close to the ugliest man in the clan."

That was why everyone was staring at her?

"Then they'd better get used to it." Charlotte tucked her arm through his. "You're my protector, remember?"

The chieftain grinned at her. "Aye, my lady."

"Fair morning, Mistress Walsh." Luthias rose from the table on a raised platform as they approached, and escorted the tiny woman with him over to Charlotte. "May I introduce my wife, Lady Emery?"

"It's just Emery," the petite brunette said, her pale green eyes lighting up with mischief as she added, "Welcome to the time-traveler's club. You and I are the only members. No highlanders allowed."

Charlotte clasped the little hand she offered, smiling politely in return. "It's nice to meet you. You're American?"

Emery nodded. "I'm from New Hampshire. We

share about fifty-eight miles of the border with Canada, so that practically makes us next-door neighbors. Come and sit here by me, and I'll tell you my Fire sword story. Or I could explain the stuff these guys eat for breakfast. They're both pretty weird."

Aware that she remained the center of attention, Charlotte gingerly took the seat beside the laird's wife, who launched into a detailed explanation of the food on the table. At first Emery's vivacious friendliness startled her, but it had been a while since she had been around any Americans. The laird's wife had a gamine quality that reminded her of the fairies she often illustrated. Yet when she looked into her pretty eyes she got the sense that there was a lot more to Emery than what she let people see.

*Not a fairy,* Charlotte thought as Emery breezily described her own rather harrowing trip through time. *You're a fighter.*

Darach, who had sat down on her right, filled a mug with a steaming, herbal-scented drink for her. Opting for some bread and fruit, she then listened as Emery described what it had been like for her when she'd arrived at Dun Lasair.

"Aside from the cool weapons they used, I thought Scottish men during the Middles Ages would have rotting teeth, body lice and boils from the lousy diet and zero personal hygiene," Emery said, chuckling as

Darach, Luthias and the other men at the table gave her appalled looks. "Fortunately the MacRoss are more like medieval male supermodels, quite clean, and very nice. Well, they're a little overprotective, their tempers have short fuses, and they like to settle arguments with fist fights. But otherwise, they're great."

Darach murmured an apology to Charlotte as he rose from the table and went to speak to three men who had just entered the hall.

"I reckon all the females from the future must do naught but ask questions and chatter on and on as my Mery shall," Luthias said to Charlotte, earning a scowl from his wife. "'Twould seem 'tis but her way."

"I'm a scientist. Questioning everything is the job description." Emery stole one of the laird's jam-covered oat cakes. "Anyway, while you're here you'll find out about the downsides of medieval life. No central heating, wool gowns, soap made from wood ash, toothpaste made from burnt herbs, and having to use a privy–" A big hand clamped over her mouth, muffling the rest of her complaints.

A tall man who smelled of smoke and metal loomed over the laird's wife. He had bizarre-looking orange streaks in his black hair, and looked like he wanted to hurt someone.

"No more whining over the privy," he said.

His brutally muscular arms told Charlotte that he could easily snap Emery's neck with one jerk. *Just another thug who thinks he can do whatever he wants to a woman.* Something dark and huge rose inside her as she grabbed the knife from the bread plate. Her chair suddenly fell over as she got up and held the tip of the blade to his neck.

"Take your hands off her," Charlotte told him. "Now."

The man uttered a low laugh and released Emery before he looked down at the knife. "You're quick to make threats, wench." He grabbed hold of her wrist. "Only you cannae cut my throat with such a dull blade."

"Want to see me try?" she countered, moving closer and tightening her grip on the handle.

Suddenly Darach got in front of her and shoved the man away from the table. "Dinnae touch her."

"I like the wench. She fights when she's cornered." The man staggered back as if he'd been punched, and his mouth started bleeding. "'Twas but a jest, Chieftain."

Charlotte hadn't seen Darach hit him, but when she glanced down at his hand she saw blood on his knuckles. How could he have moved that fast?

"Enough." Luthias got up and stepped between

the two men. "Camdyn, go and dine with the guards. Chieftain, attend to your patrollers."

For a moment it looked as if both men would ignore him, and then with one final, ugly glare at each other they went their separate ways.

"It's okay, Charlotte," Emery said, touching her rigid arm. "That's Camdyn, our armorer, and he really was just joking with me. He and I are good friends." She glanced over at the chieftain. "He and Darach, not so much."

"My thanks, Mistress Walsh," Luthias said, new respect in his eyes as he regarded her. "The threat, 'twasnae real, but 'tis good you'd choose to fight than run."

Charlotte stared at the knife in her fist, really seeing it for the first time. She hadn't even consciously decided to pick up the blade; she simply grabbed it like a reflex. The thought that she could have stabbed Camdyn didn't dismay her as much as it should have, either. She made herself put the knife back on the platter and reached down to right her chair before sitting in it.

"Do you have some fighting experience?" Emery asked.

"None at all." She wasn't embarrassed by what she'd done, only angry. She forced herself to smile. "I suppose it was a delayed reaction from being attacked. I don't plan to be in that position ever again."

"Me, I always kick first," Emery assured her. "They never expect that, and it really hurts if you hit their shin bones—or certain parts north of there. Then I either talk my way out, or run away fast and hide. When you're my size those are pretty much the only follow-up options."

"You're lucky." Charlotte glanced down at her food, but her stomach had tied itself into a knot. "I never knew I could be a violent person."

"Well, don't kick yourself for it, okay?" Emery put her small hand over Charlotte's. "From what Luthias told me you've already been through hell. Also, Camdyn shouldn't have done that. He only acts like a big jerk because, well...think of him as being twelve years old and hating girls. That helps explain most of what he does."

Charlotte glanced over at the armorer, who sat eating a bowl of stew. His mouth looked swollen on one side where Darach had punched him. He did look like a sulky boy, but that didn't make her any happier about what she had done. "Excuse me for a moment."

She got up and went over to Camdyn, who rose and looked at her hands as if making sure she didn't carry a knife.

"Truly I didnae mean any harm to our lady, Mistress," he said, sounding a little ashamed of himself now. "'Tis but a long standing jest between us."

"Yes, Emery told me. I'm sorry that I assumed otherwise. My name is Charlotte Walsh." She held out her hand. "I understand that you're the clan's armorer."

"Aye." He clasped her fingers firmly but gently as his gaze shifted over her face. "If you're in need of a weapon or armor, I'm the man to see."

She recalled how good it had been to hold the bread knife in her fist. "I would like something I can carry with me while I'm here. I don't think I can manage a sword, but can you spare a dagger?"

Camdyn smiled, turning his sullen face into a stunning work of art. "Come to the forge when you've time, Mistress, and we'll find one that suits you."

As Fyn Carack entered the garrison hall at Dun Deigh, he saw most of the whiners and complainers gathered before the hearth with their nightly jugs.

"The great hunter returns from stalking the

cleaning wenches," a bitter voice called out. "Come and drink with us, wee brother."

*Wee brother. Wee piglet. Wee, wee, wee, always and ever, eh?*

Fyn allowed his steps to grow unsteady as he gave the group of clansman a sloppy grin. "The no'-laird bid me go to my chamber and mourn the dead laird."

"Aye, 'tis ever all we shall do." The guard drained a goblet before slamming it down on the table. "Pray the Gods dinnae forever curse us for no' taking vengeance on the facking MacRoss."

As Fyn passed them he took note of the face of the one who had called him wee, and then stumbled around the corner. When he saw no other Carack in sight he straightened and moved quickly to open his door, which he took care to slam loudly before he lit two candles inside.

*Home comes the master hunter, home from the killing fields.*

The flames flared, dancing in the polished stone eyes of the fox, boar and stag heads he had stuffed and mounted on his walls. Since going on his first hunt he killed too many animals to display them all—the lot would cover every wall in the stronghold—but he kept the heads of those that had been particularly memorable. The fox had bitten his wrist as it struggled to free itself from the snare, and the stag Callum had failed to take down, which Fyn had hunted for weeks just so he could present the antlers to the laird.

*Keep them, Brother,* Callum had said. *'Tis your trophy, no' mine.*

The boar, his favorite, had taken even longer to die. Sometimes all Fyn had to do was stare into its pebble eyes for a few minutes as he remembered that kill, and his cock would spurt in his trews.

Fyn smiled at the dead things and their eternally silent snarls. Hunting their kin would also please him, but he had other prey to track now. Slipping out of the stronghold unnoticed, and returning without anyone realizing he had gone, however, required some canniness.

*You cannae be seen away from Dun Deigh,* his master had warned him.

Pretending to be pished on whiskey had at first entertained Fyn, for nearly everyone ignored his antics and spoke more freely around him. When he wished to leave the stronghold, however, he had to resort to an elaborate scheme to fool his brothers into believing him sleeping off the drink he never swallowed but poured out the windows and down the drains.

First Fyn had to make a show of drinking too much, and then feign passing out in some place inconvenient for the rest of the clan. One of his brothers would carry him to his chamber and dump him on his bed. Once he was left alone Fyn would arrange a few wads of linen under his coverlet to resemble his sleeping body, pour a bit of the spew he'd collected from the privies on the floor (the smell and sight of the puke would chase off the nosiest vassal) and then use the narrow passage between the stronghold's walls to descend to the back passages. Being forced to wait there for sunset before he crept out like some rodent made him impatient, as did avoiding Struan's patrols and the watchers until he could reach the entrance to the mines.

Once the miners left for the night, however, Fyn could use the shafts to go wherever he wished.

He might have tolerated a few days or even a week of the ruse, but after refusing to be named the new laird Struan had declared the entire clan would remain at the stronghold and mourn Callum in the old way, from one full moon to the next. Only patrols, guards and the household vassals would be permitted to carry out their daily duties.

*What of mine?*

The prospect of being unable to return to his work made Dun Deigh seem more like a cage than a castle to Fyn. He found himself picking fights with the youngest scullery lads and tormenting the wenches, all of whom feared him, but even that secretive toying wasn't enough to satisfy his needs. He wanted a spear and net in his hand and a mount between his legs, and the cool shadows of the forest caressing him as he stalked his prey. He wanted to drive something terrified into one of his hollow traps, and watch their eyes close as they succumbed to the dreamstone he had strewn in the pits.

*Aye, and put their flesh and blood in my hands.*

Leaving one candle burning by his bed, Fyn carried the other over to the pelt rack in one corner. Setting it aside, he slid back a panel of wood he'd painted to resemble stone to reveal the opening behind it. He had been only a lad when he'd found the passage, thanks to being locked away by his bitch *màthair*, who likely would have left him to starve if the old laird had not missed the ptarmigan he always brought for the winter meals.

*You're no' like the other lads, Fyn. You're quick and keen, like my boot knife. 'Tis why I named you thus.*

His slim build permitted him to walk through the narrow space between the walls as if it were a passage made specially for him. Although he had stood much taller, the old laird had shared the same narrow shoulders and hips, so Fyn knew he had first used them. They had allowed him to suddenly appear where his sons and vassals had least expected him.

He passed a post in which he had carved as a lad.

Instead of FYN he'd chiseled into the wood what he considered now his true name. Forever he had vowed to be his sire's finest hunter, hiding himself from everyone so that he could strike as the old laird had, as silent and cold as death.

Fyn listened before he opened another false-fronted panel door and stepped out into the back passage used for deliveries from the mines. The stone floor sparkled with bits of crystal ground beneath the cart wheels that had trundled over them for centuries. He eyed a bit of dreamstone that had fallen into a crack in the stones, and crouched for a moment to pry it loose and pocket the gem.

*You neednae a sage's elixir for the pit traps,* his master had assured him. *You've but to grind the dreamstone to powder, and scatter it under a layer of dead leaves. When your prey falls into the hollow, they shall breathe in the dust and soon fall into deep slumber. Only take care to remove them before rain comes. Any moving water that touches their lips shall revive them at once.*

Creeping out of the stronghold, Fyn checked for any guards before hurrying over to the shed built over the ore hoist for the Carack mines. There he listened to be sure none of the clan's vassals or sages had lingered before he climbed down the rope and moved into the shafts.

Aside from the forest, Fyn most loved the stone

tunnels of the mines, and how their walls glittered with tiny traces of the wealth his clan had dug out of them. He decided to check on the recently-dug shaft where new dreamstone had been found, and saw that the men had removed nearly all of the gold discovered with it. He took out a small pick, and used it to dislodge several chunks of the rainbow-streaked crystal, which he dropped in his pocket. The miners would notice the missing crystals, of course, but believe one of their own had filched them, and say nothing to the overseer. Indeed, some of them might even begin tucking some gems in their beards and boot sole gaps to do the same.

Who would suspect a Carack to be the one stealing from the Carack?

Once he had the dreamstone he needed, Fyn left the shaft and walked down the oldest tunnel to a second level that had been abandoned after proving devoid of precious gems and metals. There he moved aside an L-shaped strut that covered a gap in the stone wall, and squeezed through it into another, far older passage.

A coldfire orb sat under a dark cloth atop the old work bench, and when Fyn removed the cloth he saw a note had been left under the ever-burning light. On one side a likeness of a female he had never seen had been sketched on the parchment, and on the other his master had left him instructions.

*The Fire sword brought another wench from the future to Dun Lasair last night. She's tall, pale haired and wounded. Bring her to the sacrarium before the full moon, and put her in the holding place. Dinnae fail me, my son.*

To keep from shrieking with joy Fyn bit his tongue, and then took out his firesteel to set the parchment alight. Watching the note burn to a curl of ash, he imagined all the ways in which he might play with the new wench. The master would first do things to her, of course, to make her confess her secrets, but watching that was almost as much fun as taking his turn.

*She'll tell you naught, you scabby gowk. Aye, for her laughter shallnae permit her speak.*

The sound of the dead hoor's whisper made Fyn draw his blade and turn around slowly. He knew she could not be there—he'd watched her corpse burn—but lately he had been hearing her voice taunting him from the shadows. He'd sown salt all over his chamber, which kept her out so he could sleep, but he'd used the last of it in the sacrarium after finishing his latest tasks for the master.

"Come out, you slut," he muttered, peering into the dark end of the tunnel. "I dinnae fear you. Struan himself scattered your ashes. You cannae hurt me again."

*You reckon you're safe?* A cackle of bitter laughter came from the opposite direction. *I wish I'd done more than kick your skinny arse. Dinnae you fear your master shall bring me back from the shadow realm to hunt you, you wee piglet?*

Icy sweat trickled down the sides of Fyn's face. "'Twasnae my desire to end you. I didnae wish you dead. I...I gave you aid, didnae I?"

*You caged me, and starved me, and made me watch you night after night while you spewed all that filth in my ears about your hunts. Then you brought me to the shearing barn, and watched him drown me in the dub. You even carried my body to the river so Callum would find what 'twas left of me.*

At one time Fyn had been convinced he'd loved her, which was why he had pleaded with the master to spare her.

"Forgive me, please." His hand shook as he sheathed his dagger. "I didnae wish you to die, nor Callum to burn. 'Twas the master's doing, and I cannae go against him, for you ken what he'll do to me."

His voice echoed around him in the empty tunnel, and for a moment Fyn thought she might have gone. Then he heard her again, this time inside his skull.

*I shall haunt you forever unless you do as I told you. Give the wench to him, but find the sain.*

"Any Carack who touches the Fire sword shall die," Fyn protested.

*No' the facking blade,* Athdara Martin said. *The other sain. The one made by Prince Kaer.*

## Chapter Five

Darach sent his senior captains to oversee the men training in the lists, and then looked over at Charlotte, who sat listening to the laird. After speaking with Camdyn she still looked too pale, and during the night the bruise on her cut cheek had spread up to her eye. He wanted to carry her back to his chamber and put her to bed, and spend the rest of the day pampering and watching over her. He also wanted very much to go to their dolt of an armorer, drag him out the lists and pound him into the straw-strewn dirt.

Yet for the first time since the two of them had begun clashing as lads he wondered if it would end with only a beating.

"Camdyn meant no harm, Chieftain," a deep voice

said. "And 'twould appear that the lady can well look after herself."

Darach regarded Taveon. "You didnae see the lady last night when she fell from the sky, her face bloodied and that facking sword in her trembling hand."

The war master glanced over at Charlotte. "She no longer trembles, Brother, nor does she cower when threatened, as now we ken." He smiled a little. "Although from what I saw she cannae hope to match you now for quickness. That clout you gave Cam, 'twas mayhap a boon from the Fire sword?"

"Aye. When I took the blade from Charlotte an enchantment swept over me. Now when I move"—he lowered his voice—"I wonder if I'll blink and end up in a loch."

"We need test the bounds of your boon, then." Taveon nodded toward the arch leading down to the castle's lower levels. "Come down with me to my training chamber."

"I dinnae wish to leave the lady alone for long," he warned.

"Our Emery shall keep her ears filled with chatter all morning." His mouth hitched. "Or should you rather learn how powerful you've become the next time you reach for Mistress Walsh, and instead knock her through a wall?"

Darach followed the war master down the stairs and past the dungeons to the big room he used for his own weapons practice. Because Taveon's weakness left him unable to touch metal, everything inside had been fashioned of wood, leather or stone. Two corded bundles of straw on poles provided targets for his solitary practices, and from the mounds of shorn hay on the floor he likely didn't often miss.

"Toss a dagger at the form," the war master suggested.

Darach pulled his shortest blade from his boot, and threw it at the straw target. It moved so fast it blurred, and yet pierced the center as it would any other time.

"Catch." Taveon hurled something at his face, and smiled as he snatched the whetstone out of the air. "So you've grown faster, yet no' especially stronger. An interesting boon." He tossed him a wooden staff. "Disarm and we shall spar."

As he pulled off his tartan and set aside his weapons, Darach wondered if Taveon meant to do more than simply test him.

"If you're angry with me for hitting Camdyn," he said as he stepped into the circle chalked on the stone floor, "you may bring him out to the lists tonight. 'Tis long past time we settled our differences."

"'Tis on you to arrange that match, Brother." The war master spun his staff in his hands, feigning a show before he tried to sweep Darach's feet out from under him. The loud clack of the staffs colliding came as he blocked the blow. "Camdyn doesnae wish serve in the forge. Never shall he."

This again, he thought, growing angry now.

"I didnae beg the laird choose me his second, nor ever once wish to command the garrison." He twirled the staff to fend off two more blows, and the wood spun so fast it blurred in the air. "Aye, and I'd be in the forge now if Luthias had named me armorer, and no doubt happier. Only I've no' Camdyn's skill with smithing, and you ken as much."

Taveon dodged a hit. "You reckon forging, 'tis the lad's only talent?"

"Ask Luthias why he chose as he did," Darach countered. "Well-forged weapons, they're as vital to the clan as commanding the men. We each of us serve where we do best for our brothers and the vassals."

Going on the offensive, he used the ends of the staff to drive Taveon backward. When the war master countered the move by spinning to one side Darach retreated, watching his brother's pale face as they circled each other again.

"You're ten times as fast now," Taveon said. "Your

control, 'tis as good as 'twas before the sain empowered you. Yet I'll wager 'tis a price to such."

"I ken ever you've favored Camdyn over me, and yet never once took you his side over mine." Darach slammed his staff into the war master's, knocking it from his grip. "'Tis why I respect you."

"Just as I ken should you truly lose your temper you'd likely kill Camdyn." He glanced down at the wood Darach had pressed to his knee. "I'd rather yield than limp for the rest of summer. May I?" He held out his hand, and when he gave him the staff he ran his palm along the length of it. "Your gift, 'tis no' without cost, Chieftain."

Darach repeated his gesture, and where he touched the wood it seemed very hot, as if it meant to burst into flame. "'Tisnae from enchantment, surely."

"'Tis the speed of your movements. The staff becomes a spindle, and the air and my staff act against it as a hearth board. Had we sparred longer, I reckon the wood, 'twould have begun smoldering." Taveon examined the length of the staff. "What of your hands and body? Your skin, 'tis feverish?"

"No." He'd barely worked up a sweat. "If I must, I shall fight only with steel. 'Twillnae melt."

"Dinnae spar with the lads until you've mastered control over this quickness. You cannae see your own moves, and may break bones before you realize how hard you've struck." The war master picked up his staff. "Camdyn shall use Mistress Walsh to bait you. You shouldnae notice his jigging nor swallow his hook, for the lady may end the one entangled."

"Aye." Darach dragged a hand through his hair. "Ken you the true cause, then?"

"I suspect 'tis Ailsa MacAnvoy, made worse when she refused to wed the Tolmach," Taveon said, looking grim now. "Luthias shall say naught, but she didnae break the betrothal because Laith's a stinking old man with a big gob and a wee tadger. 'Twas for love."

He frowned. "You pair Camdyn with Ailsa? He hates females."

"'Tis all on Ailsa. The laird didnae wish me to ken thus, but she's sent a scroll in secret every week for the last year, begging Luthias accept their love, and permit Cam wed her." He sighed. "Aye, and she's vowed to wait for him until he seeks her sire's blessing. 'Tis driving the armorer mad."

Of all the excuses for the armorer's frayed temper, that was not one he would have guessed. "Why should Camdyn give his heart to the MacAnvoy's daughter?"

"He vows he never did," the war master said. "He swore to Luthias he's but seen the lass once at a clan gathering a decade past, and then only from afar. He's never spoken a word with her. Yet to read those scrolls she sends, 'tis as if they've been lovers in secret these ten years. The laird believes him, as do I."

Darach winced. "Ailsa's off her head, then."

"She's lived a sheltered life, thanks to her sire," Taveon said. "I reckon she lost her heart to Cam at first sight, and convinced herself he had done the same. Regardless, she wants no other man but our armorer, who cannae wed her, nor ever wished to."

"The laird need only speak to Ramsay..." He stopped as he saw the larger issue and rubbed the back of his neck. "Och, for fack's sake."

"Aye, you now recall how the MacAnvoy worships his daughter with uncommon ferocity, and would go to war with any who speak against the lass, as he nearly did the Tolmach," Taveon said, nodding. "'Tis why Luthias forced Laith settle with Ramsay over the broken betrothal, and doesnae punish Cam for his foul moods."

Darach's anger turned to a grudging sympathy. "How can I help?"

"You're the other thorn in Camdyn's side," the war master pointed out. "Dinnae prod him. I shall do what I may and keep him far from Mistress Walsh and you."

What Taveon had told him stayed in Darach's

thoughts as he returned to the great hall to find the men gone and the maids clearing the tables. A cluster of young sages stood beneath the empty crystal crypt where the clan had kept the Fire sword for centuries, and came rushing toward him as soon as they saw him.

"Hold, lads," he told them as they all tried to speak at the same time, and pointed to the one who looked calmest. "You, tell me what 'tis the matter."

"We went to the spring this morning to collect moss for Elder Sgur, Chieftain," the sage said. "He wishes make torch heads that never burn out." He held out a large, strapped black bag with toothed pockets. "'Twas there we found this hanging from a branch over the water, and reckoned 'twould belong to the lady brought back by the sain."

Darach took the bag, which weighed more than he expected. "You've no' poked about inside, I hope?" As the sages all hung their heads he sighed. "Did you put back everything you removed?"

"Oh, aye, Chieftain, we wouldnae filch from the lady." The sage grimaced as he held out a large book with a fine coil of metal binding the pages. "Only we cannae fathom how she made this."

He opened the book, which contained page after page of delicately-tinted, finely detailed paintings. Some depicted animals dressed like people; others showed fantastic scenes with young bairns at play. Some smaller sketches had been clipped to some of the pages, and some other glossy images that had to be what Emery had called photographs. One showed Charlotte standing in front of a window filled with books.

"That one, Chieftain." The sage tapped the photograph. "'Tisnae painted nor drawn, and yet 'tis like a tiny window through which we see the lady in her time. Reckon you 'tis some form of magic?"

"The future holds many wonders that we cannae ken," Darach told him as he closed the sketchbook and tucked it back in the bag. "Dinnae fear such things. They're harmless, I promise you."

"We're no' afraid," another sage said. "We wish to ken more of Mistress Walsh and her bag of wonders." He leaned close and whispered, "Please ask her speak with us, Chieftain. We've so many questions."

He chuckled and shouldered the bag. "Aye, so you do."

CHARLOTTE WALKED WITH EMERY THROUGH THE kitchen gardens, admiring the bounty of vegetables, fruits and herbs being grown by the clan's vassals. The abundance provided a rich spectrum of deep greens, reds and yellows; in this time everything seemed to grow much bigger and brighter than in the future. If she stayed she might be able to make her own paints from the local botanicals.

*I'm staying.*

As the sun warmed her shoulders and she breathed in the pure, cool air she still found herself watching for any sudden movement around them. She knew the monster in her own future remained at a very safe distance—the Moss Park Butcher wouldn't even be born for another seven hundred years—and yet she couldn't shake the sense that someone was still watching her.

"Penny for your thoughts," Emery said. "Which are currently made of silver, by the way, and worth about five hundred bucks each in our time."

The laird's wife had been unrelentingly friendly, and seemed sincere about wanting to help her adjust to life at Dun Lasair. She was probably also lonely, and happy to have someone to talk to who understood everything she said. That thought made Charlotte wonder how Emery had grown so at home in such a primitive era, surrounded by people who had no idea what her life had been like in the twenty-first century.

"How long did it take you to get used to all this?" she asked.

Emery smiled. "All this as in living in the Middle Ages, or being dragged through time to save the clan when you don't have a clue how to do that?"

The way the petite scientist put things made Charlotte wish she could laugh, but the killer had taken that from her, too. "Ah, both."

"I assimilated pretty fast, but I studied this time period for years before the Fire sword grabbed me," the other woman admitted. "Medieval Scottish highlanders were also integral to my thesis, so I was plenty prepped for them and their way of life. You're still not a hundred percent sure this is happening, right? Don't worry about that. I was the same way for the first week or so."

Charlotte stopped in front of a bed of vibrant crimson flowers. "I illustrate fairytales, so magic isn't entirely unfamiliar. It always seemed a bit like religion to me. Unfortunately I'm not a believer—or, at least, I wasn't."

"Starting to acquire some faith, huh?" Emery wrinkled her nose. "I struggled most with embracing what is completely outside all science and logic, but actually living through this experience has a way of convincing your skeptical side. You'll definitely get what I mean as you experience more Middle Ages perks, like the joy of the privy."

"I discovered that perk this morning." She

stopped and stooped down to watch a fat bumblebee alight on a broad red petal. "Why do you think the sword chose me? Other than very general skills I don't have any practical or useful knowledge. I doubt I can save the clan by painting something. It doesn't make any sense."

"It won't, and then suddenly out of the blue it will," Emery told her. "You came here because you can do something no one else can—that's according to the clan's Fire Sword legend, anyway. When it's time for you to do your thing, you'll see what it is. For me, I had to use my forensic knowledge to prove a suicide was actually a murder. There's just one thing I need to warn you about when it's wish time. Don't ask to go to a time in the future that is earlier than when you left."

"I don't want to go back at all." She frowned. "Why do you think I would?"

"You might be tempted to try and warn yourself, or prevent your friend from being murdered." The laird's wife sighed. "Being anywhere near an earlier version of yourself would create a temporal paradox. Theoretically it's not possible, but with Fae magic nothing makes scientific sense. It's the kind of thing that could tear reality apart."

"Just like in the movies, I suppose." Charlotte

nodded. "What started all this time-traveling, anyway?"

Emery told her briefly about the long-standing rivalry between the MacRoss and a hostile neighboring clan called the Carack, and how a killer had manipulated both lairds into nearly going to war. Emery credited everything to the forensic evidence she had uncovered, but Charlotte got the sense that there was a lot more to the story than she was telling her. She also knew she wouldn't get her to be more candid by accusing the other woman of withholding information.

"Your area of expertise is art," the laird's wife said, "so it's logical that however you can save the clan would be related to that skill set and knowledge."

"I keep thinking of that book I illustrated." She straightened and glanced back at the stronghold. "I painted the Fire sword and a character who looked just like Darach, and that can't be a coincidence. Some fairytales like Snow White and Bluebeard are based on real people, and some actual events."

"You said a historian wrote the book, right? Maybe she based some of it on what's happening now or in the near future. You're also the only person in this time who has read the book." Emery snapped her fingers. "There's one way to check. Do you remember the story well enough to write it down?"

"I believe so. I'll need pen and ink and paper, or the medieval equivalent." Charlotte heard footsteps approaching and turned around to see Darach with her messenger bag on his shoulder. "Or maybe not. Chieftain, that's mine. Where did you find it?"

"Some sage lads spied the bag hanging from a tree by the spring, my lady." He stopped and handed it to her. "I'm sorry to say they first looked through your belongings, but they promised me they didnae take anything."

"That's all right." She hugged the bag against her chest. "Emery, is there someplace with a desk or a table where I can work?"

"Sure. The clan's map room is nice and quiet, and there's plenty of light." The laird's wife regarded Darach. "I promised Luthias I'd ride down to the village with him right after I gave Charlotte the gardens tour. Would you take her there and set her up with whatever she needs for her work?"

"Of course, my lady." The chieftain bowed.

"Good man." Emery winked at Charlotte. "See you later."

"I'm sorry," Charlotte said as she walked back into the castle with Darach. "Once I learn my way around Dun Lasair I won't impose on you so much."

"Ah, so you wish to avoid me now." He nodded as if he'd expected as much. "I reckoned you'd soon grow weary of my company." He gave her a sideways look. "Or mayhap 'tis my face that tries your patience."

"Lady Emery tires me out," she said, opting for blunt honesty over politeness. "I'm more comfortable around quiet people like you. I also know you have better things to do than serve as my personal escort."

"I'm your protector, Charlotte, for as long as you stay," he reminded her. "I promised you that."

She wanted to tell him to assign her to someone else, someone who didn't have so many responsibilities. Yet in her heart she wanted to be selfish, and have him stay by her side for as long as she could. Just being close to him made her relax, and when she looked at him she forgot about the terrors and horrors that she had faced in her time. With Darach she could be herself, the way she had been before this nightmare had begun.

"If this becomes unmanageable, please tell me," Charlotte said as he led her through a passage to a tower staircase, and then followed him up. "I don't want to be a nuisance."

Darach didn't say anything as he opened a door halfway up the stairs, and gestured for her to go inside. Small glass balls filled with blue glowing light illuminated the chamber, which had several tables and many racks and shelves of scrolls. He closed the door as he came in, and then went to uncover the narrow windows.

"With all the parchment we cannae bring any flame inside the chamber," he told her, and then rolled up a map on the center table and set it aside. "The sun, 'tis past zenith, so the windows shall provide good light until sunset. I shall return when 'tis time for the evening meal."

*Does he have to be in such a hurry to get away from me? Maybe I am nothing but a nuisance to the man.*

A strange irritation came over Charlotte as she set down her bag, and then went around the table to stand before him. "Don't bother. You can just send one of the maids to get me. Emery said there are plenty."

"'Tisnae any trouble for me to escort you, my lady," he said, and took a step back.

"I'm already a problem for you, aren't I? Because of other issues I don't know about, and whatever else you've decided to keep from me." She waited, and when he said nothing she nodded. "Just admit it."

His jaw tightened. "You've endured too much, and I dinnae wish add to your troubles or worries."

"You offer one truth to avoid another." She moved closer, until only a few inches separated them. "I'm not as stupid as you think. There is more to this than what you and the laird told me. Emery explained about the hostility between your clan and the Carack, and the murder of that jewel-setter being blamed on Luthias so the clans would go to war. You still haven't caught whoever killed her, right?"

Darach shook his head.

"I can't force you to be honest with me." She stepped back. "I can look after myself from now on. You can go, Chieftain."

He didn't move for a few moments, which she understood. She wanted badly to apologize for being so unpleasant and pushing him away. She also wanted to smack him for keeping her in the dark.

Still not saying a word, Darach reached out and pulled her into his arms.

Charlotte froze. When he bent his head and kissed her, she just stood like a statue. This sort of thing never happened to her, so she had no idea how to react. Should she shove him away? She should. Just because he had held her and soothed her and carried her around he had no right to manhandle her whenever he wanted.

The hot hunger of his mouth on hers melted through her shock and surprise, making all of her senses come alive with a vengeance.

Darach held the back of her head with his hand as he kissed her so deeply the heat of him seemed to surge down into her breasts and belly. She was a modern woman, not some medieval ninny too ignorant to stand up for herself, only she could not turn off her body. She wanted his hands as well as his mouth on her. Her thighs knotted as she went wet between them, and her sex swelled and throbbed like the sweetest, most unbearable wound.

*He wants me as much as I want him, but we can't do this. Not here, not now.*

The kiss ended by some strange unspoken agreement, with first their lips parting and then their hands dropping and their bodies moving back from each other. For a moment the chieftain looked as if he didn't recognize her now.

Inside she reeled, aghast and ablaze. *One kiss and he destroys me like this.*

"Forgive me," Darach said, his marked eye looking like a bloodstained coin as he walked past her and left the room.

"Oh, Darach." Charlotte abruptly sat down at the table, her mouth still tender and hot from the ferocity of his, and propped her head against her hand. "I don't think I can do that."

After a few minutes she regained some of her composure, and unzipped her bag. Taking out everything to see if anything had been damaged during her trip through time, she soon discovered she'd been lucky again. The box in which she kept her watercolor pans, brushes, pencils and pens remained intact, and water hadn't gotten into the bag, so her sketchbook and field journal hadn't been ruined. The notepad she used to jot down notes during meetings with publishers wasn't the one she'd used when she'd met with Seona Kerrich, but it had plenty of blank pages. She even had a handful of ballpoint pens for writing.

She unzipped one bulging pocket she didn't remember stuffing with anything, and found a bundle of toffee bars with plaid wrappers, along with a note.

*Blondie,*

*I know you always forget to eat when you're out and about, so here's a stash of my fav candy. It's as hard as a rock, so smash the bar on something before you open the wrapper to break it into pieces.*

*Also, don't freak out about this chucklehead who's been harassing you, okay? You've done nothing to deserve his crap. The OOP will nab him and he'll go to jail, and then you and I will party until dawn. If you'll lend me your black boots to go with my gray leather mini-skirt. I don't have legs that go on forever like yours. Wait, why do I hang out with you, anyway?*

*Right—because you're the best friend I've ever had in my whole life. Maybe I'll start stalking you.*

*XOXO,*
*Z*

CHARLOTTE STARED AT THE NOTE FOR A LONG TIME. All the guilt that had been crushing her slowly dissolved, thanks to the reminder of how much the other artist had cared about her. She would always regret how Zoey had died, but she had been a loving friend. If the situation had been reversed, and her friend had found her dead, Zoey would never have blamed herself. The horrors the stalker had inflicted on her had made Charlotte forget that.

*All right, so we're good now, Blondie,* her friend's ghost whispered from her memories. *Just remember what's important: I loved you.*

She placed the candy back in the pocket along with the note. "Love you, too, Zoe."

Chapter Six

༺❦༻

In the laboratorium at Dun Deigh, Master Sage Reothadh gazed at the ruins heaped atop the largest work table. Most of the distillation bottles and tubes had melted during the making of the disaster; a sizeable pile of glittering white sludge produced by it still gave off wisps of steam. Here and there he saw cooling stones had been dropped to contain the spillage, each crystallized now like rough diamonds. The work he needed done would now have to wait until this disaster could be remedied and the fixtures replaced.

The smell of the mess had mostly dissipated, but a trace of scorched metal, singed hair and panicked sweat lingered.

"Alert the other guards," Reothadh told the two

Carack who had rushed into the chamber with him. "The stench doesnae come from a fire."

"Master," a hesitant voice said as a young sage with soot-strained robes approached him. "I can explain."

"My uncle had no head for alchemy," Reothadh said as he bent down to pick up a piece of shattered tubing. "He near poisoned the other apprentices when he passed around the only tonic he ever concocted. Every scroll he handled became torn, smudged or lost. He wasted so much crystal the losses set back the enclave's work for a full season. Yet for all the chaos he caused before leaving the enclave to shepherd, my brother never destroyed all that he touched." He finally looked at the anxious young man beside him. "Should I send you tend sheep, when I ken you're likely to kill off a full herd?"

"Too much sun gives me rash, Master," Geamhradh said in an uncharacteristically timid tone. The tall, heavyset apprentice stood an arm's length from Reothadh, and shifted his considerable weight from one foot to the other as he spoke. "Permit me explain. I reckoned to blend an elixir to crack stone. 'Twasnae meant to dissolve glass and crockery."

"They're the same as stone, you eejit." His younger brother, Fuachd, made a contemptuous sound. Short, thin and rather unkempt, he came to the master sage's other side to peer at the table. "I told you dinnae add the borecrystal to the white gold when 'tis roiling, but would you listen? As ever, no."

"You ken naught of my methods," Geamhradh snapped. "Nor could you, with your nose ever stuck in a scroll while I–"

"Guards," Reothadh called out, and glanced over at the door as two Carack sentinels came in. "Drag these two dolts to the dungeons. Lock them in the same cell, for they may do me the favor of strangling each other before they starve. Then leave their bodies there for the rats and voles."

As one of the men grabbed him Fuachd uttered a squeaking cry of alarm. "Master, please. I took no part in Geam's nonsense."

"'Twas by Lord Struan's bidding I attempted the blend, Master, I vow," his brother added quickly as the other guard clamped a hand on his shoulder. "He wished the elixir made."

"Only he bid you tell the Master, no' make the blend yourself," Fuachd said.

Geamhradh swatted at the smaller sage. "Hold your tongue."

Reothadh rubbed his brow, and then recalled a very good reason not to send the pair down to the dungeons. To the guards he said, "I've changed my mind. Take these eejits to the stable master. Say they're now his, and set them to muck out the stalls and attend to any other work he wants done."

"For how long should he use them thus, Master?" one guard asked.

"Until I no longer wish to kill them." He looked at the table again. "Winter next, mayhap."

Once the quarreling brothers had been marched off, the enclave's wrights came in with several apprentices to clean up the mess and salvage any equipment that remained undamaged. For a time Reothadh helped, but what the stout sage had said kept echoing in his thoughts.

"I must go and speak to Lord Struan," he told his wrights. "Dinnae discard the mixture yet. Once it cools place it in a wooden bucket. I wish to examine the stuff later."

From the laboratorium Reothadh made his way down to the lower levels of Dun Deigh, where he followed a narrow passage to a room between two large cisterns kept full by channeling water from a nearby loch. They also cooled the chamber between them, where he knocked on the door and waited until a flinty voice bid him enter.

Inside the chamber Struan stood studying a map

pinned to one wall. Covered in sweat, the war master wore only a pair of damp trews. Nearby several buckets of cold water stood, with sponges floating in them.

Reothadh pitied the war master, who had to spend three moons each year closeted in this chamber during the days. From his sire he had inherited a weakness that left him incapable of tolerating heat; during the summer months his pale skin would blister the moment he ventured outside the keepe.

"Forgive the intrusion, my lord," Reothadh said. "I should wait until nightfall, but 'tis been a mishap in the lab. The younger lads attempted to blend the rock-cracking elixir themselves before informing me of your request."

Struan used a sliver of charcoal to mark a spot on the wall map. "The younger lads being those two sage brothers ever at each other's throats, I'll wager. I heard them bickering just after I told them ask you."

"They've good intentions," he said, sighing. "'Tis what shall end me, I reckon. But why ask you for a stone-cracking wash? The miners, they've hit granite again?"

"'Tis no' for the shafts they now work." The war master stepped back from the wall and gestured for him to come closer. "We once mined in the places

I've marked, only my sire abandoned them all just before he died. Callum reckoned they'd filled with blackdamp, but I'm no' so sure 'twas the reason."

"Over time near every mine amasses so much bad air that they become unsafe for the men," Reothadh murmured. "Just as the coal miners must beware of firedamp in their shafts. You ken that time doesnae improve such conditions, my lord."

"Aye, 'twould be dangerous to send teams into the old tunnels, unless we might first vent them. Yet we cannot dig down with picks and chisels, else the shaft collapse." Struan tapped one mark on the map. "If we weaken the overlying stone in a small spot, mayhap no' bigger than a hand, we might drill down to make vent holes."

"With care, 'tis possible." The sage hesitated before he asked, "Why should you wish again work shafts abandoned long ago? 'Tis unlikely they yet hold any veins of value, and most border the boundaries... ah. The MacRoss ken them to be long abandoned. They'd never expect them used again."

The war master gazed at him for a long time. "Repeat naught of what I've said, Sage, else I relieve you of your duties—and your head."

His throat tightened, and he bowed low. "Aye, my lord."

After leaving the map room Darach asked a guard to stand watch at the base of the tower stairs, and then returned to the lists to see the last of the day's matches. A battered Kyal had a bleeding Wal in a grappling hold, and both panted heavily as they kicked at each other in vain attempts to sweep a leg. The taste of Charlotte still lingered on Darach's mouth; he could still smell the maddening womanly scent of her on his hands and tunic. He pretended to watch the bout while he fought the pounding need to return to the tower, drag her onto the table and bury himself inside her.

"'Twould seem an even match, Chieftain." Ameron came to stand beside him, and wiped some sweat from his upper lip. "Our lord and lady, they've no' returned yet from the village. The war master, he's in the forge with the armorer. Since the morning meal most of the clan's fallen in love with Mistress Walsh."

He grunted. "They're but tickled to watch a lady put a blade to Camdyn's neck."

"Ah, no, Chieftain." The guard gave him a wry look. "You've no' looked at Mistress Walsh in the light of day?"

Darach wondered if clouting the back of his head would end his prattling. "I ken she's lovely, lad."

"Had I a chance to win her heart, I'd kneel at her feet and confess my devotion now." Ameron winced as Kyal went down, but then grinned as he rolled and pinned Wal beneath him. "None would go near Lady Emery, for she's wee and adorable, like a young sister to us. Aye, and we saw from the start she wanted none but our lord."

"Say what you mean," Darach demanded.

"'Tis said Mistress Walsh doesnae wish to return to her time," the guard said. "She's tall and fair and as fetching as a Fae princess. Should she wish to stay with one of us, and become immortal like Lady Emery, well." He moved his shoulders. "What lad among us wouldnae leap at the chance to wed such a lady?"

Darach took a step toward the circle to call an end to the match, and heard something like a bow string twang, and then a whistle. On instinct he reached out and grabbed an iron-tipped bolt out of the air a moment before it buried itself in the guard's eye.

"By the Gods." Ameron stumbled backward, his expression horrified.

"Who fired a crossbow in the lists?" Darach demanded as he strode forward, looking at all the men. None held any weapons, so he looked up at the top of the curtain wall and shouted, "Watch captain, attend me."

The captain of the wall sentinels looked over the edge at him.

"Aye, Chieftain." He frowned at the bolt Darach held up. "We've no archers on the inner wall or towers. They man the outer wall and gates." His eyes narrowed. "That, 'tisnae a MacRoss bolt."

"Kyal, Wal, Cinead, Tamhas, arm yourselves and search outside the gates. The rest of you, to the walls. Check every trail from the stronghold into the woods. Bring in anyone you find, crossbow or no'." Darach turned to Ameron, who looked ashen now. "Go into the hall and wait by the hearth, lad. Muir, go with him and keep your blade at hand."

"Aye, Chieftain." Muir took the shaken guard inside, and the other men scattered.

Darach returned to the spot where he and Ameron had been standing, and looked carefully in the direction from which the bolt had flown. No one should have been able to shoot into the lists because the wall blocked it off on two sides, and the stronghold did the same on the others. Whoever had fired had been concealed inside the lists.

He ran to the straw targets lined up against the wall, and began pulling them down one by one, tearing them apart. The third seemed too heavy, and smelled of something burnt.

Taveon trotted up to him. "Someone attacked us inside the wall?"

"A bolt, fired at Ameron from here." Darach ripped the target in half, exposing the crossbow concealed inside the straw. It had been fired, and the catch and part of the stock appeared scorched. He went behind the target pole, where he crouched down over a small pile of glittering ash.

"Dinnae touch the bow or the ash," he warned the war master as he joined him. "Kindling stone, 'twas placed on the crossbow to slow-burn the catch so the bolt 'twould fly only after the bastart left the lists."

"Who should wish Ameron dead?" Taveon asked.

"'Twasnae meant for him. Look." Darach straightened and regarded the spot. "Ever I stand in that position while watching the matches. 'Tis where I may see all the sparring circles. Ameron walked up to me a few moments before the crossbow fired."

"Such treachery stinks of Carack scheming," the war master muttered. "I'll tell the laird. Until we find the assassin, you should remain inside the keepe." He rubbed the back of his neck. "And it begs me ask again: Who should wish you dead?"

"Every enemy we count. My death, 'twould dishearten the garrison, challenge the truce, and distract you and our brothers from..." He stopped and looked at Taveon. "Charlotte."

They both took off at a flat run into the stronghold.

AFTER THE EMOTIONAL OVERLOAD OF BEING KISSED by Darach and finding Zoey's note along with the candy, Charlotte gratefully focused on writing what she remembered of The Rose Knight, Seona Kerrich's fairytale. Vaguely she recalled the strange dedication—*from the last of my line to those who may someday wonder*—and the opening paragraph, which she wrote on her notepad.

*Long ago in a land where magic was as real and pure as sunlight and water, a fairy prince and a beautiful lady of the highlands fell in love. Although they knew they could not stay together forever, for only the prince was immortal, they could not bear to be parted. After they married in the prince's garden, which he filled with enchanted flowers, they gathered all of their dear ones to live in the prince's castle. In time, when the prince's wife gave birth to his son, their dear ones brought flowers from the garden and lay them all around the boy in his cradle.*

Charlotte stopped there, set down her pen and rubbed her temples with her fingertips. Although she was sure of that much, she drew a blank on what came next. On impulse she took out her sketchbook and started recreating the drawing she had done for the first illustrated page, which showed the prince and his wife standing over their baby's flower-filled cradle.

"You weren't tattooed with the flowers," she murmured as she drew the tiny baby's face, and placed a large rose next to his left eye. "When everyone put them in your cradle they covered you, and became part of your skin, and shielded you with their magic. Right. Seona added that to the story to explain why they were all over your skin and face."

The more details she added to the drawing, the more she wanted to paint the illustration. She knew she didn't need to do it, but she had her watercolors. She also sensed it would help her remember the story if she repeated everything she'd done the first time she'd worked on the book.

She took out the sealed bottle of water she always carried in her supply bag, and set up her travel palette with its little brush bowl. Dampening the paint pans, she selected which brushes she wanted and removed the sketch from her book before taping it down to the table's wooden top.

As Charlotte began to paint, the room around her faded to a background blue, and the distant sounds coming from outside muted. With a brush in her hand all her senses focused on the art; the floating dreaminess of working with watercolors creating a new world from the endless fountain of her imagination. She had often tried to define what happened to her when she painted, but words simply couldn't do justice to the experience. Nothing in reality compared to what her art made of her.

"You have someone here who looks just like you," Charlotte told the baby as she delicately tinted the rose blooming over his left eye. "He's much bigger and older, of course, but you'd like him. I do."

A small throb in her lip reminded her of how Darach had stalked out of the room after kissing her. He'd apologized, but he'd been just as angry as she had. She'd never had a sweeter, hotter first kiss with any man, and she wanted more. At the same time she wanted to throw a tantrum and call him every bad name she could think of.

*He said he can't lie. Why can't he tell me the truth?*

The clamber of heavy steps approaching on the stairs outside made Charlotte stop working and set aside her brush. A moment later Darach and a very tall, dark-haired man burst into the room. Both appeared sweaty and grim.

"You're well, my lady?" the chieftain asked, looking everywhere but at her.

"Of course, I am." She glanced at the other man, who had dark eyes that seemed to look right through her, and saw how he was staring at her hand. She put down the pair of scissors that she hadn't realized she'd grabbed. "Is something wrong?"

Darach nudged his companion.

"An arrow went astray in the lists, Mistress Walsh. We wish only to assure the stronghold's safe." The dark-eyed man bowed before he turned to the chieftain and murmured, "I'll search the rest of the tower."

After he left, Charlotte watched Darach close the door and lean back against it, his face turned away from her. When he regarded her again he gave her a slightly sheepish smile. If he apologized again for kissing her, she thought, she really would lose her temper. Suddenly she realized why the dark-eyed man had answered her question instead of the chieftain— so Darach wouldn't have to.

*I wonder how many ways you use to lie without actually lying.*

"You don't have to stay here with me." She started cleaning up her supplies. "You can go and help your friend."

"He's Taveon, our war master. I shall introduce you when we've a moment." He came to the table and looked at the half-finished illustration. "'Tis beautiful work you do. I've never seen such paints as you use."

"They're called watercolors. They're one of the oldest types of paint, but the sort I use won't be popular for another century or two." Since the illustration had already dried she removed it from the table top and placed it in her sketchbook. "Why did you run up here like that?"

"We reckon the arrow, 'twas shot by an intruder as a distraction. I wished only to assure you safe." He grimaced. "I'll prepare a work room for you in the garrison. 'Tis safer."

He meant safer for him, Charlotte thought. He'd never kiss her in front of his men.

"That's unnecessary," she assured him. "This afternoon I'll be moving into the guest room that Emery used when she first came here. It's just down the hall from her and the laird. I'm sure I can ask for a table and paint there."

From the way his expression darkened he didn't like that idea. "Anyone may roam the halls of the keepe. Only clansmen may enter the garrison."

"Do you know what I learned while I was being stalked in my time?" she asked him. "If someone wants to get to you badly enough, no place is safe. That, and relying on others to protect you is foolish."

Darach put his hand over hers. "I want you closer to me, my lady."

"For all the wrong reasons," she muttered, and

then jerked her hand out from under his and rose from her chair. "I'll be fine, Chieftain."

"I ken why you're angry, Charlotte." He touched her bruised cheek. "'Tis been the same for me since you fell into the spring. You put yourself in my arms. You undress and ask me look upon you. You beg me lay beside you. No woman's ever regarded me as other than the ugliest man in the clan."

So she was some kind of novelty for him, Charlotte thought, and hid her hurt with a shrug. "I thought I might be breaking some cultural taboos. I'll be more careful to maintain a proper distance. I don't want you to—"

"I want you." The words hung between them like a threat before he said, "When you touch me I wish do the same to you, and run my hands over your silken skin, and breathe in your sweet, soft heat. You're strong and lovely and last night I couldnae sleep for watching you, and wishing, and wanting. And now that I've kissed you, 'tis that and more."

"Then it isn't just me. Good." Charlotte closed the gap between their bodies. "I shouldn't be the only one suffering."

"You cannae ken what you desire, lass." He smoothed his palm over her hair before he curled his fingers over her nape. "'Tis been no' even a full day since you came to Dun Lasair. 'Tis unseemly to want such when we hardly ken each other."

"All right, I agree with that in theory. The problem is that I don't care about that, or being seemly, or doing what I should. Nearly being beaten to death does that to you." She watched the emotions flicker across his face. "There's something else you haven't told me about yourself, isn't there?" When he didn't say anything she knew he was trying again to dodge the truth. "Maybe you're the one who doesn't know what he wants, Chieftain."

As someone knocked on the door she stepped back, breaking the contact, and shouldered her bag. Emery came in, looking a little exasperated, and scowled at Darach.

"Taveon said to tell you that the tower is clear, and you should meet him in the great hall. I am now officially done being your personal messenger." She turned to beam at Charlotte. "Ready to check out your new small but very comfortable accommodations? You get your own fireplace and wash stand, plus maid service by authentic Scottish maidens."

Charlotte gave Darach one last look before she followed the laird's wife out of the map room.

"I know it's not much," Emery said a few minutes later as they walked over to look out through the narrow windows of the guest room. "The feather mattress will take some getting used to, but I've made sure that it and the bed linens are clean. This is also probably a good time to tell you that the tower rooms aren't sound-proofed, and I heard some of what you and Darach said to each other."

Charlotte stiffened. "Some?"

"Well, everything from he wants you closer to him to you accusing him of keeping things from you." She grimaced. "Honestly, if it does work out, don't knock the man to the floor and have your wicked way with him."

Would her humiliation ever be complete? "I won't."

"It's just that most of the castle floors are all stone, and they're ice-cold unless you're right in front of a blazing hearth, and even then you have to throw down a fur or blanket first. Which men tend to forget to do in the heat of passion. Or maybe that's just Luthias." Emery rolled her eyes. "Anyway, stick to the feather bed. No chance of bruises or chilblains."

"That's good to know." Charlotte looked down to see the guards on the curtain wall below. "Can I see the garrison tower from here?"

"No, that's on the opposite side of the stronghold." The laird's wife came to stand beside her, and pointed to the left. "Darach spends the morning training the men in the lists, which are over there outside the great hall. They basically beat the crap out of each other every day, but it helps if you think of it as the medieval version of working out, or physical therapy. In a way it's kind of both."

"Is that all he does?" Charlotte couldn't help asking.

"He's second in charge, so he has to be Luthias whenever my guy leaves the stronghold for long periods of time," Emery said. "Darach also assigns patrol and guard duties, listens to their reports and then gives a condensed version to the war master. Then he and Taveon meet every day with the laird to decide if they need to do anything different. The garrison has over five hundred men, and every time they have a problem, they go to Darach. Then there's overseeing the weapons stores, the stronghold's defensive capabilities, and a whole list of the other little things he does."

Like the general of an army, Charlotte thought. "He handles all that by himself?"

The laird's wife nodded. "Taveon's been covering for him today, but our war master has his own responsibilities. Everyone works in this time, no days off or vacations."

"I already told the chieftain that I didn't want to keep him from his work." She saw how Emery was frowning. "What's wrong?"

"You really do like Darach, don't you?" Before Charlotte could reply she held up her hands. "I get that it's none of my business. It's just that he's been like a big brother to me since the night I landed here, and I wouldn't be happy if anyone stomped on his heart. I thought I should say something before, you know, you two stop avoiding feather beds. In a fight I definitely couldn't take you, but I'd still try. Plus you have lots of leg for me to kick."

Charlotte suddenly understood why everyone in the clan adored the tiny woman. "Please don't worry. Darach has been very kind, but the clan comes first with him, and I don't want to interfere. I also need to find out why the Fire sword brought me here, and deal with that. You understand my situation better than anyone."

"Of course. Been there, done that, dodged Luthias for weeks, told him we couldn't, swore I wouldn't, etc. You can see how well that worked out." Emery held up her left hand and tapped her wedding ring.

"Even if Darach and I got involved, I'm not looking for a husband." Charlotte thought of her mother, and how heartlessly she had treated her father. She knew she had too much of Leona in her to ever be a good wife. "I'm not interested in getting married."

"Neither was I, but in the end I chose my guy over everything else. I'll never regret that, but there are tons of things that I had to give up that I miss. Indoor plumbing, certainly. I loved my work, and studied for years to qualify, but my career was over before it even started. Sometimes it kills me to know that I'll never even finish my doctorate." Her eyes widened, and she said quickly, "I didn't mean to put it like that."

"It's all right. I can't forget that the only thing waiting for me in our future is a horrible death. It makes staying in this time very easy." Charlotte leaned against the stone wall. "Once I've paid my debt to the Fire sword, I'll look for work and a place to live somewhere else."

"Now I'm a huge jerk." Emery reached out and touched her arm. "Listen, I may be little, but I'm still the gal in charge around here. You'll always have a home at Dun Lasair. If you don't want to stay with the clan, we've got farms and the village and friends all over the highlands. When it's time we'll find a safe place for you to start over and make a happy life for yourself, okay?"

After the laird's wife left, Charlotte pulled back the blanket on the bed and wrapped herself in it before she sat on the floor in front of the hearth.

*You really like Darach, don't you?*

How could she answer that, even just to herself? 'Like' seemed such a lukewarm word; she liked French coffee and arugula salads and dark chocolate, all of which she'd never taste again because she'd decided to stay in this time period. Her skills as an artist might translate into some kind of decorative trade—she'd taken classes in weaving and pottery in art school—but she'd never again see her paintings hung in a gallery or published in a book. All the conveniences and technology she'd enjoyed in the twenty-first century were likewise lost to her.

*Like any of that really matters.*

Her emotions had been frozen since Zoey's murder, but from the moment she'd fallen into the spring everything inside her had thawed out and come back to life. Darach was her ideal man, and not just physically. He embodied everything she had wished she could find in modern men and never had. But although he was attracted to her, he was keeping something from her. It had to be related to serving as Luthias's second-in-command. Maybe he didn't want to tell her that the MacRoss would always be first in his life, and she'd never be as important to him as his clan.

*Men lie and call it love, but it is only desire,* Leona had told her when she'd given her the talk. *Sex is the only thing they want from you, and the only power you will ever have over them. Never mistake what they do as love. Only you can love yourself.*

As much as she hated her mother's pitiless logic, Charlotte knew in this situation she happened to be right. *I'm just here to save his clan, and he's the one who has to protect me until I do. That's all we can ever have together.*

## Chapter Seven

In the slightly musty confines of the MacRoss enclave's scriptorium, Master Sage Duine sat and patiently listened to his apprentices' reports. They eagerly recounted every detail of the outing that resulted in recovering Mistress Walsh's bag, and all the items they had found inside it. To them it had been a treasure chest of magic wonders that included small windows into other worlds and brushes so fine they might have belonged to a master illuminator.

"The blocks of thin brick wrapped in wee flat tartans smelled so good, Master," one of the apprentices said. "Like burnt cream and honey, but sweeter." He held up a hand. "I vow we didnae unwrap them."

"Very good. You put back all that you removed from this bag?" Duine noted the uneasy glances between them and held out his hand. "Mayhap you forgot something you've brought to me with your apologies. A thing you should give me now, before 'tis missed."

The boys shuffled their feet and looked at the eldest among them. He grimaced as he took from his belt pouch a slim oval made of a dark polished shell, which he opened before handing it to Duine.

"'Tis a mirror, Master," the lad said reverently. "Made of flawless glass, and we reckon backed by pure silver. 'Tis wondrous clear."

Duine flinched as he saw his own reflection in the glass circle. He had never before beheld his own face with such detail, and reached up to touch his rather bulbous nose, which appeared to be covered with freckles. Why had no one ever mentioned he had so many?

"As you say." He made himself close the two halves again and then examined the outside. "I shall return the mirror to Mistress Walsh with apologies." He gave them all a stern look. "And tell her we reckon the thing fell from the bag as you put back her possessions, and only now discovered such. Do you agree?"

The boys ducked their heads and murmured "Aye."

"Now go and attend to Elder Sgur for the

remainder of the day." As the apprentices groaned over the prospect of looking after the oldest and most troublesome member of the enclave, Duine hid a smile. "Do you wish instead I should send you aid the gong-scourer?"

After the threat of having to clean out the stronghold's privies sent the apprentices hurrying from his chamber, Duine opened the mirror and took a longer look at himself. As a young lad he had been among those considered handsomest by the stronghold's maids and village women, but for the first time he realized just how much time and troubles had aged him. He had never realized how heavy the burdens of his position would weigh on him, either. The many silver hairs gleaming in the dark brown of his cropped fringe, and the deep frown lines around his nose and mouth attested to that. He looked so much like his sire now it dismayed him.

*You must protect every sage under your charge, my son. Whatever that requires, see such done.*

Remembering those long evenings of instruction with his sire always made Duine bilious, but it was thanks to the elder master sage that he had carried on his order's sacred duty to protect life with his own. He'd also disappointed his sire time and again when he'd failed to meet his stern expectations. Each night after finishing his work he would go to the laboratorium to recount his efforts as an apprentice. He never received praise for his successes, but for every misstep his sire would cane his palms. The greater his failures, the harder the caning. Some nights he had left with hands so swollen and bloody he could hardly use them the next day.

Now he looked at the old scars that crossed his palms before he curled his fingers over them to hide the reminders of his unpleasant, painful boyhood. If nothing else his sire had taught him what never to do with the lads in his charge. They were not his sons, of course, but because of his own suffering Duine would never raise a hand to hurt any of them. He had told his sire as much as the old master sage lay in his deathbed.

*I shall protect all life, Father. Whatever I must do, I ken 'tis my true calling.*

He splashed cold water on his face and changed his robe to a finer one before he left his chamber and went down to the great hall, where Lady Emery sat with the seamstress and a mound of linen.

"As tall as Charlotte is, stable lad trews will look like capris on her. Ah, I mean they'll be too short for her long legs." Emery pursed her lips. "Do we have someone in the clan who is tall but slender?"

"Nearly all the MacRoss, they're giants, my lady," the seamstress said, and puffed out her cheeks. "Aye, and they're strapping to a one, particularly the senior clansmen. I yet must let out the seams in Armorer Camdyn's sleeves each time I sew a new tunic for him. You'll no' find what you seek among the clan."

"Is there such a thing as too strapping? I'm thinking no." Emery chuckled, and then noticed him. "Fair day, Master Duine. Do sages wear trews?"

"Only in winter, and then under our robes, my lady. Fair day, Mistress." Duine bowed to them. "Forgive me for intruding, but my lads found something by the bathing spring that belongs to Mistress Walsh. May I meet with her, my lady?"

"Sure. I was just going up to her room to get some measurements for clothes." She picked up some strips of linen and said to the seamstress, "You know, I think one of the gardeners is kind of a beanpole— the one who's always tending the vines near the back of the garden. Would you ask the groundskeeper if he's around, and if we might borrow a pair of his trews? I'll be right back."

As Duine accompanied the laird's wife up to the guest chamber he became somewhat nervous at the prospect of facing another woman from the future. Emery herself had always been sharp-eyed and intelligent, and she often noticed things that even Luthias missed. Her comfort in speaking about subjects unseemly for a woman regularly intimidated him. At the same time he took some encouragement from their presence. At least Emery and this new lady proved that mortal kind had continued on for at least seven centuries, which surely meant his efforts to protect life would prevail in the end.

"I confess, I've yet to meet Mistress Walsh," he said. "What think you of her, my lady?"

"Don't worry, Master Duine, you'll like her," Emery said, patting his arm. "Charlotte is Canadian, and they're just about the nicest people who live in my time. She's not at all brazen and ill-mannered like me."

He coughed to cover the laugh she startled out of him. "Who should call you such, my lady?"

"Except you and Luthias, I'm pretty sure everyone in the fourteenth century does." The laird's wife winked at him as she stopped in front of a door and knocked. "Hey, Charlotte, it's Emery again." She waited a moment for a reply, and then said, "Are you all right? Can I come in?"

Duine listened, and shook his head. "Mayhap she yet sleeps."

"This late in the day?" Emery opened the door and peeked inside before closing it and frowning. "That's odd. She's gone."

Fyn glanced down at the gardener's garb he had donned, which smelled of lye soap and sunshine, and then pulled his broad-brimmed straw hat lower on his brow to hide his features. The master had told him to keep to the back of the gardens, where he would not be noticed. That would give him access to the granary, the windows of which lay directly across from those of the garrison hall. There, his master promised, he could remove the hindrance to their plans.

*Do as I've told you, and finally we shall prevail over the MacRoss.*

While spying on Darach, Fyn had caught glimpses of Charlotte Walsh, the wench the Fire sword had brought back from the future. She stood taller than him, and had the look of a Norsewoman. He had spent many nights imagining her as she would look in the sanctorum's cage, naked and terrified as he plied his blade for her. No one would hear her screams; they had never once heard Athdara Martin while she had been imprisoned there. Perhaps when he had finished questioning her the master would allow him a night alone with Mistress Walsh. Fyn had discovered of late that he enjoyed playing with mortals even more than animal prey.

*We shall ken such fun together.*

Fyn lifted the hatch and crawled out of the tunnel

into the bean patch that concealed it. He had to drag the grain sack he'd brought with him, which proved heavier than he realized, and made a loud scraping sound on the ground. For a moment he lay still and listened before he dared to lift his head to look around him. Once he'd assured no vassal could see him he stood and walked behind the thickest part of the gardens, where the tall stalks of ripening beans provided sparse but adequate cover. At the same time he took hold of the cloaking charm he wore around his neck, which his master had given to him long ago.

*Wear this always, my lad, and when you wish to invoke the spell, clutch it and think yourself a shadow. 'Twill cause anyone who beholds you see only darkness.*

Using the cloaking charm in broad daylight came with great risk, Fyn knew. Nightfall or moving through the forest made his shadow blend in with the rest of the surrounding darkness; sunlight in an open place would show the black patch that shrouded him moving on its own. The darkness that covered him only lasted as long as he held the charm in his hand; the moment he released it he would reveal himself. That was why he slowed his steps and kept watching for the MacRoss's gardeners and servants, so that he might go still if he encountered them.

"Hey, there," a cheerful voice called, making him freeze.

Fyn looked over to see Emery Parker walking straight toward him. Had the charm failed? He looked down to see the shadow that enveloped him still intact, and drew his dagger. *Do I take the slut as my next kill? Shall he praise me for ending her?* He knew the master particularly despised Luthias's filthy hoor for ruining his last scheme.

A tall, skinny young vassal suddenly stepped in front of Fyn, blocking his view of Emery.

"Fair morning, my lady," the lad said. "You wished speak with me?"

Fyn wanted nothing more in that moment than to bury his blade in the boy's spine, but as the pair talked about garments his temper subsided. The master would grow very angry if he again strayed from his task, and he feared his punishments.

*Serve me, wee piglet,* Athdara Martin's ghost whispered in his head. *Steal Prince Kaer's sain and you shall rule the mortal realm at my side.*

"I just need one pair," Emery said to the boy, and walked back into the stronghold with him.

Fyn closed his eyes, sheathing his dagger as he pushed Athdara from his thoughts. *Go back to the shadow realm, demon hoor.*

*Once he's finished using you, the master shall send you here to me,* she said, her laughter filling his skull before fading away.

His belly shrank, and a sour taste filled his mouth. He could not boak here, where the gardeners might hear him retching. To calm himself Fyn silently repeated the assurances he had been given.

*The master needs me at his side. I'm his chieftain as well as his hunter. When we prevail, I shall be named laird of the Carack. He cannae destroy the MacRoss without me.*

The litany allowed him to move past the terror and continue his work. Once he slipped inside the granary Fyn released the charm, set down the sack and went over to the window slits to pull down the covering slat and peer outside. For most of his life he had been sneaking onto MacRoss land, but never before had he dared breach the stronghold. Walking about directly under the noses of Luthias's guards made him strong and confident in ways his furtive poaching and spying never had.

*I may do whatever I wish and they shall never stop me.*

As he watched the men entering and leaving the garrison hall Fyn took the crossbow out of the grain sack and loaded it with a bolt. He should have insisted they do this from the beginning. He had known that hiding and rigging the first bow to fire by itself would likely fail, but since the suicide scheme had gone wrong his master had been acting with an overabundance of caution.

*If you're caught by the MacRoss, they shall chain you in the dungeons and torture you until you tell them all.*

With the crossbow loaded Fyn propped it on the sill of the window, and checked along the shaft of the bolt before centering the arrowhead at the foresight. Aiming at the entry to the garrison hall would mean shooting a moving target, but thanks to hunting he had a good eye for envisaging where his prey would be in the moment after he released an arrow.

Fyn took time to get into a comfortable position by pulling some grain sacks over to the window to make a perch, and securing the crossbow with his shoulder sling. The rich scent of old death drifted around him, pungent and welcoming, thanks to the master's cleverness. Now all he had to do was watch and wait for the ugly facker to show himself.

And then Darach would become the first MacRoss loss in the clan war to begin.

CHARLOTTE HEARD THE SOUND OF LOUD BANGING coming from the other side of the big door as she approached the forge, and for a moment she wondered if she should just go back to her room. Yet after several days of following Emery around the castle she was reasonably sure no one working inside would get angry with her for visiting. Taking a deep breath, she opened the door.

Heat wafted in her face, and as she walked inside she saw an enormous hearth made of pale bricks that had a large metal door standing open. In front of it a bare-chested Camdyn stood hammering a gigantic sledge hammer against the glowing red tip of a long sword. Sparks flew as he worked, and his muscles gleamed with sweat.

The scene reminded her of an illustration she'd painted of the smith-god, Vulcan, for a book of children's mythology. She also suspected most women would have been mesmerized by the armorer's godlike physique, and imagine what he'd look like without the rest of his clothes. All it did was remind her of seeing Darach climb out of the spring, his wet trousers clinging to his long legs and the gorgeous curves of his buttocks.

*That's who I want to see naked. The man who doesn't want me.*

"Unless the Carack attack the keepe, or 'tis burning to the ground, get out," Camdyn said. "And tell Luthias I'm no' a facking druid, and his blade shall be done when 'tis done." He lifted the hammer and gave the red-hot steel another mighty whack.

"Do I have to use those words exactly?" Charlotte asked, walking up beside him. "I'd rather not curse at the laird. He might kick me out." As he finally looked at her she offered him a polite smile. "Hello again."

"You've a bold tongue, Mistress Walsh." Camdyn put the blade he'd been hammering into a barrel of water, which immediately sent up a plume of steam. He then regarded her with a flattering amount of wariness. "You ken every female in the stronghold fears me."

"Emery seems to like you well enough." Charlotte waved a hand to dispel the steam wafting into her face. "Do you want to be feared?"

"No' especially," he said. "Only ken that Darach shallnae approve of you coming here alone, Mistress."

"I wasn't aware I needed his permission. Please call me Charlotte." She glanced around the big workroom. "If you'll tell me where you keep the smaller blades I'll have a look at them, and you can go on working."

"You truly want a knife?" The armorer held up another blade to inspect it in the light from one of the narrow windows before placing it in the furnace and setting aside his hammer.

"I'd truly prefer a gun, but Emery tells me they won't be invented until the end of this century." She watched him pull on a tunic. "You don't have to stop working. Just point me in the right direction."

"'Tis more to choosing a dagger than you ken."

Camdyn took a large bundle down from one of the shelves over a long table, where he unrolled it. "Then, too, I dinnae forge them for the wee hands of wenches."

"I have fairly large hands for a wench, I think." Charlotte took a moment to admire the long row of polished knives. "You do beautiful work, Camdyn."

"I dinnae forge them for admiration. Show me your palms." When she did the armorer selected three different blades, and set them in front of her. "Pick up each one, and let the weight of the dagger rest on your palm. Choose one that seems right to you."

She did that with the first, which seemed almost too heavy, as did the second. The third, the lightest of the trio, should have been the most comfortable. Yet once she set it down she went back to the first blade, and picked it up again. The heaviness of the weapon was unfamiliar, and yet seemed to fit her hand better.

"This one," she told him.

"Good. 'Tis the one I'd chosen for you." He eyed her wrist before he said, "Now hold the hilt as you would to use the dagger to stab me."

Charlotte smiled a little. "That's easier."

Camdyn watched her grip the blade, and then reached for her hand.

"If I may change your hold?" Once she nodded

he adjusted her thumb so that it wrapped over her index and middle finger. "Always keep all four fingers curled tight around the hilt, and secure your grip with your thumb thus. 'Tis proper for fighting, and your hand shallnae slip. Once you draw the blade from the sheath, ever hold on tight as you may."

She tightened her grip on the hilt, and suddenly the weapon seemed very lethal. "What if I don't want to hurt anyone?"

"Then dinnae carry a fighting dagger." Camdyn plucked the blade out of her hand and tossed it onto the table. "'Tisnae shameful. Most females wouldnae choose to wound by purpose. 'Tis for a man to do such work."

"What do you think a woman's work is? This?" She touched her injured cheek. "Should I just stand there the next time I'm attacked, and let myself be beaten while I wait for a man to come and rescue me?"

"No, Charlotte." His gaze shifted over her, but not in an insulting fashion. "You should run away and scream."

"There are some things you can't outrun." Charlotte grew furious now. "So yes, I need to carry a knife for fighting, and I want to learn to use it properly. Because next time anyone attacks me or tries to hurt me, I'm going to fight for my life. I won't just wound him, either. I'll kill him."

In the silence that followed the echo of her last words, which she'd shouted, the armorer reached for the dagger she'd chosen before and offered it to her.

Charlotte took it, wrapping her fingers around the hilt as he'd shown her. "I'm sorry that I yelled like that."

"'Twas likely deserved, and never shall I attack you now," Camdyn said. "Extend the blade out so I may look at your hold again." After she did he studied her hand, and then picked up a chunk of something white and touched it to three spots on the side of the hilt. "I need make a new grip wrapping to better fit your palm, and carve a wooden dagger the same size and shape."

She frowned. "Why would I need one made of wood?"

"'Tis for practice. You said you need learn blade fighting, and wood, 'twillnae wound nor kill your trainer." He took the blade from her and placed it on another table where strips of leather in various widths hung neatly coiled on a low rack. "Ask Darach teach you. He's better with short blades than most in the clan."

Charlotte saw the scowl that went along with the reluctant praise. "I thought you two didn't like each other." When he didn't say anything she sighed. "He's busy with his duties, and I've already imposed enough on him. Do you have time to give me a few lessons?"

"Mayhap, if 'tis worth my effort." Camdyn deliberately let his gaze wander over her, this time in a more obvious manner.

"It's not worth what you're thinking right now." She suspected his interest had more to do with provoking Darach than any attraction to her. "Do you ask everyone you train to pay you back with sex?"

Instead of being offended he made a rude sound. "I cannae fack my brothers."

"I'm sure they'd be relieved to hear that. Let's see, I can barter something else for the lessons." She walked around him, making a show of inspecting him in the same way he had her. "You're quite good-looking—when you don't scowl—and you have a very nice body. Have you ever had a portrait done?"

"Never, and I'm no' so vain I'd wish one. You shall instead owe me a boon. What Emery calls a favor," he added when she started to shake her head. "Or ask the chieftain for training, which he shall refuse, for to him you're but a helpless wench who ever needs coddling."

Camdyn could teach her mother a thing or two about how to subtly insult, Charlotte thought. "All right, I'll owe you a boon in return for training, with two conditions. Don't use my training to provoke another shoving match between you and Darach."

He moved his shoulders. "I shall say naught to the chieftain. What more?"

"The boon needs to be reasonable to me," she told him. "I want the right to refuse if you ask for too much."

"You're a canny wench." The armorer gave her a stunning smile. "Agreed."

Charlotte held out her hand. "All right, let's shake on it." As he clasped her forearm instead she frowned. "What's this?"

"'Tis how we put bond to our vows," he said.

Camdyn went over to retrieve the sword he'd been hammering from the furnace, and then pulled off his tunic before he placed the red-glowing blade on his anvil. "I shall ready your practice blade by the morrow. We'll begin your training after the evening meal. Meet me in the lists." He glanced at her. "Shall you tell Darach, then?"

"If he asks, I will." She had to end her dependency on the chieftain. "Thank you, Camdyn."

Charlotte left the forge and walked back in the direction of the great hall. Along the way she passed a pair of teenagers wearing long robes that fluttered as they rushed toward her. Between them they carried a large crock brimming with what appeared to be black and brown hockey pucks. They slowed long enough to gape and then bow to her, and in the process spilled some of the crock's strange contents on the floor.

"What's this?" she asked, stepping aside as the pucks bounced around her feet.

"Your pardon, Mistress." One of the boys tried to catch the rubbery objects, but they ricocheted off the walls higher and higher until they stuck to the wooden braces overhead. "Oh, no, Sradag. The spores, they're rooting again."

"Go and fetch Master Duine, Losgadh," the other boy said. He grimaced at her. "Forgive me, Mistress, but you shouldnae stand beneath them. They spawn very fast."

"What are they?" Charlotte asked, and then blinked as the pucks sticking to the ceiling began to swell and turn red.

"I meant to dry them to serve as torch heads," a querulous voice said, and a bald elderly man came hobbling up to them. "Fair day, my lady. Your pardon." He gently nudged her aside to stand beneath the pucks, which were now the size of basketballs and glowed yellow-orange. "Och, 'tis too late."

The pucks burst, raining down dozens of tiny black and brown pebbles onto the elderly sage. The little spores bounced like jumping beans on the passage's stone floor and walls, but they were too small to reach the wooden braces overhead.

"Gather them up quickly, lads," the old man said as he peered at the floor. "Else they grow large enough to plant themselves in the rafters and swell again." He smiled at Charlotte. "I reckoned the mushrooms that grew in the crystal caverns should have some special use, and when one fell in the hearth I saw the thing burned but it didnae char nor stop burning. I reckoned they'd make torch heads to last for eternity."

"I see." Charlotte actually didn't understand, but she crouched down to help him gather up the rubbery spores anyway. "They seem to grow very fast."

"Och, aye, for they dinnae have wood in the caves. 'Tis like clootie dumpling to them, and makes them jump like randy hares." Sgur gathered up the last handful and dumped them into the crock. "Lads, we must take them back to the cavern before they escape the castle through this passage and find the forest at its end."

Charlotte glanced at the other end of the corridor, which went past the forge. "You can walk out into the forest from here?"

"Aye, for the passage leads under the walls and

opens onto the walking trail," the old sage said. "Only we mustnae, for should even one spore find a tree, well, 'twould end with the highlands buried beneath a mountain of the same."

"I hate to agree, Elder Sgur." Emery appeared with a broom and a bucket, and a small army of maids following her with the same, as well as large crocks. "Hey, Charlotte. I see you two have already met." She leaned closer and murmured, "Sgur is the oldest member of the enclave, and kind of the medieval version of John Dalton. If Dalton were a mad scientist, I mean."

"Yes." Charlotte saw the old man hurry with the two younger sages as they chased some escaped mushrooms down the hall. "I got the same impression."

"He's mostly harmless, and we all love him." The laird's wife glanced up just as the last mushroom overhead burst and showered her with pebbled spores. "Well, most of the time."

## Chapter Eight

"The men need occupation, my lord," Eamon, the chieftain in charge of the Carack garrison, told Struan during their morning meeting in the great hall. "They've spent weeks drinking and whining while mourning for the laird, but 'tis making them soft. Soon I wouldnae trust them to face a pair of sages, much less the facking MacRoss."

Although it angered him to hear the chieftain's claims, Struan knew he was right. The clan's grief over Callum's death had dwindled, and left idle the men had grown surly and morose. If he continued to enforce the mourning period the clan would end brawling in the chambers and halls.

*Och, get on with life, Brother,* Callum would say. *The dead can do naught but sleep.*

"Very well. You've my permission to drill them from dawn until dusk. I shall come at noon to watch individual bouts." He looked up as the chieftain continued to hover. "'Tisnae enough?"

"'Tis the garrison that concerns me, my lord. Some of the lads, they're no' easy facing Hunter Fyn," Eamon admitted. "You ken how foolishly he behaves in the lists. He draws blood and wins every match, but of late..." He stopped and sighed.

"Naught you say shall astonish me," Struan assured him.

"The lad's harming himself." The chieftain grimaced. "I've seen him bite his lip or tongue so he may spit his own blood in the face of the maids, my lord. He doesnae limit such torments to the vassals. Some days past I saw him pacing the hall and gnawing at his fingernails until they bled. I dinnae ken why he'd do this, and I'm no' inclined to ask."

Struan had always known this day would come, so it wasn't a surprise. Still, he hated what would have to come next.

"Go to Fyn's quarters and remove all the weapons, and then escort him there after the evening meal. Tell him only 'tis punishment from me for setting the fire in the hall, and that I shall speak with him on the morrow." He knew giving the hunter any hint of his fate would only make him run. With his knowledge of the Carack lands and the many hunting blinds he'd made Fyn could spend years eluding capture. "Once he's inside bar the door from the outside, and put two guards to stand watch for the night. That shall be enough."

The chieftain nodded, and bowed before he backed out of the room.

Only after he had gone did Struan rub a tired hand over his face. He had spoken to Callum in the past about Fyn's unstable nature, and what they might do once his madness became unmanageable. His brother had always favored indulging the hunter for as long as possible, but agreed that in time it would be too dangerous to permit him to roam free.

"He's like a wild thing himself," Callum had said. "'Tis too cruel to lock him away in the dungeons or anywhere secure enough to hold him. We cannot exile him, nor hand him over to the magistrate to be imprisoned with the other lunatics. In the end Fyn's Carack blood would expose us all."

"When the time comes, and you give me leave, my lord," Struan said, "I shall send him along to our sire."

The laird had put a hand on his shoulder. "I but beg you keep his end free of pain and fear. I dinnae wish Fyn suffer for what 'twas never his fault."

Callum had already gone to join their sire in the

next life, however, leaving Struan in charge of Fyn and the rest of the clan. Tomorrow he would ride out with the hunter to his favorite spot up in the slopes, and there share a meal and some tales he had never told him of Callum. Then, as Fyn gazed out at the beautiful forests surrounding Dun Deigh, he would plant his dagger in the hunter's heart, and keep his promise.

Struan looked up as a knock sounded on his chamber door. "Enter."

The new kitchen maid came inside, a tray balanced on one arm. "Eventide, my lord." She tried to bob, thought better of it, and brought the food to him. "Cook bid me bring your evening meal to you."

"Put the tray there." He nodded toward a side table, and as Revna turned away inspected her gown. It looked newer than the one she had been wearing in the forest, although he could see it had been made from cheap hemp cloth instead of wool. Contrary to the laundress's claims she also wore a shift beneath it. Her feet remained bare, however, and the sight of her dusty toes annoyed him. "Didnae the steward give you new boots to wear?"

"Aye, he did, my lord." The tray clattered as she put it down. "I dinnae wish to dirty them."

Struan saw her hands twist the sides of her apron,

and then he understood. "You've never worn shoes or boots, have you?"

"No, my lord." Revna met his gaze, her own shamed. "'Twas no coin for such when I lived with Da. I didnae mind." Her nose wrinkled. "They're pretty, the new boots, only they make my feet itch."

Struan heard a rusty sound come from his mouth, and realized it was a chuckle. How long had it been since he'd laughed?

"You'll be glad of them when winter comes." He saw a handful of dark purple berries on the plate by his bread, meat and cheese, and a mug of cider. "Who prepared the food?"

"I did, my lord." She glanced at the tray. "Cook said you wouldnae want stew or pottage. If 'tisnae what you wish, I may fetch more—"

"I dinnae favor berries, nor hot foods," he told her. "I drink only cold water."

As he watched her set out the food on the table Struan wondered what they were feeding her in the kitchens. Likely scraps from the clan's meals, as she was new and as such had no status among the other servants. The thought of sending her back with an empty belly made him think of Fyn. Like the maid the hunter had ever been helpless to escape his lot in life.

At least Struan could do something to change that

for Revna. "You'll eat the berries, and drink the cider. Sit down."

Her pale eyes widened. "Oh, I darenae sup with you, my lord."

"'Tis my command. Do as you're told, wench." Struan watched her gingerly perch on the other chair at his table as he placed the plate of food between them, and put the cup in her hand. "How fare you in the kitchens?"

"I'm learning, my lord." She took a tiny sip of cider. "I dinnae ken any of the other maids, but they seem kindly. The pantry keeper, he's teaching me my duties with great patience. Even Cook doesnae shout or beat me when I've a mishap."

She knew well enough not to criticize the other vassals, another sign of her innate cleverness. He tore a piece of bread in two and offered her half. "Did your sire beat and shout at you?"

"Da? Only when he'd come home well-pished from drinking." She hunched her shoulders. "I favor my mam, and sometime he'd mistake me for her. She died birthing me."

Learning that she had been raised without a mother made sense of her strange behavior; she'd never been taught how to properly speak to a man, or what might happen to a maiden wandering through the forest alone at night.

"You've no other kin?" When she shook her head he cut a wedge of cheese and put it in her hand. "Eat."

Revna kept chin down and nibbled like a mouse as he ate the rest of the meal, but now and then stole a glance at him. The coldfire orb in the forest had painted her in a blue glow, but now his chamber lanterns revealed the soft golden-brown shade of her hair. Her dark eyelashes had gilded tips, and thin rims of gold encircled her pale blue eyes. He could see the delicate veins showing plainly through her pallid skin, as well as the narrow fineness of her bones. She would never be regarded as comely, as his male vassals preferred their wenches plump and well-curved. She reminded him of a dandelion.

*All wishes and wisps, this wench.*

Because Revna didn't resemble any of the strong, sturdy female vassals who served the Carack, her differences would likely cause her some grief. He could tell from the way the laundress had spoken of her she'd already stirred disapproval among the other females. Then too, every member of the household came from families who had served his clan for many generations.

For being born to poor villagers, and abandoned by her only blood-kin, Revna would always be considered an unwanted outsider.

Struan commanded an army of battle-hardened warriors, had more wealth at his disposal than any other highland laird, and enough important allies among the nobility and court to do whatever he wished when he wished. Yet he could do nothing to help Revna make a place for herself at Dun Deigh. Any favor he showed her would only cause resentment among his other vassals, who would see to it that the maid suffered in a hundred ways.

He could send her away with enough gold to make a fresh start somewhere far from Carack land, but living alone in a strange place with no one to protect her would likely end badly for the lass. What she truly needed was a husband, but since her father had run off and left her penniless a marriage seemed unlikely.

"You've had no word from your sire?" he asked.

Revna cringed. "No, my lord."

Struan had questioned the groundskeeper and several other vassals who had known the trapper; they all claimed that while sometimes too fond of drink the man had been steadfast with his work and devoted to his daughter. The villagers grudgingly accepted Revna because her sire's parents had been well-respected, but all seemed uncomfortable with the girl. None would say why, but Struan's steward thought it might have to do with her resemblance to her mother, who had also been an outsider.

Struan wondered if he should intervene further in the girl's life. "'Tis someone you wish to wed?"

Revna dropped the berries in her hand onto the table, where they rolled around his plate. "I cannae marry, my lord. I promised my da I wouldnae."

A strange pledge to make, although he could see the sense of it. Her sire had not married again, so he obviously had wanted his daughter to stay and look after him in his old age. Yet if that were the case, why had he abandoned the girl?

"Your sire's gone. You may do as you wish." When she said nothing Struan leaned forward. "'Tis someone you care for, then?"

"The midwife in the village, she said I'm too small in the hips." Revna wouldn't look him in the eye now. "If ever I birth a bairn 'twill likely end me. My da's run off. I've no dowry, and naught to tempt a man to offer for me."

"'Tisnae what I asked you." As she got up and started putting the dishes on the tray he reached across the table and took hold of her wrist. "Who would you wed?"

Revna's bottom lip trembled, and then she turned her hand in his grip so that her cool fingertips brushed across his forearm. "Who should want me, my lord?"

In that moment Struan knew with one tug on her arm he could have her against him. She would not resist him, either. Three strides to his bed, and a few moments to strip her out of that cheap gown. Thanks to her thinness he wouldn't even have to douse her skinny young body with icy water to cool down her skin so he could fondle her and suck her breasts and sink his heavy, aching cock into her virginal quim. He'd be the first man to take her, and by the Gods then would he be the last, for he'd keep her as his bed wench.

*Until she grows old, and loses what bloom and beauty she possesses,* a voice that sounded remarkably like Callum's murmured inside his head. *All while you remain young and handsome and strong.*

Struan jerked his hand from her arm and pushed the tray into her hands. "Return to the kitchens now, wench."

After she had fled he spent a long time trying not to think of her, and failing. He wanted to blame it on Callum for dying, for if he had still been laird, Struan might have done as he pleased. His bedchamber grew stifling, so he stalked out and walked the passages until he found himself climbing down the stairs into the dungeons.

Instead of seeking the cool, quiet space where he spent the hottest part of the day Struan went to the cells and walked down to the door at the end of the big chamber. It had been secured with a crystal lock his sire had enchanted to assure that only the hand of the laird of the Carack could open it. Since he had refused the title Struan wondered if the vault would open for him, and yet as soon as he placed his palm into the lock's recess the white-blue crystal flared with cold light, and hidden gears turned.

*You must never open the vault,* Callum's ghost whispered in his ear.

A waft of icy air came out of the chamber on the other side of the door, so frigid that Struan saw frost crystals forming on his eyelashes. His sire's magic had always been thus, thanks to his elemental power over ice. The luxury of the pitiless cold pouring over him nearly made him howl with frustration. Why had Callum never told him of the chamber's qualities? He might have retreated here during what were for him the long, unbearably hot summer days—and then he realized that his brother couldn't have known. Only the prince had, and kept this secret to protect the sain.

*Shall I never suffer enough for you, Sire?*

Bitter now, Struan stepped inside. As a lad he'd always wondered what lay behind the bespelled door, and now that mystery would be revealed. He found himself in what appeared to be an empty room, the stone walls of which had been thickly covered in frost and ice. Snow covered the floor everywhere except for an area of crystal inlay in the very center. The temperature hovered so low he could see every breath he released hover like wood smoke in the air.

As he approached the crystallized floor center the glittering circle also became illuminated, and the stone panels inside it sank down and slid back. White and blue sparks of Fae magic floated up as a stele made of blue-streaked white quartz rose slowly from within until it loomed over him, and then turned completely transparent as glass.

Locked within the stele lay a war hammer unlike any Struan had ever seen. Forged from steel, silver and ice-clear crystal, the long handle had been etched with the spell that empowered it along with his sire's spirit. Seeing the head, which had been carved from a single, enormous chunk of icestone, the rarest of Fae crystals, made his gut knot. The prince had shaped the hammer's head like a giant fist.

*Never should a Carack take up the Ice Hammer,* Callum had warned him during their only conversation about the sain. *'Twill destroy all we ken and love.*

Struan walked around his father's weapon to examine it from all sides. Some perverse part of him wanted to reach out and wrap his hand around the wickedly beautiful handle, perhaps because the only other person who had ever held it had been Prince Kaer. Callum had claimed that their sire had forged the hammer in this very vault before stumbling out, enchanting the lock and then falling dead at the feet of his personal guards.

*Trust you, Sire, to create the most nightmarish of weapons,* Struan thought.

Like the MacRoss Fire sword, the Ice Hammer had also been created to protect a Fae Prince's sons. Unlike the time-traveling blade, however, the enchantment empowering it did only one thing: shatter anything struck with it. According to the legend a man struck by the sain would literally fall to pieces. So would any other weapon it touched. If wielded against any structure, the entire building would collapse. Stone and steel it would break like glass, as it would villages, forests, curtains walls and strongholds.

If a Carack deliberately struck the Ice Hammer against the ground, it would shatter and crumble away, along with the rest of the mortal realm.

The wintry chamber helped cool Struan's overheated temper, but beholding his sire's sain did the same to his emotions. As a lad he had desired the approval and affection his sire had instead lavished on

Callum, but he had never understood the price his older brother had paid for his position. Each day the Carack laird had to defend and rule over the clan while knowing that thanks to Prince Kaer's sain he held the fate of the world in his hands.

Callum had called it lonely, but in truth it seemed unspeakable that one man should have such power.

Now Struan understood why Callum had been so enthralled by Athdara Martin. The jewel-setter had likely seduced his brother only to use him for her own purposes, and perhaps Callum had even known that. After nine centuries of loneliness what man could make himself turn away once he'd fallen in love? That obsession with Athdara had driven his brother to folly, and her death had killed everything but the hate inside him. If Callum had declared war on the MacRoss, he might have taken the Ice Hammer from the vault to assure a Carack victory.

As he left the vault and secured the enchanted lock, Struan knew he had to be smarter than Callum. No love, however much desired, would be worth destroying a world.

During the evening meal Charlotte considered confiding in Emery about the knife-fighting lessons she'd arranged with Camdyn, but then Darach came and sat across from her, making that discussion ill-advised. He again wore his hooded tunic, which along with his long hair covered most of the marked side of his face. As the maids brought platters of food out to the tables he kept his face turned, she noticed. Still the women avoided looking at the chieftain, except for one who gave him a quick, openly fearful glance. Seeing the way he was treated made Charlotte angry and wretched all at once.

*Why can't they see past the surface to the man beneath the birthmark?*

"It's pretty obvious that every woman from the future isn't a chatterbox like me," Emery said, dragging Charlotte's attention back to her. The laird's wife eyed the men at the table before letting her gaze settle on the chieftain. "So if you want to know something, you need to ask. That okay with you, Charlotte?"

She smiled back at her. "Of course, please do."

Darach picked up his mug to drink, but over the rim gave Emery a pointed glare.

"I'm curious, Mistress Walsh. Your blood-kin, they're from a northern land, mayhap?" Taveon asked.

"My father's family is from Canada, which is a country in the north," she said. "My mother and her family are French."

"Allow me to interpret for you, Tav," the laird's wife said, patting the war master's shoulder before she regarded Charlotte. "What he really wants to know is if your ancestors were Vikings."

"Not that I'm aware of," she told her. "My father's great-grandparents were Welsh, but the rest of his family are Québécois. I'm fairly sure there were no French Vikings."

"Technically speaking, though, the Normans... Well, let's not go there," Emery said, and then turned to the war master. "She's mostly New World Francian, with a dash of Brittani, Tav, so you don't have to worry about her raiding and pillaging. I'm kidding," she added when she saw Charlotte's expression.

Completely bewildered now, she asked, "Why would it matter who my ancestors were?"

"Since the Vikings were driven out of the Western Isles in the last century, just being Scandinavian is a polarizing issue. In this time they're still regarded as the bogeymen by the Scots. That's why anyone tall and blonde like you makes them nervous." Emery patted her hand. "If anyone asks, just say your people are Francian. Simpler."

"Okay." Charlotte saw how Darach was watching her. "Can I ask a question about the clan?" When he nodded she said, "The only women I've seen at the castle are servants from the village, and there seem to be no children or elderly people here. Where do your families live?"

Three of the men quickly got up from the table and left. Darach suddenly wouldn't look at her, and the laird grimaced. Only Taveon seemed amused.

"Good question." Emery sat back and folded her arms as she glared at her husband. "Maybe you want to answer that one, honey, a little sooner than you told me."

"The MacRoss cannae age, for we're no' entirely mortal," Luthias said. "The clan, we're the half-Fae sons of Prince Ross."

"All of you?" When he nodded Charlotte did some mental calculations. "That would make you all brothers, and...immortal, unless you have some magic elixir you're drinking to stop from aging and dying."

"No elixir," Emery said. "They're immortal. They don't marry because they don't age, and one of the other downsides is that they can't have children."

She looked at Darach, who avoided her gaze. "I see."

"The Carack are the same because they're all the sons of Prince Kaer," the laird's wife added. "Unlike full-blooded Fae these guys can be killed, but it's pretty tough. Half-Fae can't drown, by the way, so if you see one of them fall off a cliff into a loch, don't worry."

Luthias leaned over and kissed his wife's cheek. "Our vassals and some of our allies, they ken that we're no' entirely mortal, Mistress Walsh. 'Tisnae something we tell outsiders, or those we cannae trust."

Did that make her an insider, or trustworthy?

"I appreciate your candor," Charlotte said, and got to her feet. "Excuse me, but I need to get some air."

## Chapter Nine

Once Charlotte escaped the great hall she followed the path to the herb gardens, where the earthly perfume of rosemary, sage and mint scented the air. The setting sun cast an amber glow over the curtain wall, turning the sentinels standing watch into gilt-edged silhouettes. She tried to imagine what life would be like for men who couldn't age or marry or have children. Bleak, endless centuries of watching the mortal people they cared for grow old and die, obviously. No wonder Darach didn't want to get involved with her.

*Then why did he kiss me like that? Like I was the only woman he'd ever wanted so much that he lost all control? And why didn't he tell me?*

"I reckon we've shocked you again, my lady,"

Darach said, startling her as he stepped out of the shadows. "Forgive me for no' telling you all."

"I understand." No, she didn't. How could he keep something this huge from her? If she hadn't cornered Luthias about the lack of clan families, would any of them have ever let her in on their big secret? "You can assure the laird that I won't tell anyone."

"I neednae." He looked away. "We trust you, lass, and I...I care deeply for you."

Just as her father had, Charlotte thought. He'd made her believe he was fine after her mother had left, and said that he loved her, while he'd been secretly drinking himself to death. Knowing Darach could do the same thing to her was the last straw.

"You care for me?" She had to clench her hand to keep from slapping him. "Chieftain, from the moment I dropped in that spring you've been treating me as if I can't handle anything. It's true that you didn't know me at first, and I did arrive traumatized, but I've calmed down. I've also accepted everything you told me about the magic sword, the time-traveling and being brought here to save the MacRoss. You should have told me the rest."

"Aye, you're right." He took a step toward her. "Charlotte, 'twas my doing. I wished only to protect you."

"It's easier for you this way, isn't it? Treating me like a helpless child instead of a woman, so you don't have to deal with this." She took hold on his tunic and pulled him close enough for their noses to touch. "You're protecting yourself, not me."

Darach took in a quick breath, but didn't touch her. "'Tisnae your fault. I'm the one to blame."

"Maybe you're right. Anyway, I don't need your protection anymore, so you can go back to being the immortal second-in-command." She saw Camdyn walking toward them and stepped back. "Excuse me, but I have something to do." She walked quickly toward the armorer, and said to him, "Is he following me?"

He frowned. "Darach? No."

"Good." She looked at the small bundle he was carrying. "Are those my blades?" When he nodded she gestured in the direction of the lists. "If you're ready, let's get started with my training right away."

As he walked with her around the stronghold Camdyn kept glancing at her. Finally he stopped her just outside the arch leading into the practice area.

"You shouldnae train when you're angry," he told her. "We'll begin on the morrow."

"I'm not angry." She wanted to scream, but that was out of frustration. "At dinner Emery and Luthias told me about the clan being half-Fae immortal brothers, so you don't have to lie about that anymore."

"Och, no wonder you're so crabbit. Follow me." Camdyn led her to the back wall, where some straw bundles shaped like human figures stood mounted on wooden poles. "Choose one you can imagine as the attacker from your time."

Charlotte studied all the forms before pointing to the shortest. "That one."

"Head, neck, chest, belly, tadger, knees, shins," Camdyn said, pointing to different areas on the target's form. "Where first should you strike with a blade?"

"I don't know," she admitted. "The chest or belly, I suppose."

"You dinnae suppose killing with a single strike. You practice." He removed a wooden dagger from the bundle and offered it to her. "Close your eyes. Remember him as he hurt you. How he moved, and what he did. Look at the target again."

She opened her eyes, and could almost see the killer's chilling smirk on the blank straw head. "Now what?"

"As he struck you, he left parts of himself unguarded. 'Tis where you shall strike him." He waited another moment, and then said, "The bastart's come for you, woman. He means to carve you up, the butcher. Shall you allow him do as he pleases?"

His taunt made others emerge from her memory, all framed with the killer's high-pitched laugh.

*Are you still trying to hide from me?*
*A hunter always knows where to find his prey.*
*Must you force me hurt you so much, precious?*

Charlotte gripped the hilt of the wooden blade as she rushed at the target. She drove the point into the side of his scrawny neck. Straw scratched her fist as she yanked out the practice weapon and rammed it into his side. She kept stabbing the form over and over, in the lower belly and the thighs and then in the upper part of the head where his beady eyes would be.

At last her arm jerked as the dagger caught on something, and she couldn't free it. Panting, she released the hilt and stepped back. Not much was left of the target; the straw she had yanked out lay on the ground around the base of the pole. Seeing it made her swallow hard. She also had white marks all over the front of the dark tunic Emery had lent her to wear.

"No attacker stands still. As you strike, so would he," Camdyn told her, and held up his chunk of chalk. "I marked where you left yourself unguarded, and you didnae once see my hand as I did thus. A blade buried in any of these places, 'twould end you."

Charlotte wiped some sweat from her upper lip and took a deep breath to dispel the nausea. "You didn't warn me to be on my guard."

"'Tis why he hurt you in your time. Ever and always must you guard yourself." The armorer pulled the straw away from her practice dagger. "That, 'tis what I must teach you. I reckon you already ken how to kill."

She saw the split in the pole where the blunt tip of the wooden dagger had lodged. "I did that?"

"Aye." He tugged the practice blade free and frowned at the splintered end. "'Twould seem I must make you another before the next lesson. I shall fetch you on the morrow at sunset." He reached out and plucked a piece of straw from her sleeve. "Until then, think on what I've told you, Charlotte."

Although dismay and shame twisted inside her she made herself look him in the eyes. "Thank you, Camdyn."

After he left, Charlotte bent down to gather the stuffing she'd hacked out of the form. If she had been fighting a real man the straw would be blood and body parts, and her own ferocity horrified her. Since she had decided to become an artist she had immersed herself in endless daydreams of magical places and amazing characters; she'd also actively avoided anything dark or depressing. The negative energy from such things, one of her teachers had told her, could be toxic to a creative spirit. That was how Charlotte had always viewed herself, as a woman who only saw beauty, and painted her dreams.

*I'll never be that woman again.*

A GUST OF WIND MADE THE WINDOW'S COVERING flap against Fyn's face, rousing him from a long and happy dream of hunts past. At first he resisted waking, as he wished to remain with all the creatures he stalked. Opening his eyes, he bit back a curse as he realized he had fallen asleep in the granary, where any of the MacRoss vassals might have found him. He looked out through the window to see the tall, pale-haired wench from the future kneeling on the ground and gathering up loose straw.

*They've left her unguarded.* This was his chance; he would end her now.

Fyn lifted his crossbow and aimed his bolt at the back of her neck, only to have his target blocked by the broad back of the man who stood in front of the granary's window, only a few inches from Fyn. A nearby torch cast enough light on him to reveal the paleness of his flesh, and the wooden cloak pin he wore.

Taveon, the MacRoss war master—an even greater prize than that slut.

Reaching for his dagger, Fyn knew he could kill both and still escape. He'd stab Taveon in the back through the window, and when he dropped he'd shoot Charlotte Walsh. Another gust of wind swept Taveon's hair to one side, but the biting cold of it stung Fyn's eyes and carried a cold dampness that settled against him.

Slowly the hunter released his dagger, biting down on his tongue to stop the howls rising in his throat.

*Wee piglet, you're caught in your own trap.* Athdara Martin's ghost appeared beside him, her transparent fingers reaching out through the window to play with the edge of the war master's tartan. *What shall you do now?*

Fyn could not say anything in return to her; his voice would give away his presence in the granary. His hand shook as he reached for the pouch of salt he kept on his belt.

*Do you reckon that shall drive me away?* Athdara's bitter laughter echoed inside his skull. *'Tisnae the place I died, and you didnae kill me.*

Fyn sank to his knees, tasting blood in his mouth as his teeth cut into his tongue.

*Dinnae despair, wee piglet.* Her misty arms came around him, hugging him with an icy embrace. *I shall ever and always be at your side now. You may never escape. Why didnae you bring Prince Kaer's sain to me?*

"You shouldnae be here," a low, melodic voice said, making Fyn jerk.

The dead woman vanished as another man came to stand beside the war master. Fyn saw the red-gold hair of the MacRoss laird, and crouched down and held his breath.

"Nor should you," Taveon told Luthias. "Now that you've come, mayhap you should go and order your chieftain down from the balcony, and your armorer back to the forge."

"I cannae nursemaid them forever," the laird said, and sighed. "'Tis time the two of them sorted out how 'twill go with her."

The war master leaned back against the granary wall, making it creak. "So you've seen how 'tis for them."

"They're no' lads anymore, Brother, and the clan, we're under threat again." Luthias patted the back of his shoulder. "You may keep watch, but dinnae meddle unless you see blood drawn."

"Oh, aye, for no blood, 'tis reassuring," the war master muttered as the laird walked away. After a moment he also left.

A large hand covered Fyn's mouth, making him grab his dagger.

"Be still," the master whispered against his ear as he disarmed him. "I see 'tis tempting, but you cannae yet end her. Only the chieftain dies tonight. I must learn why the Fire sword chose her, and what she brought with her from the future."

He sagged back against the big, strong body. "You'll permit me watch you torment this one, aye?"

"Of course, my beloved lad." The master's hand stroked over his snarled hair. "I'd never deprive you of your delights. Now, wait until the chieftain stands alone, and then you may kill him. If no' tonight, then in the morning—and Fyn." His fingers grabbed a handful of his locks, tugging on them painfully. "Dinnae disappoint me again, else I cast you into the shadow realm, where you shall forever be tormented by those you ended." He held in front of his nose a glittering slice of icestone etched in black.

Tears of pain and fear burned in his eyes, but something in Fyn's twisted heart grew as cold as the Fae charm. "I shallnae, Master."

From the balcony above the lists Darach watched Charlotte, who stood staring in disbelief at the target she'd hacked apart. The gentle scent of the flowers climbing the wall beside him perfumed the air, but even their sweetness could not soothe him. Her back had been turned toward him when she had used the practice blade, but the ferocity of her strikes and complete lack of hesitation told him she had been in a blind fury. He suspected Camdyn had said something about her attacker to trigger such rage. As soon as the armorer left the lists Darach drew back and then stalked down the passage to intercept him.

As soon as Camdyn saw him he stopped in his tracks. "Eventide, Chieftain."

Two guards at the other end of the passage looked over at them, and one nudged the other.

"'Tis naught, lads," Darach called to them, and then shoved open the door to a storage room. "A word in private with you. Now."

Once inside the armorer leaned against a wall and folded his arms. "Before you again clout me, I told the lady to ask you train her. She didnae wish to trouble you, and chose me."

"So you looked upon her face, yet bruised and cut from the bastart who near beat her to death, and said aye." Darach unbuckled his belt. "Disarm."

"I shallnae tussle with you," Camdyn said, straightening. "'Twas at her bidding. I'm bound to protect her, the same as any MacRoss."

"No, you reckoned 'twould anger me to learn you'd train her. Or you wished watch the lady make a fool of herself in the lists, so you'd crow on her as yet another useless wench." He removed his hooded cloak, and set aside his sword and daggers. "You may despise me all you desire, but Charlotte came to us to save the clan—to save your unworthy arse."

"You reckon since you found her she's yours?" the armorer countered, bunching his hands into fists. "You're no' the laird. She's no' Emery."

Darach eyed him. "I'm her true protector, chosen by the sword."

"Ever you've been a fool for wenches," Camdyn said, sneering the words. "To what avail, Brother? None may even look upon you without shuddering."

Suddenly he knew something the surly armorer didn't wish him to see. "Aye, but she's kissed my ugly face, and confessed she wants me. You she but bids train her, and you so handsome a lad." He smiled. "Och, well, there's yet Ailsa, eh?"

The armorer's expression turned ugly, and he threw a punch that Darach easily avoided. Using his lightning speed he hooked Camdyn's leg and sent him sprawling, and then hauled him to his feet. This time the armorer brought up his fist, intending to strike his jaw, but Darach flung him away before he could land the blow. Camdyn fell against a table that collapsed under him, but pushed himself up and wiped a streak of blood from his chin.

"Never moved you so fast," he said, taunting. "You'd use the sword's boon to prevail over me, and at last prove yourself to her the better man? You shame yourself."

"Shut your facking mouth." Darach seized his arm and wrenched it behind his back as he shoved him face-first into the wall.

"The truth makes you squirm, I ken." Camdyn grunted as he twisted, trying to free himself. "She'd rather train to fight than rely on your protection. What should your Charlotte think of you now as you beat me bloody for helping her, Chieftain? Shall she beg you make her yours?"

"You eejit," Darach said as he fought to keep him pinned. "I've belonged to the lady from the moment she dropped out of the sky. Since she held the Fire sword at my throat. Since she looked upon me and didnae shake with fear. I ken you covet my place beside Luthias, and command of the garrison, but Charlotte, she's no' mine. I'm hers. Aye, and so I'll be forever."

The armorer suddenly went still. "Now you shame me."

Although he still wanted to smack his head into the wall, Darach realized that was as close to an apology as he could expect. He also suspected Camdyn struggled with the same penchant for Charlotte as he did. He had never known the armorer to want any woman.

Anger and sympathy warred inside him as Darach released him and stepped back. "What next, Brother?"

"How should I facking ken? With your boon I cannae proper brawl with you anymore." Camdyn turned to face him, his nose bleeding and his mouth sullen as he stalked toward the door. "Go and look after the lady."

Darach followed him out, and went down to the lists, where he saw Charlotte bent over and gathering up the straw that had fallen from the target. This close he spied dozens of cuts on her fingers and the sides of her palm; beads of blood gleamed on one long scratch across her knuckles. She had struck the target so hard she'd hurt herself, and yet hadn't shown any sign of pain. He'd trained men long enough to recognize what was happening to her. Her anger had grown so much that soon it would drown her heart.

Darach went over to stop her from using the wash barrel.

"Dinnae, my lady," he told her. "The men change the water only just before they train in the morning. 'Tisnae clean."

"Thank you for the warning." She hid her wounded hand behind her back as if it were something that disgraced her. "I'll go and wash up in my room."

"My chamber, 'tis closer." He gestured toward the garrison hall. "And I've salve for your cuts."

She looked down at his boots. "I can't ask for your help, not after the way I spoke to you."

"You didnae ask. I offered." Darach smiled. "Dinnae fret, lass. I've a short memory. 'Tis needed when serving as a chieftain with five hundred hot-tempered half-brothers. As for what you said, 'tis truth. Only ken my silence, 'twas truly meant as a kindness."

"I know, and I wish I had chosen my words better." Charlotte sighed as she looked down at her hand. "I don't know why I'm like this. It's like I want to pick a fight with the world, and I've never been like that."

A surge of relief made Darach relax; at least she realized the change that had come over her.

"Training to fight, 'twill help release such anger." He hated that Camdyn would be the one to teach her, but he had to accept that she would make her own choices. "Come and we'll see to your hand."

Charlotte didn't say anything more as she went with him to his chamber. While he fetched clean water, the salve, and some linen for bandaging, she moved to stand by the window. As she looked out at the night sky moonlight poured over her, silvering one side of her face while the glow from the lanterns gilded the other. In that moment she looked so lost and alone that Darach wanted to enfold her in his arms.

*'Tisnae the only reason you wish embrace her.*

Of course her beauty dazzled him. For centuries he had admired lovely ladies like her from afar, perhaps because he had always been so unsightly to behold himself. The few women he'd taken as lovers had looked away from his face or asked him to extinguish the lanterns so they could fack in complete darkness. Yet Charlotte had never regarded him as disfigured. Indeed, she had treated him as if he were as handsome as any other MacRoss.

"Come and sit by the fire," he said, and brought everything he needed for her hand to the table there.

When she lowered herself into his chair he placed the empty basin on her lap, placed her hand over it, and slowly poured water from the jug over her cuts.

"You've no' the callouses and thick skin of a fighter," Darach said. "You should wear gloves when you train."

"I've always taken good care of my hands," she said dully. "In my time I wore gloves when it was cold outside, and used a healing balm to protect them from drying and chapping."

"Mayhap we've a salve that may do the same," he said. "I'll speak with the sages on the morrow."

"I didn't know how much I've been holding in since I came here." She stared at the small wounds as he bathed the blood from them. "Camdyn said to imagine the straw target as my stalker in the future, and that was all I could see. I couldn't stop myself. But when the practice blade got stuck in the pole, I realized how furious I was—I am—and just how much I want to hurt him. I want to kill that monster. That made me sick."

"You're at war with your heart, lass." Darach wrapped her hand in a dry cloth before he set aside the basin. "You desire vengeance for the wrongs he did to you and yours, but 'tisnae in you to harm another. The true battle, 'tis inside you."

She looked into his eyes. "You've been through the same thing?"

"Aye. I told you of my brother Kendric who saved me from the storm." He removed the cloth and began applying the healing salve. "Some years ago we discovered him stealing from the clan. He lied to the laird and claimed 'twasnae him, and I set out to show him innocent, only to find proof of his thieving. When I confronted him, he again lied, and I lost my temper, and we beat each other bloody. When they pulled us apart, he called me a blind fool and then left." Wrapping a bandaging linen around her hand, he added, "I've no' seen him since."

"You must have suffered a lot since then," Charlotte said.

Darach nodded. "Kendric's ever been my favorite brother. As a lad I wanted naught more than to stay at his side. Each morning now I wake wishing I could find him and make him pay for what he did, and yet hoping to hear news that he's alive and well. How I regard him shall ever battle on in my heart." He tied and tucked the ends of the bandage in the folds, and then loosely clasped her wounded hand between his. "You're no' wrong to wish dead the bastart who hurt you. Only ken 'tis a wont against your true nature."

"I'm sorry I took it out on you." She leaned forward, putting her arms around him, and rested her cheek against his shoulder. "I shouldn't have done that."

Embracing her proved more torture than comfort for Darach, but he held on, sensing that she needed to be held. Charlotte's determination to rely only on herself tore at his heart; in her time she must have always lived that way.

"Dinnae trouble yourself, my lady," he assured her. "I'm your protector, and stronger than you reckon."

Charlotte drew back. "I'm not so sure that's a good thing."

"You've naught to fear, my lady." He frowned. "I'd never permit anyone harm you."

"You let everyone depend on you—me, the laird, his wife, your clan—but it seems like you don't have anyone to be there for you since you lost Kendric." She rose to her feet and briefly touched his shoulder as she moved past him. "Why isn't there anyone for you to rely on, Chieftain? Who protects you?"

She left his chamber without another word.

Darach waited for a moment before he tidied up and carried the basin to empty it outside. Seeing the water stained pink with her blood sink into the charcoal pit where they emptied their wash basins made his gut clench. Remembering what she'd said tore at him, as every hard truth did. Kendric ever had been his strength and shield against the harshness of the world. He'd believed the bond between them a thing that could not be broken. Yet so easily his brother had abandoned him when he'd run off to be a mercenary. He'd never once admitted to his betrayal of the clan or made any amends for what he'd done. Since that terrible night when Kendric had left, Darach had never again relied on anyone, and while he had always known that, he'd never reckoned why.

How had Charlotte seen that so clearly? Darach

turned to look up at the garrison tower, and the basin fell from his hands as he again endured the pain of losing the brother he had loved most. After so many years that wound remained open and raw, and so it likely always would.

"Eventide, Chieftain," Taveon said as he came to stand by the pit. "'Twould seem you're in need of a new wash basin."

"What?" Darach glanced down and saw the broken pieces of what was left of his. He hadn't even realized he'd smashed it. "Och. Aye."

The war master crouched down and began gathering the largest shards. "'Tis good to smash some crockery now and again, if 'twill keep you from doing the same to Camdyn's ribs or head."

"I'm no' angry with him." He didn't want to say Kendric's name, or dwell anymore on the harm his turncoat brother had done to the clan and him. Instead he bent down to help clean up the mess he'd made. "Did you see Charlotte training?"

"Aye. She did well. So did you, for no' stepping in as doubtless you wished." Taveon carried the smashed pottery over to a rubbish barrel and dropped them inside. Once Darach had done the same he said, "The laird sends me on the morrow to haggle with Ramsay MacAnvoy over some nags he desires for less coin than they're worth."

"Bid him buy his mounts from the lowlands," he suggest. "He'll pay half what we ask, and spend twice more on feeding and doctoring such poor beasts."

"I shall borrow your words to persuade him loosen his purse strings," the war master said, sounding unworried. "Or you might ride along with me to his stronghold. 'Twill do you good, and we'll stop at that tavern you like on the journey back."

He shook some tiny shards from his fingers. "You neednae coddle me, War Master."

"If I wished to play your *màthair*, I'd be speaking to the lady." His mouth hitched. "She doesnae want Camdyn, Brother, nor he her. Dinnae see what 'tisnae there."

"As you say." Darach glowered at him. "I cannae go with you to MacAnvoy's, but ride with at least two guards. We've yet to capture that fack bone cobbler, and your broad back makes a fine target."

As he walked up to the entry to the garrison hall, he saw the war master walk back to the pit and bend to pick up something. Not wishing to see more proof of his foolishness, Darach went back inside.

## Chapter Ten

By the time Charlotte returned to her room her hands wouldn't stop shaking, but she couldn't blame it on the cool night air. She added some wood to the fire and after washing up stood before it to undress and put on the lightweight linen shift she'd been using as a nightgown. The radiant glow of the flaring flames caressed her skin, but the growing chill inside her seemed immune to the heat. Every time she thought about the target she had hacked apart, she wondered what she would do once she held a real blade in her hand. She also remembered how fast she had put a knife to Camdyn's throat when she'd thought he meant to hurt Emery.

*Is that who I really am underneath it all?*

She climbed into bed, huddling until her body

warmed the linens. Ever since her mother had abandoned her Charlotte had been more relieved than hurt, but Leona had never tried to hide who she was. Her complete disinterest in being a mother had firmly established the boundaries of their relationship. She'd never once seen her parents touch, much less kiss or hug. For his part, her father had loved Leona with the fawning, perpetually dismayed eagerness of an acolyte about to be excommunicated. He must have known he couldn't keep her happy, as that was exactly what had happened to him when her mother had run off with her rich lover to France. After the divorce her father had become like a ghost of himself.

Charlotte would not do that to Darach. Even if he couldn't marry a mortal woman, he deserved to be loved by one who wouldn't prey on his emotions so she could use him like a body shield.

Slowly she began to drift off, her thoughts untangling as she thought of the public gardens near her apartment, and the woodland walks she often took to gain inspiration from the birds and flowers in spring. She found herself climbing up a broad series of stone steps to a terraced area that had sloped beds bursting with blooms. As she walked along she let her fingertips trail over the delicate petals and breathed in their sweet scents. Now and then she would pass a worker, and their stares made her uncomfortable, so she kept heading up toward the highest terrace.

*I don't need a blade. I need a paintbrush.*

The warmth of the sunlight didn't quite dispel the chilliness biting at her, but she ignored that as she climbed higher. The gardeners that she passed kept staring at her, and some muttered things that buzzed a little in her ears. She didn't know why they disliked her presence; all of the gardens were on public land. This was where she was supposed to be. It was her first and best retreat from the world, since the day her mother had heartlessly made it clear that she'd neither wanted or cared about her, and set her father on the path to committing slow suicide. Until she had escaped into art, Charlotte had drifted aimlessly, unable to find any place for herself. That was why she had begun creating new worlds: so she could live in them.

*I'm an artist, not a killer.*

At the top level all the beds appeared bare, as if they hadn't been planted yet, but Charlotte saw an overlook at one end. She had to hoist herself up onto a ledge to get the best view of the woodlands, but once she stood there she understood why she had come to this place. They couldn't see what she did: the shadowy spaces in and around the gardens, where things that hated the light hid themselves. That was what she needed to do in the other place, the place where they had offered her sanctuary. She needed to see for them.

"I'll find you," she murmured, her hair blowing and her shift billowing as the wind picked up and tugged at her. She closed her eyes as they stung. "I know you're still in the future, but you're here, too. I can sense it."

"Is that really what you think, my precious?" a soft voice asked. "Or are you pretending you're not a killer like me so you can have him?"

She glanced over her shoulder at the hooded man standing behind her, a bloody knife in his hand. Suddenly the gardens vanished and she was on the rooftop of the hotel where he had attacked her, and he was striding toward her. She didn't have the sword in her hand, or any way to defend herself.

"This time you cannot escape, you stupit bitch," the killer said, and smiled so broadly she could see his teeth gleaming in the darkness shadowing his face. "Once I have that blade, all time shall belong to me."

Charlotte backed away, and then turned and ran. Her heart pounded in her chest so hard she wondered if it would burst. She had to step on a mechanical box to climb onto the ledge at the very end of the roof, and when she looked down she saw a bunch of white-faced tourists staring back up at her. They seemed strange, and so small, like dolls.

"You cannae face what you're becoming, my precious." The killer gazed up at her, but he had no face, just a mouth filled with sharp-looking teeth. He held out his hand. "I understand, for I did much the same. Come and permit me end your suffering."

She turned away from him and looked up at the stars. She'd always wondered if people really meant it when they claimed they weren't afraid to die. Now she knew.

*Charlotte, dinnae move.*

Why did she hear Darach's voice even here, seven hundred years from his lifetime? Maybe it was wishful thinking, and she had only imagined him. Everything about him, the clan, Dun Lasair and even Emery were like stories from a book. Was it even real, any of it? Or had she somehow ended up in an afterlife made from her own illustrations?

"Charlotte, dinnae move." This time Darach's voice sounded very real, and much closer. "Stay still, lass. I'm coming for you."

*I'm not dreaming this.*

Charlotte opened her eyes to see nothing but the night and the sprawl of the forest. Cold wind swirled around her, and she looked down to see her bare feet on a narrow stone ledge. Far below she could make out the pale faces of several men gazing up at her, and the cloak they held around the edges like they were preparing to spread it out on the ground.

*Or trying to catch something. Like me.*

She reached out with her hands on either side, but there was nothing around her she could hold onto. Above her she saw only the night sky. Her balance, the one thing that had probably kept her from falling off the ledge, started to become wobbly.

"Where am I?" she asked, centering her weight and holding as still as she could.

"You're on the watch tower ledge, lass," Darach said, his voice very soft and gentle. "I'm climbing up to you. Stay there, and dinnae move."

It seemed to take forever, during which time Charlotte wondered if it might be better if she did fall. At least that way she wouldn't take him with her. Then boots appeared on either side of her bare feet, and a cloak fluttered around her. The hard, solid heat of the chieftain's body pressed against her back.

"I'm tying a rope around us both, Charlotte." As Darach did that, his breath warmed her cheek. "Kyal and Muir hold the other end, and they shallnae drop us should we lose our footing."

"We've got you, my lady," one of the guards called from someplace below them.

"How high up are we?" she couldn't help asking.

"Higher than you should stand in the night wind, lass." Darach took hold of her arms. "I'll step down now, and then turn you toward me. Put your arms about my neck, and your legs about my middle."

Charlotte thought she would be too afraid to move, but as he dropped down a step his hands guided her, and then she was clinging to him as he made his way down a ladder. When she looked up she saw she had been perched on the top of a ten-foot wall, and shuddered.

"Good work, lads," Darach said as he stepped off the ladder. When she did the same, he swung her up in his arms. "Tell the guards below we're safe."

He carried her inside and down the tower stairs, but instead of taking her to her chamber he went to the garrison hall.

"You don't have to do this," Charlotte told him. "I can walk. I'm not hurt."

"'Tis good, for I'm scared witless." He took her through a throng of clansmen who looked at her as if she were crazy before he strode into his bedchamber and kicked the door shut. He grabbed a tartan and brought her over to the fire, where he sat down with her, holding her on his lap just as he had the first night she'd spent in this room.

"Dinnae," Darach told her when she tried to get up. "'Tis for me, no' you."

"I wasn't trying to kill myself," Charlotte told him as he wrapped her up in the plaid. "I had a nightmare where I was standing on the roof of the hotel. The stalker had chased me to the edge. I was trying to decide if I should fight or jump. I don't know how I got there. It was all a dream."

"You didnae dream yourself onto the ledge, my lady." His mouth tightened. "A guard saw you walking the passage toward the tower. He called your name many times, but you wouldnae answer, so he came and fetched me."

"I was sleep-walking?" That astonished her as much as finding herself about to jump off the tower, but then she remembered waking up in front of the windows and another time in the great hall. "All right. I think it's happened before, but I never went outside. I'll have to start locking myself in my room at night."

"No. You'll sleep here, with me," he said, his tone almost savage.

Charlotte found it suddenly hard to breathe. "Is that an order, Chieftain? You seem to forget that I'm not yours to protect any longer."

"You're too important to the clan." He tucked a piece of hair behind her ear. "I'll assure you'll no' escape again."

"Are you planning to tie me to your bed?" She

meant to make that sound like a joke, but her voice went low and husky. She saw the flare of heat in his eyes and an answering surge bloomed in her middle. "I'm kidding, of course. You can just bolt the door. I'll sleep on a cot."

"After tonight I shallnae sleep unless you slumber at my side." His gaze shifted to her lips. "'Tis a big bed, and I'll be your blanket. I'm a light sleeper, so any move you make shall wake me. Naught more shall happen."

Charlotte had made up her mind to stay away from him, but after what had just happened she realized how dangerous that was—and how she needed him for more than her personal protection. She also wanted to kiss him so much her whole body throbbed with longing.

"I don't want to sleep with you so I can keep warm." She turned her head and pressed her lips to the side of his neck. "You're not a blanket to me."

"Wait, my lady," he said, his voice dropping low. "Wait and ken you're sure, for if you come to me, I shallnae resist. Nor shall I let you go again." He turned to look into her face. "I darenae even kiss you now, for I fear I'll drag you to the floor."

"Emery advised me against that." It should have been funny, but seeing the desire in his eyes made her curiously solemn, as if she stood poised to cross a threshold into a place that might be wonderful or terrible. "But you can kiss me any time that you want to."

"I want more than kisses." He bent his head, close enough for his breath to warm her mouth. "You ken that, aye?"

"That's the problem." Whatever distance she'd hoped to keep between them collapsed under the weight of her wanting him. "So do I."

He turned his head so that his lips brushed across her cheek. "Then I'll give you as much as you wish of me. You've only to reach for me, my beautiful lady, and I'm yours."

TAVEON STOOD OUTSIDE THE LAIRD'S BEDCHAMBER, listening for a moment before he lifted his hand to knock. A light trill of laughter made him lower his hand again; he would not interrupt what he knew to be the only time Luthias and Emery had for themselves. Silently he walked down the passage to return to his quarters, and then changed direction and headed for the forge.

He found Camdyn banking the fire in the furnace, and glanced at the lengths of wood he'd set out on his work table. The presence of so much steel and iron around him made Taveon's skin itch. He took care not to touch anything, for thanks to his weakness even momentary contact with any metal would burn and blister his flesh.

"I'm finished for the day," the armorer said without looking at him. "Return on the morrow."

"I saw you with Mistress Walsh, and I wish to ken something." He picked up the wooden dagger she'd splintered, which was made of larch instead of the oak Camdyn always used for such pieces. "You gave her a practice blade made of softwood?"

"Aye, I whittled it from a piece of old cladding I found down by the loch. I reckoned 'twould soon snap in her hand." Camdyn turned around, and the light from the lanterns showed his swollen nose and a deep cut on his chin. "While I make another, 'twill give Darach time to persuade her to cease training and find a pursuit better suited a wench."

Taveon wondered who had given Camdyn's face a pounding, and then saw the set of his jaw and decided against asking. "You're a devious bastart."

"High praise from the MacRoss master of trickery." He closed the furnace door and removed his heavy gloves. "You didnae come to tirl my arse or speak of Mistress Walsh."

"I found Darach out by the charcoal pit. He'd smashed his wash basin, or so he reckoned. I said naught of what did." He removed the broken crossbow bolt he'd removed along with the shards and showed it to him. "'Twas knocked from his hands."

Camdyn took the broken shaft and held it in the lantern light. "Someone wishes to end him. You didnae show him the damn thing?"

"He went inside before I spied it. I couldnae tell the direction or time of the shot, or if the assassin yet lingered. I've guards searching outside now, but 'tis likely he'd fled." Taveon tapped one of the carved wooden fletches. "I've never seen such on crossbow bolts. You?"

"We fletch ours with leather, as do the Carack. To carve them thus takes time, and 'tis foolish, for most bolts may only be fired once before they're ruined or lost." He turned it over. "'Tis quality work, the broadhead. Only the forging, 'twasnae done here in the highlands."

Taveon shook his head. "You cannae ken thus."

Camdyn gave him a narrow look. "I'm the clan's facking smith, and I ken the work of every other from here to the border of the lowlands. We forge swallowtail broadheads for battle, as the barbs cause more injury if they're pulled from the wound. Your assassin's bolt, 'tis a far simpler bodkin, and half a hand longer than highland smiths forge." He inspected it again. "'Twas meant to pierce armor or chain mail, but 'twould do the same to an eye or heart."

Taveon frowned. "Who could forge such, then?"

"'Twas a Norseman, or a smith taught by a Norseman. 'Twould explain the carving of the fletches as well." He handed the broken bolt back to him. "Your assassin purchased these far from here. Out in the islands they've villages of folk who name raiders as blood-kin, and even still trade with them. Mayhap there, or in the Norse-held territories across the sea."

"My thanks." Taveon sighed. "'Tis the second attack on the chieftain. How could the bastart gain entrance to the stronghold so easily? I've spoken to every guard, and they've seen naught."

"Arrange a signal for the guards to close all the gates at once," Camdyn suggested. "Then if the intruder tries yet again, we may trap him inside the walls and corner him."

Taveon considered that. "'Twould mean awaiting another attempt, which may never come."

"After two such? You may expect another." He pulled off his work apron and hung it by his bench. "Tell Darach your scheme, for he should ken someone's hunting him."

"I tried persuading him ride out with me to barter with Ramsay, but he shallnae leave Mistress Walsh unprotected." He saw Camdyn's scowl and suddenly put everything together. "So 'twas Darach bedecked your face."

"He's too quick now for me to repay the favor." He hesitated before he said, "When you go speak with the MacAnvoy, guard your words. If he desires see the nags himself, say you'll bring them to his stables. Dinnae for any reason invite him to Dun Lasair."

Taveon didn't need the armorer to tell him why. "Ailsa schemes to come here and demand in person the laird's permission for you to wed her, then."

"She vowed as much in her last dozen scrolls. Ramsay shallnae permit her come here alone, but if invited he might bring her along with him. Then we shall never be rid of her." Camdyn wiped his hands on a rag before he regarded him. "Luthias reckons soon he shall stop burning her messages, and instead deliver them to her sire so he may ken his daughter's foolishness."

Taveon winced. "Mayhap 'tis for the best. The MacAnvoy should send her to her mother's people in the west. They've a fine clan, and plenty of strapping young warriors. Surely one shall catch her eye and replace you in her heart."

"Or out of love for that bampot wench, Ramsay shall declare the MacRoss his enemy and attack us."

The armorer eyed him. "Be ready for such, War Master, for I reckon Ailsa's madness didnae come from her *màthair*."

"And what of Mistress Walsh? Shall she drive you and Darach to such madness?" When Camdyn said nothing he knew Luthias had been correct in his suspicions. "Since Kendric left, you and Darach do naught but quarrel and fight. Should you drag the lady into the clash between you, 'twillnae end in just another brawl."

"We've already come to blows over her. Darach claims she wants him." The words came from the armorer as if dragged out by trawling lines. "Only ken should she change her mind and come to me, I shallnae refuse her. Once she's mine, I'll kill any man who touches her."

"No' that you're counting on such." Taveon watched him stalk out of the forge, and rubbed his aching head. "Fack."

## Chapter Eleven

Being safe in Darach's arms after another brush with death made Charlotte imagine herself as a rescued princess, but her Rose Knight had been a fairytale character. Her deep attraction for the real man took a decidedly erotic turn as his teeth nipped her earlobe, and the velvety dampness of his tongue stroked the flesh beneath it. Nothing had ever aroused her as much as the way he touched her now, his work-roughened hands rasping against her skin as he forgot to be careful and instead caressed her like a woman he meant to pleasure.

*This is why he was afraid.*

Charlotte could sense herself changing, as if every touch stripped away some façade she had worn all her life. Darach's heat and desire melted away the cool, collected woman she had been to reveal her primal female self. She had never experienced emotions so powerful or fearless.

*Can I do the same for him?* The lukewarm encounters she'd had in the past didn't reassure her, but no man had ever made her want to tear down all the barriers she had spent a lifetime building around her.

*Yes. This night, me, and the man I've been waiting to find. That's all I need.*

Darach moved his arms under the plaid, one hand curving over the top of her thigh and the other stroking her arm. She shifted her legs apart in silent invitation, and closed her eyes as he caressed the sensitive skin on the inside of her thigh.

"Does this count as reaching for you?" Charlotte asked as she slipped her hand around his strong neck. "I don't think I can wait until we're in bed."

"Aye, 'twill do." He brought her hand to his mouth and kissed her fingers. "Only I want you naked for me."

"I'm not wearing anything under this shift." She rubbed her hot cheek against the thick softness of his bronze mane. "But you knew that when you picked me up and carried me here, didn't you?"

"Aye. I didnae wish anyone to see how thin this wretched garment 'tis on you—save me." He nuzzled the side of her neck. "Nor do I wish to love you in a chair. Permit me turn down the lanterns, and then we shall take to my bed."

"Leave the lights on. I want to see what's under your clothes," she told him, looking directly into his eyes as she shifted off his lap and onto her feet. "And if you really want me naked for you, you'll want to look at me, too."

"Show me, then," Darach told her.

Charlotte unwrapped the plaid, folding it to give herself a little more time to gather her courage. She'd always been passive during sex, probably because she'd never experienced any significant arousal from foreplay. Now she had grown drenched between her thighs, and all Darach had done was pet and nuzzle her a little. What would happen when they made it to the bed?

*I don't care if I come apart at the seams and embarrass myself. It doesn't matter, not with him. I want to be real with him.*

"Charlotte, wait," Darach said as he got up and came to her. "'Tis been a long day for you, too, my lady. I wouldnae press myself on you if you're weary."

"You're still trying to be polite." Reaching for the hem of the shift, Charlotte pulled it up and over her head. "That has to stop."

Although she knew she had an attractive body, standing naked in front of him required more daring than she imagined she had. Yet she pushed past the doubts about herself for Darach. She wanted him to think of her as beautiful and sexy, so much so that he would forget to be polite. She wished she could drive him so crazy that he would pick her up, toss her on the bed and do whatever he wanted to her.

Darach looked at her body, reached for her, and dragged her up against him. He bent his head and kissed her, his hands stroking down her back to cup her bottom. As he ravaged her lips Charlotte whimpered with need, and he lifted her up and carried her a few steps, putting her down atop a table beneath the window.

"This is not your bed," she murmured against his mouth.

"'Tis too far, and you're naked for me. I cannae wait another moment." He reached back to jerk at the laces of his pants, and then pushed them down before pulling her hips to the edge of the table. "I'll take you now, or go mad."

Before she could catch her breath he pulled her closer, rubbing her bare breasts against the muscle-paved wall of his chest as he reached down between them. Charlotte gripped his shoulders as he fit his broad cockhead between her folds, and then pressed in. Looking down at his thick, heavy shaft as he came into her made a surge of sensual excitement jolt through her; sending another gush of wetness that enveloped him with her own liquid heat.

"Darach." Charlotte had never watched herself being penetrated, and knowing he was doing it while the sensations from the heat and stretching and friction spread through her made it all the more thrilling. "I think my heart is going to explode."

"Ken I wished do thus to you when I saw the moonlight on you here, that first night," he told her, his voice growling the words. "You'd been hurt, and needed gentleness, so I couldnae do more than be kind. Only touching you and carrying you and seeing you undress, 'twas torment. 'Twas all I could do no' to strip you, hold you to the wall and put myself inside you."

"That would have been better for me than the gentleness, I think." Charlotte brushed her cheek against his as she curled her arms around his neck. "I wanted you, too, from the moment I saw you climb out of the loch. I wanted you inside me." She leaned closer, and whispered, "I do every time I'm near you."

Darach made a rough sound and tangled his hand in her hair. "Have me, then." He pulled her head back as he thrust deep inside her, his mouth catching the gasp of delight that burst from her lips.

From that moment the man simply took over her body, his thick cock plowing into her while his hands caught and squeezed her breasts. Darach's strength could have made all of that painful, but he knew exactly where and how to touch her. No other lover had treated her as if nothing else existed outside of the two of them joined together. He kissed her just as wildly as he touched her, his passion bordering on brutal and desperate. Yet everything about him like this excited her, being impaled on his rampant shaft and unable to run away as he abandoned all that polite distance. As he fucked her she couldn't control herself; the last of her defenses and pretenses dissolved into nothing. She wrapped her legs around him so she could lift her hips and take him deeper, and arched her back to rub his chest with the hard peaks of her breasts.

"Please, yes." She heard herself begging him in a voice she didn't recognize, deep and husky, and filled with ragged longing.

"Aye, Charlotte, take my cock," he muttered, watching her eyes as he stroked deeper and harder into her softness. "'Twill be spilling inside you soon. I want to see my cream painting your thighs. I'll watch you quake with your bliss before you slumber in my arms. Each night, every night."

"Then I'm never leaving your bed." She let her head fall back as her body began to shake from the onslaught of sensations. "Oh, please, Darach."

"Aye, 'tis what I want," he crooned, putting his mouth against her throat and sucking at her delicate skin before he kissed her ear. "Give me that pleasure on my cock, so you grip me sweetly, and I fill you." He moved his hand to the top of her sex, pressing his thumb against her clit and rubbing it in time with the hammering thrusts of his shaft. "Give all to me, my lady."

Inside her clenching pussy his cock swelled, and Charlotte uttered a startled cry as his fucking and caresses pushed her beyond wild sensation into a climax that made everything pale around her. She held onto him as he jerked and jetted inside her, the soft warmth of his seed triggering a second wave of joy. She had her hands tangled in his hair and her mouth frantically kissing his, and she didn't care. He had done this to her; drawing her out and making her reveal her secret self. He had uncovered her, the real Charlotte, and the consequences would change both their lives.

*Now he belongs to me.*

Darach pressed his brow to hers, his panted breaths mixing with her own. "Charlotte, never shall you rid yourself of me."

She brushed her swollen lips against his. "I was thinking the same thing."

She held onto him as he lifted her off the table

and carried her over to the bed. He lay her atop the coverlet before straightening and stripping off the clothes he'd neglected to remove. Charlotte stretched as she watched him, her limbs still shaking a little with the aftershocks of becoming his lover. He had a magnificent body, all long limbs and thick, bulging muscle. Even now his penis remained half-erect, slick and reddened as it was from pumping inside her.

Charlotte reached out with a strange but welcome confidence, and trailed her fingers along his gleaming shaft. "You look good with me all over you."

"Do thus and I shall come in you again," Darach warned, his eyes narrowing.

"You keep making me promises like that and we'll never sleep." She sat up and put her hands on his hips, urging him closer to the side of the bed until his erection nestled between her breasts. "Look at how nicely you fit right here."

"Aye." The word rumbled out of his chest as he cupped her breasts, pressing them against the sides of his cock. "You've the loveliest chebs."

"Is that what you call these. I like that word." She smiled, and then dipped her head to kiss the satiny dome of his cock. "I've never done this, but I've always wondered what it would be like."

"To hold a man thus?" he asked, and then caught his breath as she parted her lips over him and slowly lashed him with her tongue. "Och, Charlotte, you'll make me spill again."

"I want you to." She pressed a kiss on his cockhead. "In my mouth this time, so I can taste you."

His legs shook as she tugged him down on the bed, and then rolled on top of his legs and nudged them apart to make a comfortable spot for herself. Darach stared at her with so much desire in his eyes she guessed it was his first time as well. A flicker of doubt ran through her mind, but remembering the sex on the table gave her renewed confidence. If she didn't get it right this time, she'd keep practicing until she could give him all the pleasure he could stand.

"Watch me," she said as she wrapped her fingers around his cock. "You're so big I don't think I can take all of you, but I'll try."

Charlotte sucked his cockhead, tugging on it gently as she worked her lips over his glans and sealed them around his shaft. The velvety skin proved so soft and warm that just the sensation of his cock moving against her lips sent a rush through her own body. Her hair fell around her face as she stroked him with her mouth, taking him a little deeper, and rubbing the swelling thickness with her tongue. Then Darach reached down and gathered her hair in his hands, holding it back as he watched and groaned.

She let him slide from her lips to say, "Guide me. Show me what you like."

For a moment he looked as if he would refuse, and then he cupped the back of her head, and brought her mouth to his cock again. Once she had him in her mouth he urged her into a steady rhythm, murmuring soft words of encouragement as she sucked him. He swelled even more as she took him as deeply as she could, and beneath her his thighs tightened and shook, telling her how close he was. Tilting her head, she slid her mouth down until she held the full length of him against her tongue, and then moaned with the pleasure of it.

Darach uttered a wrenching cry, his hand tightening in her hair as his cock pulsed in her mouth. Charlotte stroked him in and out, swallowing each jet as he pumped into her, caressing the length of him until he'd given her his all. Releasing him slowly from her mouth so he could see that as well, she licked her lips and then rested her cheek against his hip as she kept hold of his shaft, his bliss pleasing her as much as if it were her own.

"My lady," he said, sounding satisfied and a little dazed. "Anything more you want of me, only say, and 'tis yours."

"I do want to tell you something," Charlotte said, stroking him gently with her fingertips. "I just don't know if I should. The smart thing to do would be to wait and see what happens. I've just never done this, so I don't know."

"I've the same quandary." He took hold of her, drawing her up beside him to share his pillow. He leaned in to kiss her lips before he said, "Tell me yours, and I'll tell you mine, all at once. Agreed?"

She took in a breath and then nodded. "On the count of three. One, two, three."

As Charlotte said "I'm falling in love with you," Darach said "I'd give you my heart." As their words tangled they stared at each other.

"I know the MacRoss don't marry or have families," she said, wanting to make herself clear. "I'm not asking you to make any promises for the future, either. I don't care about those things. I just want to be with you."

"Then from tonight we shall be together." He kissed her so tenderly it made her heart ache. "Until you bid me go, I shall stay by your side, my beautiful lady."

EARLY IN THE MORNING LUTHIAS RECEIVED A scroll from a laird he seldom saw but still considered a friend, thanks to some mutually profitable livestock trading as well as the more unusual aspects of rule that they shared.

"'Twould seem the Mag Raith mean to expand their herds this season," he told Duine as the master sage sorted through his own messages. "Lord Domnall wishes to pay a visit to see our young mares, mayhap to purchase some for his new breeding scheme."

"He's a strange one, with his old Pritani ways and that golden ink." Duine shook his head. "Mayhap you should advise him wait, my lord. The vassals, they've noticed that the Carack watchers and patrols on the boundaries, they've doubled of late."

"Aye, we've spied the same. Doubtless Struan wishes a show of strength. 'Twillnae affect Domnall's visit, as he travels alone." Luthias tucked the scroll under his belt before he noticed the sage looking uneasy. "'Tis something more amiss?"

"'Tis a message from Mairi, my lord. She and her family shall stay on Skye another moon to attend to some matters with their kin. 'Tis likely some dispute over her sire's holdings." He looked up at him. "I'm no' easy with the long absence of the clan's healer. Some of the elder sages, they're in growing need of her care. Sgur grows more reckless and absent-minded of late as well."

The oldest of the MacRoss's sage enclave had

always created more chaos than order with his trials, but Luthias recalled what Emery had told him about the latest and most dangerous endeavor with the ever-multiplying mushrooms he'd taken from the Fae crystal caves. Had they escaped and infested their forests, the consequences would have been disastrous.

"I shall ask Domnall to bring his clan's shaman," Luthias assured him. "'Tis but a day's journey for them to reach Dun Lasair, and Edane's a fine healer."

After writing the reply to the Mag Raith, Luthias went to the lists in search of Darach to warn him of the impending visit. There he found Ameron monitoring the sparring circles while Taveon stood peering into the window of a nearby granary.

"The chieftain accompanied Mistress Walsh for a walk this morning, my lord," Ameron told him. "Before he left he ordered everyone stay clear of the spring, so I reckon they went there."

Luthias nodded and thanked him for standing in for Darach before he went over to join the war master. "You grow very fond of inspecting our stores of late."

"Someone tried again to shoot the chieftain last night," Taveon said. "The only spot that provides concealment is inside this granary. I'd ask your lady to inspect the inside for any trace of the bastart."

"His lady says no problem at all." Emery appeared and wriggled between them to peer inside the window. "I'm going to need some more light, parchment, clean shallow bowls and everyone to stay outside." She sniffed the air. "What is that smell? It's like wet concrete."

Luthias breathed in. "'Tis fresh mortar."

"I'm guessing you make yours out of lime, right?" When he nodded she stepped back. "The clan stores sacks of grain in here, right?"

"Aye." He moved to look over her head. "What of them?"

"Some of the sacks over there have dark stains on the bottom. It could be mold, I suppose." She made a frustrated sound. "I need to go in to take a better look, but this is making me flash back to the shearing barn."

Taveon called for the guards to bring torches as Luthias looked for any sign of tampering before he went inside. The scent of mortar grew strong as he ducked under the low overhang and looked over the interior before allowing her to enter.

"It's better if you stay by the door, honey," Emery told him, and then called out, "I don't want to bring torches inside, Tav, so have your guys hold them by the windows." She made her way forward carefully, examining the floor before taking a step.

Luthias drew his sword as his wife crouched down by a bulging sack. "What see you?"

"I smell decomposition now. I'm going to look inside this one." She removed the small dagger she carried on her belt and cut the drawstrings, and then pulled open the top of the sack. She made a low sound of distress that tempted him to go and pull her away. Only knowing his wife and her methods kept him still.

"Tell me what you see," he said softly.

"There's a corpse in here. All I can tell is that it's female." She let out a long breath. "She's completely covered in dried, light-colored muck. I'll assume that's the mortar."

"I'll have the men carry her out," Luthias told her. "You can examine the body in the infirmary."

She turned around to look at him, her mouth tight. "Her hands are missing."

After searching all the sacks they discovered two more nude bodies plastered with mortar, and one of those also had no hands. Luthias directed the guards to carry the dead to the infirmary while Emery finished inspecting the granary's interior for evidence.

"There's nothing," she finally said, and walked outside to take several deep breaths before she regarded her husband. "Ask someone in the kitchens to send a big jug of vinegar to the infirmary. I need to clean off their faces so we can identify them."

As Taveon joined them, Luthias touched his wife's shoulder. "You neednae do such. I shall ask Duine."

"He'll probably faint when he sees them," Emery said, and sighed. "I used to love my work. Now sometimes I really hate it." She patted his hand before she headed into the stronghold.

Luthias watched her go, and then turned to the war master. "I wish to ken how anyone could hide three dead in a granary under the noses of a dozen of our sentinels."

"'Twas likely done at night, and with the bodies concealed in sacks, none would reckon such odd. We send grain to the mill but twice a moon, and that 'twas delivered a week past." Taveon glanced up at the inner curtain wall. "I dinnae reckon the dead as our vassals or clan. We maynae miss one, but three? They're villagers, mayhap."

"Or Carack." He thought of how Athdara Martin's body had been left for Callum to find on MacRoss land. "I shall attend Emery in the infirmary. Send for Darach, and put guards on Mistress Walsh."

"I shall fetch them myself." The war master nodded to two of the guards, who followed him out through the gates.

Luthias found his wife donning an apron and

gloves as his men left the infirmary. She had pushed together two work tables, on which his men had placed the dead, and draped the bodies with blankets from the neck down. Behind him a lad appeared holding a large crock.

"Bring that to my lady," he told him, and the boy carried the vinegar inside.

"Put it over here on the bench, thanks, Tom." Emery lit several lamps and brought two over to place beside the bodies. "Luthias, can you give me a hand with this?"

"I'll aid you if I may, my lady," Tom said. When she nodded, the boy put on an apron and the gloves she handed him. He paled a little as he glanced at the mortar-smeared corpses.

Emery removed the lid from the crock, releasing the sharp smell of vinegar, and then soaked two cloths in it before handing one to Tom.

"Dab the vinegar on their faces. It'll help loosen the mortar so I can remove it," she told him before meeting Luthias's gaze. "This will take some time. We need to find out if any of our people have gone missing."

"We've lost two men from the village, my lady." Duine appeared in the doorway, and covered his mouth and nose with his sleeve as he averted his gaze from the corpses and regarded Luthias. "Forgive me, my lord, but the headman came to the hall just now to ask our help. His blacksmith went to Dun Deigh to purchase ore yesterday and hasnae returned. A carpenter who oft works for the MacRoss also vanished while out marking trees for felling near the Carack boundary."

"I've only got one male body here," Emery said as she wiped her cloth over the dead man's neck. "The other two are female."

Duine flinched. "I've word from the Carack enclave that Lord Struan searches now for two maids and a trapper gone missing from his stronghold as well."

"Two missing from our village, and three from the Carack." Emery straightened and turned to Luthias, her expression grim. "Seems like someone is playing the Let's Have a Clan War game again."

"Go to Cook," he told the sage. "Bid her account for all the maids or female vassals in the stronghold." Once Duine hurried off, Luthias went to his wife. "Can you tell me how they died, my lady?"

"I need to complete my examinations before I can, but..." She hesitated, glancing at Tom before she drew Luthias out into the hall and closed the door. "The male only had a little mortar on his neck. I'm seeing what looks like rope burn and fingernail scrapes around a ligature mark under it, all indicating he was hanged. Both females have had their hands and hair cut off. There's mortar inside their mouths, and from what I can see, their throats."

His gut tightened. "Does that mean what I reckon?"

"The women may have been drowned in it," Emery said, and leaned against him for a moment. "Someone executed these people like they were criminals, and then put their bodies in our granary, maybe to make it look like we were hiding them."

"As 'twas done to make Athdara Martin's murder appear a suicide." Anger swelled inside him. "I must send a message to Struan and warn him."

"Tell him everything, and ask him to look for our missing people," his wife suggested. "Because if this plays out the way I think it will, he'll find their bodies on his land."

AFTER HE PLACED THE FIRE SWORD WHERE Charlotte could easily look upon it, Darach spread his tartan on the grass for her. "You're certain you wish to draw what happened the night you came to us?"

"I might rearrange the elements a little." She glanced at the blade. "It was nice of you to bring the sword, but won't the laird get worried when he sees it's missing?"

"The guards shall tell him 'tis with me." Darach sat down beside her as she began sketching the spring in front of them. He grew fascinated by how quickly she worked, and somehow made what should have been a jumble of lines into trees, water and rocks.

"You can talk to me while I do this," she said, smiling a little. "I usually listen to music when I work in my studio."

That startled him. "You hire musicians to play for you?"

"In my time we have wonderful things called sound systems and MP3 players that record musicians and play their music at the touch of a button, so we can listen to them over and over." Charlotte turned slightly and darted some glances at him as the stick in her hand flew over the drawing. "Music always inspires me. So do gardens and fountains. Songs, the smell of flowers, and hearing the sound of water fill up my soul with beauty. When I draw or paint I just pour it all back out. Everything right here is perfect."

He wondered if she knew how lovely she looked with the sun dappling her hair and face. "You must miss so much from your time."

"Not really. All I've ever needed as an artist is inspiration, and I've found plenty of that wherever I go." She set down her drawing stick and turned her book around to show him what she had sketched. "Today it's you."

Darach peered at the drawing, which showed him as he sat by the spring just now. She had drawn him precisely, detailing everything about him but the disfiguring splotch on his face. She'd made him look as he might have if he'd been born like any other man instead of the ugliest of the MacRoss Clan. It also dismayed him a little to realize for the first time how much he and Kendric resembled each other.

"When I look at you I don't notice your birthmark anymore." Charlotte set aside the sketch and took hold of his hand. "I just see you. The man I've been imagining and saving my heart for and hoping to find for years. For me, that's the real magic of your Fire sword. It brought me to you."

"You've said you shallnae return to your time." He brought her fingers to his chest and pressed them over his heart. "I cannae give you bairns, nor all you possessed in your time. That weighs on me as a dozen millstones, yet I'm selfish enough to ask. When 'tis time for the Fire sword to grant your wish, would you do as Emery? Would you wish to stay with me?"

"You're assuming I'll earn that privilege." She set aside her sketchbook and stood up, shrugging out of his tartan and folding it before she pulled off her tunic. "I have to save your clan first, and we still don't know how I'm going to do that. Making a promise I may not be able to keep is a bad idea."

He had mapped every inch of her long, lovely body with his eyes, hands and mouth, and yet to see her undressing still made him tremble like a lad. "Do you want a bathe?"

"No." Charlotte bent to remove her boots and trews, and then straightened, clad only in her underthings now. The morning sunlight cloaked her lovely body in a veil of soft light. "I want you." She waded into the spring, sinking down and slowly swimming toward the center.

As Darach stripped down to his skin he watched her stroke through the gently steaming water, her movements languid and graceful. Before last night he'd wanted to brand every moment he spent with her in his memory, to amass for the lonely nights he expected to endure once she left the clan to start her life anew.

He'd always been afraid to hope for more than he had, for he'd already been granted immortality and useful purpose. The birthing mark he'd suffered could have ended his life before it had even begun. Had he been born fully mortal, his sire would have likely smothered him and his *màthair* as soon as he'd seen the hideous blight on Darach's face. He should be grateful simply to be a MacRoss.

*'Tisnae enough simply to protect her.*

He dove into the spring, swimming out to where Charlotte floated, and pulled her up into his arms.

"I dinnae care about the wish, or the blade, or why it brought you to me," he told her, splaying his hands against her back. "I want you to stay with me. Whatever comes, I want no other. Take me as your husband, my lady. Wed me."

She linked her arms around his neck. "Even if I don't get a wish, and remain mortal?" When he nodded she hugged him. "I should tell you how crazy that is, saddling yourself with a woman who will age and die on you. I can't even give you a child to stay with you when I'm gone." She drew back to look into his eyes, her own shimmering with tears. "It's horribly unfair to you, but still, I can't give you up."

"Then say aye, and wed me as soon as we may, for there shallnae be another for me." Darach cradled her face between his hands. "I love you, Charlotte."

Kissing her sealed the vow in his heart, but tasting her cool lips and sweet mouth made heat and wanting explode inside him. He kept his mouth on hers as he clamped one arm around her and swam to the nearest edge, where he lifted her from the water and lay her on the grassy bank. She looked up at him, her gilded lashes sparkling with tiny water droplets, and bared her breasts. He watched her nipples bead as he pulled down her little trews to bare her pretty quim.

Cupping the tight curves of her bottom, Darach shifted down and lifted her to his lips, keeping his gaze locked with hers as he parted her with his tongue. She tasted of the spring and her own sweet slickness, and when he laved the little pearl between her folds she released a soft, needy moan.

"Oh, Darach." As he pressed his fingers inside her softness her head fell back and her hips arched. "I can't take much more of this."

Mastering her pretty little quim with his mouth made him understand why she had sucked him with such pleasure; this way he could watch and hear and taste every moment of her delight. His stiff, swollen cock pulsed and ached to be inside her, but denying himself while loving her slowly gave him a different sort of joy. He could tell from the sounds she made what pleased her most, and as he licked and lashed and stroked her he thought of all the nights ahead that he would no longer have to spend alone.

Charlotte's body writhed on the grass as she reached her peak, and Darach came up over her, sliding his heavy cock into her drenched sex. The desire stoked by loving her with his mouth and her clenching tightness made him spill almost at once, which made her cry out and shake a second time. He rolled onto his back and held her, convinced he had found an Elphyne of his very own in her arms.

After a long while she opened her eyes and lifted her head. The velvety dark brown of them took on a faint golden sheen from the sun as she regarded him like a cat basking in the sun might. "Can we get married today?"

He had been hers from the first night, but now he could see the same love in her eyes in that very moment. *She's mine.*

"If you dinnae mind only taking vows before the clan, aye." As she smiled and nodded Darach kissed her brow, and then her lips before he lifted her and carried her back into the spring.

The sun had gone well past its zenith by the time they finished bathing, loving again and then basking in its rays on the bank while their bodies dried. Once they dressed Darach combed her damp hair with his fingers before braiding it.

"Do you have to ask the laird for permission to marry me?" Charlotte asked.

"He did not ask mine when he wed Lady Emery." The sound of approaching footsteps made him turn to see Taveon jogging on the trail, and he went to intercept him.

As he saw the taller man's grim expression Darach's gut knotted. "What now?"

"Three dead vassals, found in the granary across from the garrison hall." The war master glanced at Charlotte before he added in a lower voice, "They've been bathed in mortar and hidden in sacks."

The twang of a crossbow made Darach grab Taveon as he dropped to the ground, and then chips of bark pelted them as a bolt buried itself in the tree behind him. He looked up and saw a shadow flitting through the woods toward the slopes, and scrambled to his feet, drawing the Fire sword.

"Take Charlotte to safety," he told him before he gave chase.

Darach drew on the speed boon as he ran, leaping over fallen trees and undergrowth that might have otherwise hampered him. He saw a cloaked figure just ahead of him, shorter and slender, and shouted for him to stop. The assassin ducked into an old oak grove and vanished just as Darach came within arm's reach.

Suddenly the ground fell away from under his boots, and he lunged across a wide pit. He caught the other side with an arm and one hand, kept hold of the sword with the other, and glanced over his shoulder. The old hollow had been dug out and then filled with so many sharpened stakes it looked like a giant black mouth filled with jagged teeth.

"You canny bastart." The bolt the assassin had fired had been only a lure to make him run after him and fall into this trap. Darach grunted as he pulled himself up and over the edge, and then rolled onto his feet and straightened, looking all around for any sign of the other man. "Come out and face me as a man, you facking coward."

He scanned the ground for boot prints, but the duff of oak leaves, twigs and moss showed no sign of being disturbed. The utter silence also brought no sound of fleeing. That meant the man had hidden himself somewhere nearby. When leaves rustled behind him he turned and nearly flung his dagger at Taveon, who stood on the other side of the pit.

"I sent the lady with the guards back to the stronghold, and she wasnae happy," the war master said, coming around the trap to join him. He scanned the forest in front of them before pointing to the base of the slopes beyond. "There, 'tis a cluster of niches in the rock."

## Chapter Twelve

The guards who brought Charlotte back to the stronghold sent other men out to the spring before they took her to the great hall. There she saw Duine having a hushed conversation with Cook and a villager. All three of them gave her bleak looks before the sage came to her and the other two hurried off.

"Mistress Walsh, mayhap 'twould be best if you retire to your bed chamber until we deal with some grievous matters," Duine said, lifting a damp, wrinkled cloth to his ashen face. His hand shook so much he appeared to be dusting himself. "I shall escort you and stay with you until 'tis safe."

"I think you need to sit down first." She guided him over to a chair and waved at a fearful-looking maid. "Could you bring some water for him, please?"

The sage uttered a groan. "I should be looking after you, lass, no' you me. 'Tis only that the Fire sword, 'tis vanished again."

"That's not true. Darach has the sword now." She sat down in the chair beside him. "Someone shot at him while we were at the bathing spring. He and Taveon chased after the attacker, but the guards made me come back here with them."

"Ah." A look of relief matched Duine's sigh. "Mayhap 'twas that fiend who killed the poor folk in the granary." The maid returned with a mug of water, which he took and drank down all at once, and then grimaced. "Forgive me. I shouldnae say more, else I frighten the wits from you as savagely as they've been shocked from me."

"I'm scared, too," she admitted, touching his arm, "but I'd like to know what's happened."

The sage's voice faltered more than once as he told her about the bodies the laird and his wife had discovered hidden in grain sacks.

"I fear 'twas the bone cobbler," Duine said, blotting sweat from his brow, "for he cut off the poor lasses's hands, and the toes from the man found with them."

Everything around Charlotte went dim for a second, and she heard a strange rushing in her ears. "Did he carve something on their foreheads?"

"I cannae tell you for certain, but from what I saw he sheared away the lasses's hair." Duine awkwardly patted her hand. "Dinnae think on such horrible matters, Mistress. The chieftain and the war master, they shall capture the brute."

*No, they won't,* she thought. "Where did they take the bodies?"

"Lady Emery, she's examining them in the infirmary," the sage said, and then looked alarmed as she got up. "'Tisnae anything you should see, Mistress."

"No one should, Master Duine." Charlotte touched his shoulder before she hurried out of the hall.

Two guards stood outside the infirmary, both holding their swords in their hands. The strong smell of vinegar and something like wet cement enveloped Charlotte's nose as she went to the open door and looked inside. Emery sat on a bench by two tables with three bodies on them, and was carefully removing chunks of what appeared to be plaster from the face of one corpse. Beside her Luthias stood with a dripping cloth in his hand.

Charlotte looked at the feet of the largest body, from which the toes had been cut off, and saw a deep red ligature mark around the man's neck. A strange sense of fate came over her as she went inside, joining the laird and his wife.

"Charlotte, you really shouldn't be in here," Emery said quickly, reaching for the shrouding cloth.

"It's all right," she said, looking down at the dead woman's face. "I have to tell you some details about the murders. Before the man was hung and the women drowned, the killer carved three symbols on the forehead. The bodies will be mutilated." Her vision blurred as she related the specific details, and she dashed the tears from her eyes before she added, "You won't find the missing body parts. He takes them with him."

The laird's wife got to her feet. "How do you know all that?"

"In seven hundred years the killer will do the same things to my friend Zoey, and six other women in Toronto, and hundreds more in other provinces. He meant to do that to me in the alley. It's how he always tortures and kills his victims."

Emery turned back to the body she had been working on, and wiped the woman's brow until the symbols appeared. "Is this some kind of signature?"

"'Tis Fae letters," her husband said. "Only they dinnae spell any word I ken."

Charlotte's stomach clenched. "For him to be able to kill in this time and the future, he must be a half-Fae immortal like you and your clan."

The laird caught her arm, making her realize she

was swaying on her feet. "Can you tell me anything of what he looks like, my lady?"

"I never saw his face, but he's slender, and about this tall." She dropped her hand in below her shoulder to give him a visual approximation. "He has an odd laugh, high-pitched and excited, like a young boy's. He also had something on the back of his left hand—a large patch of discoloration, dark blue with white streaks. It looked like a botched tattoo."

"'Twas a Carack birthing mark." Luthias's expression darkened. "Did he move oddly, lurching when he walked, as if crippled? Was his head dented, as if missing a large piece of his skull?"

"He wore a hood that covered his head, but he's not disabled. He's strong and agile, and moves very fast." Charlotte forced herself to recall the moments she had spent close to her stalker. "His breath stank of whiskey, and he also smelled like he hadn't bathed in a while. He kept talking about hunting and being a hunter, as if his victims were animals instead of people. He called me 'my precious' and spoke with no accent until he got angry, and then he sounded exactly like you and your men do. Does that sound like anyone you know?"

"Aye, mayhap." The laird appeared puzzled now. "Callum never permitted his youngest brother, Fyn Carack, go among other folk or to battle. I've no' seen the man, but 'tis long rumored he possesses a stunted body and feeble mind. They call him the master hunter, but that 'twas by Callum's command. He spends each day in the forest chasing game, but I've heard he's brought naught back to the clan for centuries. He's useless to his clan."

"That's because he's doing other things with his kills." Emery removed her gloves and set them aside. "I've seen precision disarticulations like this in some of the remains we found in the sheltering cave. Get out the parchment, honey. We need to let Struan Carack know that Fyn is probably the bone cobbler, which means he murdered Athdara and Callum, and tried to kill us. You should also mention that he could be hunting and killing people from both clans now."

While they were talking Charlotte quietly excused herself and walked toward the garrison hall. Darach and Taveon were out there hunting the madman who would someday become her stalker, Charlotte thought, and they had no idea what he could do. She doubted the guards would let her leave the stronghold to go and warn them, and then thought of what Elder Sgur had told her about the passage by the forge leading under the walls and out into the forest.

*I don't have to ask the guards.*

Darach advanced slowly toward the base of the ridge, checking the trees on either side of him before he reached the spot Taveon had indicated. There he found drag marks on the ground, and followed them up to what appeared to be a narrow rockslide. The moment he reached out and touched the stones they should have slid away; instead they remained in place. He took hold of one rock and tugged, and the planks of wood to which the stones had been glued fell over onto the ground. That revealed the entrance to a narrow space, from which the stink of rot came.

"Wait," Taveon said as Darach started to go inside. "'Tis mayhap another trap." He bent and picked up a stone, and tossed it into the space. It clattered against rock and something within fell with a strange hollow thud.

He looked down as a knob of bone rolled out of the shadows. "'Tis another of the bone cobbler's hiding places."

Darach found a fallen, sturdy pine branch, and used his dagger to cut a split in one end. Wedging a pine cone wrapped in browned needles in the split, he set it alight with his firesteel. He then held the makeshift torch inside the space as he and the war master stepped inside.

Neat stacks of bones sorted by type lay within, along with balls of twine and candle stubs set atop flat stones. The narrow cave extended back some distance, and flickers of light revealed the silhouettes of more bone piles, but no sign of the assassin. The blackened cave floor sparkled with tiny bits of a white crystal, which Darach guessed to be strewn salt.

"'Tis where the demented bastart fashions his gruesome trophies." Taveon kicked one of the bone piles, which fell over and revealed a small bundle of cloth.

Darach picked it up and unwrapped a small chest. Inside lay a locket, two thick braids of red hair bound in ribbon, and a small ring carved from horn, as well as enough gold coin to feed a family for a year or better. "He didnae keep only bones as trophies, Brother."

The war master took out the finely-made locket, which had been set with tiny crimson and green stones, and opened it to reveal the painted miniature of a golden-haired woman clad in blue and black tartan. "Stolen from some noble's lady, mayhap."

"Or 'twas never delivered. Athdara Martin set jewels in such baubles for the Carack." Darach replaced the locket and handed him the chest. "We must track him to where he hides now before we lose the light."

"I'll show this to the laird, and gather more men for the search." Taveon tucked the chest under his arm. "Mistress Walsh truly didnae wish to leave with the guards. You should take a moment to find and reassure her."

On the way back to the stronghold Darach kept watch for any sign of the assassin while pushing away thoughts of what might have happened if he'd fallen into the trap. It seemed the bone cobbler wished him dead, but he could not fathom why he'd been chosen as a target. Luthias or Taveon would easily command the garrison in his place; even Camdyn could take over his position. The only thing that set him apart from the rest of the clan was his finding Charlotte and the Fire sword, and becoming her protector.

*With me out of the way mayhap he reckons he could get to her with ease. But why should he want her?*

Darach recalled everything Charlotte had told him about the killer in her time, and how he had demanded she give him the sain just before the blade had transported her back through time. He glanced at the weapon in his hand. Only a MacRoss or a Carack would know that the Fire sword had been enchanted by Prince Ross, so how could someone born seven centuries in the future discover such?

*Charlotte's fairytale book.*

He stopped Taveon just outside the gates. "The bone cobbler, he trapped Emery and the lairds in the barn, and set it afire, aye? And killed Athdara to stage her death. All to start a war between the clans."

"So we reckoned." The war master frowned. "What matters that now?"

"Charlotte may ken something the sick fack doesnae wish revealed. His aims, his schemes, something." Darach thought for a moment. "'Twill be in the story that 'twas written in that book she illustrated."

"Emery said Charlotte hadnae finished remaking the book. I'll go up to the map room, and collect what she's done thus far," Taveon said. "You must speak with her at once, and bid her tell you the story."

Darach ran into the stronghold, finding Duine and some of his younger sages gathered in the great hall, but no sign of Charlotte. After sending the guards out to scour the lists and gardens for the intruder he went to ask the sage where she had gone.

"Mistress Walsh went to the infirmary, Chieftain," the master sage said, his voice shaking slightly. "She wished for some reason to see the bodies of the dead."

As he hurried through the passages, sending every guard he found out to aid in the search of the grounds, Darach thought of what Charlotte had told him about the madman in her time. She must have known something that she wished to confirm by looking upon the victims.

*Why didnae I ever ask her tell me the story?*

As he turned a corner in the passages he saw some torches had been extinguished, and then something moving in the shadows. Suddenly a crossbow twanged, and a bolt came flying at his chest. He caught it easily, but a tiny glass ball on the point broke, spewing a puff of glittering powder up in his face. He tossed it away, but as he stalked toward whoever had fired it his legs and lungs grew heavy, and his eyelids drooped.

"You may dodge my bolts, but no' my sleeping draught," a sly voice taunted him. "I've added something special to silence you, Chieftain."

Falling to his knees, Darach opened his mouth to call for help, but no sound would come from his throat. As a cloaked figure emerged from the shadows aiming a crossbow at him, he fell forward, completely unable to move now. The figure loomed over him, bending down to caress his face with a gloved hand before taking hold of his hair.

"Come now. I cannae spring my next trap without you and the facking sain," the intruder said as if on the other end of a tunnel, and then began dragging him into the darkness.

CHARLOTTE FOLLOWED THE PASSAGE TO THE FORGE, where she hurried past the open door, only to stop and backtrack. Once she was sure Camdyn wasn't working inside she went in to look for the dagger he had promised her. Fortunately he'd left it and the splintered wooden blade on one of his work tables; he'd also put a new wrapping around the hilt. As soon as she picked up the dagger the weight of it made her fingers clench. It fit her grip perfectly now.

*I'm supposed to hold graphite and brushes and palettes, not this.*

She kept hold of the blade as she turned and nearly smacked her face on a broad chest.

"Fair day, Mistress." Camdyn glanced down at the dagger. "As you ken I finished fitting the new hilt to your blade. The bootmaker shall fashion a sheath for it on the morrow. Why do you look ready to swoon?"

"I just saw the bodies that were found in the

granary." Charlotte was tempted to tell him the rest, but the armorer wouldn't understand. "Emery believes whoever killed those three people is the bone cobbler."

"Indeed." Camdyn's eyes narrowed. "Why did you come here, then?"

"I'm scared." That much was true. "I don't want to walk around unarmed anymore."

He reached out and touched her arm. "If 'twill give you ease, take the blade."

She thanked him, and walked out into the passage as if to go back to the hall. As soon as she heard him adding wood to the hearth she changed direction and went the other way, keeping her footsteps as quiet as possible. Soon the sound of hammering came from the forge, and she was able to run.

*Stay alive until I get there. Please.*

The passage had a barred door at the end that opened in the forest. Charlotte looked around until she remembered the direction of the bathing spring, and hurried in that direction until she found the trail to it. For a moment she hesitated, and looked back at the stronghold. Only the thought of Darach at the mercy of the killer made her turn her back on Dun Lasair.

*This is why the sword brought me here. To save him.*

By the time she reached the spot where they had

made love by the water her heart hammered under her breast. At the same time she sensed a strange certainty growing inside her, as if some part of her knew this was exactly where she should be. She saw the crossbow bolt still buried in the tree, and the broken branches in the brush where Darach and Taveon had gone after the intruder. She followed their trail to the slopes, where she saw a narrow recess in the rock. Flickering light came from within the dark place, and deep, fresh marks on the ground in front of it indicated something large had recently been dragged inside. The smell of blood and rot that came from it reminded her of the moment she'd walked into Zoey's house to find her friend butchered.

Charlotte tightened her grip on the dagger as she went inside.

A dying torch cast feeble light on the piles of bone that littered the cave floor, where the drag marks continued back into the shadows. She took down the torch and held it in her free hand as she moved forward, her throat and chest so tight now she could hardly breathe. The passage seemed to constrict around her until both of her shoulders brushed the sides, and then it suddenly opened into a much larger open space.

*This is where it began,* Charlotte thought as she took in the gruesome view. *Where he became a monster.*

All over the cave hundreds of thousands of bones of different sizes and shapes had been twined together in ghastly sculptures. Some formed spiraling columns, and others had been shaped into the animals from which they had been taken. To one side the torch illuminated a work area with tables fashioned from bones that had been mortared together, and long bones driven into the walls on which he had hung knives and other tools. In the back of the cave, a large, blackened pit of ashes sat beneath a hole in the cave roof high overhead. From the sheer number of constructions, Charlotte guessed the killer had been using this cave for a very long time.

Everywhere—on the bones, the walls, and even the floor of the cave—the three Fae symbols had been carved over and over, a silent yet screaming litany.

She turned, and looked across the small pool of murky water at a flat-topped boulder, on which a shrouded body lay. "Darach? *Darach*."

"You came too early," a familiar voice said, and shrill laughter echoed through the cavern. "I've no rope to hang the bastart, so he yet breathes."

"You don't need him." Charlotte walked forward, holding the torch higher as she tried to see where he was. "You have me and the sain. Wasn't that the point of all this? Let him go."

"'Tisnae what my master wished," the killer said, and a strong hand seized her wrist from behind, gripping it so tightly her bones ground together. "I've plans of my own now."

She bit her lip as he jabbed her in the back with the tip of a blade, and dragged in a shallow breath. "What do you want from me, Fyn Carack?"

"Drop that dagger, my precious, and I shall tell you." When she did, he chuckled and released her hand. As he touched the tip of the Fire Sword to her neck, he snatched the dagger from the ground. "You shall wish Nyf become the laird of the Carack."

*This is why it brought me back, because I'm the only one who could recognize the way he killed,* Charlotte thought. *So that I would expose him as the bone cobbler, and the MacRoss could stop him from killing. This all ends with me and him.*

As if confirming her suspicion the flame-shaped hilt began to glow.

"Did your master tell you to kill those people in the granary?" she asked, hoping to stall him as she tried to think of a way out.

"Aye, for 'tis the true sacred work." He put his other hand in her hair, twining it around his fingers. "Before the master took me in hand I'd only ended the lives of the creatures I hunted. He taught me that mortals, they're no different from deer or hares or boars. I've had such fun this past moon, chasing them and putting them to sleeping and bringing them here. I wish I'd killed that hoor Athdara."

Charlotte had to save Darach as well as the clan, but how could she? "They're people, not animals."

"They're flesh and blood and bone, like you. The sain, 'tis alight, so you've a wish to make now. What shall you choose?" He cackled. "Doubtless you desire my end, but then I'll cut your throat, and we'll both die. Or do you wish save your lover? Mayhap that 'tis the wiser choice. I doubt the clan shall soon find the chieftain, and until running water touches his lips he shallnae again wake. Creatures creep in here in the night, you ken—the smell lures them. They shall dine well on him, aye?"

She stared at her lover's shrouded body. "You're a monster, Fyn."

"My name, 'tis Nyf," he said into her ear, and tightened his grip on her hair. "Give your wish to me, and I shall spare you and the chieftain."

No, he wouldn't, she thought, and then calmed. Protecting Darach and his clan required her to do only one thing. It would be a terrible thing, and the pain and suffering she faced terrified her, but it would end this. Knowing she would save his life as well as the MacRoss made strange sense of what her dreams had told her.

*I see everything now.*

"I'll wish whatever you want me to, but first I want to say goodbye to him." When the sword started cutting into her neck she added, "Or you can kill me and get nothing but another corpse."

Fyn shoved her, knocking over one of the deer he'd cobbled together from bone. For a moment Charlotte thought he would kill her anyway, but then he clamped his sweaty hand on her neck as he marched her toward the altar.

"Say your farewell, then," he told her, sneering the words.

Gently she drew back the dirty linen covering her lover's face. In the flickering light the birthmark over his eye looked like a dark red rose. Her heart ached, and her face grew wet as she leaned over to press her lips to his left eyelid, and then his lips. She tasted the salt of her tears on them.

"I love you. I'm sorry I couldn't stay." Charlotte didn't resist as Fyn dragged her back from Darach and shoved her hand into the glowing hilt of the Fire sword.

"Wish me to become laird of the Carack Clan," he demanded.

Fae magic spread through her hand and into her

arm, and Charlotte took one last look at the altar. Darach's eyes opened, and then she realized that her tears were a form of running water. For a moment there was nothing but the two of them. She smiled at him, wanting that to be his last memory of her.

How lovely her life would have been with him, she thought, remembering every moment they'd shared. "Please take us to my time."

## Chapter Thirteen

"No," Fyn bellowed as her wish echoed in the cavern, and he tried to wrestle the blade away from Charlotte.

She held onto the hilt with all her strength, just as Camdyn had taught her. As the sword's magic swirled like a tornado of light around her she caught a glimpse of Darach stumbling away from the altar. He looked so frightened it wrenched at her heart, and then the darkness descended, swallowing her and Fyn.

*Good-bye, my love.*

A moment later Charlotte stood in the alley where she had been attacked, and looked around until she saw Fyn huddled against one wall, his eyes almost bulging out of his head. Over by the crates where she had dragged Detective Logan some torn strips of crime scene tape fluttered in the breeze, and dark blotches stained the ground, but no body. Then she looked over as someone came out of the nearby hotel stairwell door, and froze.

"I've been waiting and watching for you every night since you vanished, my precious." The hooded man strode directly up to her, a dagger in each hand. His voice echoed oddly in the alley, as if the sound were somehow delayed by a split second. Her hands tightened on the hilt of her weapon, but a dagger was instantly under her chin. "I knew you'd return." His gaze shifted down to the Fire sword. "And you brought the sain back to me. Such a good lass."

Sirens screeched somewhere close by, and a smear of red and blue lights hovered in the sky. Behind her the hunter wailed.

"I brought you another present," she told him. "Fyn Carack, the bone cobbler."

For a moment the killer went still, and then he began to laugh. His mirth blended with the sounds of the hunter's terror, and the air in the alley began to ripple as if giant heat waves were rising from the ground.

"Oh, I do like you, Charlotte," the killer said. "No one but a dreamer like you might have solved the mystery and made such a wish. Well done." He leaned to one side to look around her. "Get up, you eejit."

"I shallnae," the cowering hunter shrieked, and then turned to her and began to beg. "Take me back now. I dinnae wish to be in the future. I must become the Carack laird. No—I—I shall warn the master, and obey him, and kill them all for him."

"You shall do naught." The killer chuckled from the dark depths of the hood. "I dinnae recall coming to the future with you, Charlotte, so you've no' yet changed my past. After I finish you, mayhap he shall return on his own, and all shall be made as 'twas. I dinnae need the fearful little numpty getting in my way."

The hunter stood and brandished her dagger. "I fear naught."

"What of Athdara Martin's ghost? What of the master, you eejit?" The killer yanked back the hood concealing his face, which was identical to Fyn's. "Do you even ken what I've endured because of you and your madness, Fyn?"

"My name, 'tis Nyf," the hunter shouted back.

They were the same man from different times, occupying the same moment and place, Charlotte thought, relieved to know she had been correct. But even as she thought it, strange ripples rolled through the air, distorting sound and color.

*Being anywhere near an earlier version of yourself*

*would create a temporal paradox,* Emery had told her. *It's the kind of thing that could tear reality apart.*

The blade dropped out of the hunter's hand and clattered on the ground. "No. No, never should I leave Scotland. Never should I come to the New World."

"'Tis called Canada, you dolt. In your time the Carack shall prevail over the MacRoss, and kill them all, and then hold a grand celebration. Only in the morning after, when our vassals come to the keepe, they shall find every Carack dead. Your beloved master poisoned our clan, to make you laird of the dead." The killer quickly sheathed one dagger and caressed Charlotte's face before she could pull away. "Do you ken why I alone survived, my precious?"

"Because cockroaches like you are impossible to kill," she said.

He backhanded her, sending a jolt of pain into her cheek and jaw. As she started to raise the sword, he grabbed her arm. "You never came to my past, you interfering slut." He brought the hilt of his dagger down onto her wrist, dislodging her grip from the hilt. "I shifted the blame for the murders of the blacksmith and carpenter onto Struan, and the maids and the trapper onto Darach." Ignoring the pain in her hand, she grasped at the Fire sword, but the killer simply knocked it to the ground. He smiled at her as its metallic clang echoed over and over. "The MacRoss attacked the Carack, beginning many months of war. In the end my clan won, but somehow Struan discovered the truth. I ran away from Dun Deigh that night, and hid in the cave. The master assumed me dead along with the rest of the Carack." The killer gripped her throat. "Now you shall use that facking sword and wish me back to that time so I may save my clan."

"I've already used my wish to come here with him," Charlotte told him, bracing herself for what was about to come. "It won't give me another."

He grinned. "You reckon you've won? Yet the sain always returns to the MacRoss Clan, aye? As long as I carry the blade, then 'twill take me back."

"You darenae return instead of me," the hunter said, drawing a thin dagger from his belt. "'Twill end us both."

"We shall go together, then, you wee coward, once we deal with this hoor." The killer sighed. "I've ever wished to watch myself at work. Ply your blade now. Begin with these clever hands."

Out of sheer desperation Charlotte made a grab for the hunter's long dagger. He grunted with surprise and then punched her in the belly.

*No,* she thought, and looked down to see him twisting the blade buried in her body. *He stabbed me.*

As he yanked out the blade a huge, hot, tearing sensation pierced her and rammed into her spine, as if he had somehow cut all the way through her body. She gulped in air, unable to avoid the next thrust of the dagger but twisting so that it ended up glancing off her hip. The agony of the steel dragging across the bone as he wrenched it out again nearly made her faint.

"Hold still, you impatient bitch," the killer said. "You need see she suffers properly before you execute her, eejit. Och, give the blade to me."

With all the strength she had left Charlotte drove her elbow backward into his diaphragm, making him double over. As his chin hit her shoulder she brought her fist up and smashed it into his face, but somehow he held onto her, his fingers tearing at her skin.

"I was always your fate, Charlotte," the killer said. "In this time and the past. You shall never escape me."

Her eyes widened as she saw Darach step out of the shadows behind the Fyn from the past. Her lover saw the blood dripping from her abdomen onto the ground and his marked eye turned completely red. He bent down and picked up the Fire sword.

*Please take us to my time,* she had wished, as Darach had been struggling to reach her in the cave. The sain had now done exactly as she'd said, and brought them all to the future. When the man she loved met her gaze, Charlotte silently shaped with her lips the three words that she always wanted him to remember: *I love you.*

"I'll cut the tendons in her legs," the past Fyn told his future self. "She'll no' run away. Then I may–"

Without making a sound Darach swung the Fire sword down, moving so fast Fyn had no time to react. The blade neatly decapitated the hunter. As his headless body toppled over suddenly the hands holding Charlotte disappeared. She dropped onto her knees and looked back, seeing only an empty space where the killer from her time had been standing.

"He's gone." In disbelief she looked over at where Detective Logan's body had lain, and the dark stains and crime scene tape had also vanished.

*'Twill end us both.*

Killing the past version of Fyn meant he would never live to become her stalker in the future. The killer had been erased from time. That would change everything back to what it should have been. Zoey, the police officers, and everyone else he had murdered would still be alive.

*In this new version of the future I'm the only one who dies,* Charlotte thought as she sank down onto the ground. Her body had grown so cold, and yet, so warm inside.

*Love you, Zoe.*

Darach dropped down beside her, putting his hands under her and carefully lifting her from the ground. She knew what he was thinking as he looked frantically up and down the alley. Her body told her it was too late for that, and that she only had a minute or two left.

"I've come full circle," she whispered. "I'm so glad you're here. I thought I'd never see you again."

"The healers in your time, Charlotte," he said quickly. "Where are they?"

She shook her head. "It's time for me to go. If you can, take me back with you and the Fire sword to Scotland, my love, and bury me by the forest spring."

"You cannae die, no' here. We've too much to do, you and I. We're to wed, remember?" Tears slid down his gorgeous face. "You've but to make a wish."

"Bringing Fyn to my time and saving the clan was my wish. You coming along was just perfect." Charlotte tried to hold onto him, but her hands wouldn't work anymore. "All of the people in my time that Fyn murdered are alive now. My friend Zoey, and all the police officers he killed will live on, too. Thank you for that. Thank you for loving me."

"No, my lady, you must stay with me," he told her, his voice hoarse now. "I dinnae ken how to live without you now. I cannae live without you."

"When it's time, wherever I am, you'll find me again. I know we'll always find each other, my love." Her lips curved. "Fyn was wrong. He wasn't my fate. You are."

She took one last breath, filling herself with the marvelous woodsy scent of him. It wrapped around her like the warmest of blankets. Death didn't frighten her anymore; the darkness was quiet and safe, and there she would wait for her love, for he was her immortality.

AS CHARLOTTE'S EYES FLUTTERED CLOSED AND HER body went limp, Darach took the Fire sword from her bloodied hand, intending to hurl it away. Then his hand slipped into the grip of the amber hilt, and the fire of Prince Ross's magic surged up his arm and into his chest.

*You must be the strong arm of the clan, my son.*

"My lady saved the MacRoss for you, Sire," Darach said. "Now I beg you save her life for me. Give her back what this Carack madman stole from her, and return us to Dun Lasair." He brought the tip of the blade to his throat. "If you dinnae, then tonight I shall die at her side."

Fiery red-brown eyes glared at him from his distant memories. *You dare end your life over a mortal?*

"No' only a mortal, my prince." He looked down at his lady's pale, still face. "As you loved the Fae king's daughter Avarel, so I love Charlotte. I'm no' like you, and I shallnae go on without her. I've lived too long alone and unloved."

*For my pride I allowed you carry the burden of blood on your face, my son. 'Twas one of my deepest regrets. For that I shall do as you ask, so that you may live on and protect the clan—with her.*

Light flickered in the carved amber, and grew so bright it blinded him. He held onto Charlotte as a pure, fiery power swirled around them, lifting them up and then hurtling them down. Darach wrapped his arms around his lover as they fell into warm water only a few feet deep. When he got his boots under him he stood and carried Charlotte to a grassy patch by the bathing spring, and gently lay her on the ground.

She opened her eyes and looked up at him, her expression one of utter confusion. "Was I sleepwalking again?"

Darach shook his head, too overcome to speak. He ran his hands over her, but all of the terrible wounds inflicted by the madman had vanished. Everywhere he touched her his sire's magic sizzled against his flesh as it sank into her body. He recalled the same thing happening to Emery when she had wished to stay forever with Luthias.

Charlotte suddenly gasped and clutched at him.

"I was dying—no, I think I was dead. Then I was standing in the most beautiful garden I've ever seen, surrounded by orange and red flowers." She gripped his hands. "There was a man there, too. He looked just like you."

"You dreamed of Prince Ross, my sire," he said.

"He wanted me to tell you something." She frowned. "You saved the clan, too, by putting an end to the two Fyns. For that, the sword granted your wish. He said something else about changing me to keep you alive." She frowned and reached up to push back his hood. "I don't believe it. What happened to your face?"

"Never say you forgot I'm the ugly MacRoss?" he chided.

"Your birthmark." Charlotte brought his hand up to his left brow, where the raised flesh glided smooth and sleek under his fingers. "It's gone."

He could count on one hand the times his sire had looked directly at his marked face. Always the prince had favored Luthias, and Darach believed it was because of the noble, flawless features the laird had shared with his elegant *màthair*. He and Kendric had been their sire's mirror image. Darach always believed his own birthing mark reminded the prince that all of his sons would never be wholly Fae, and ever condemned to live in the mortal realm. As such he'd been sure the prince had never once loved him.

He had been wrong.

Helping his lady to her feet, he put his arm around her. "Come, my love. Come home with me."

Seeing most of the MacRoss gathered in the great hall filled Charlotte with so much happiness she thought she might burst with joy. Although her life would never be the same, she had found the love of hers. She and Darach had a future now, and it looked more beautiful than any garden she had ever imagined.

She glanced up to see Camdyn standing at the railing looking down at her and her lover, and his bitter expression struck at her like a slap. The smile he gave her in the next moment made his handsome face look unearthly and beautiful, and yet in his eyes was such sadness it made her heart wrench.

*Seems that you didn't see everything after all, Blondie,* Zoey would say.

As the clan noticed them and began shouting

Darach pulled back his hood to show his unmarked face to his brothers. That silenced everyone, and Luthias came down from the dais to inspect his chieftain's changed features.

"Who's the handsome swain you brought to us, Charlotte?" Luthias asked her. "Surely he's no' my second, the ugliest MacRoss in the clan?"

Darach laughed, setting off everyone else, and pulled the laird into his arms for a long hug. He then gazed around at the other MacRoss, his smile wide and his eyes filled with merriment.

"Dinnae be deceived by this pretty face, lads," he warned them. "I'm yet the Chieftain of the garrison, and more than ready to drill you until you drop." His gaze shifted up to the gallery level. "My lord, I need a word in private with you about the bone cobbler and what happened to me and my lady in the future."

Charlotte saw the armorer turn and walk off, and put her hand on Darach's arm. "I'll be right back, okay?"

He scowled for a moment, but then nodded. "Hurry. We've much to tell the laird."

She had to go all the way to the forge to find Camdyn, who sat in front of the furnace holding the wooden dagger she had splintered while training with him. He looked so miserable she almost turned around to go back to the great hall, but she knew she couldn't avoid this forever.

"I fought with my heart instead of a blade," Charlotte said, closing the door and leaning back against it. "You were right about me. I'm never going to be a killer."

His eyes glittered as he looked up at her. "And if I'd been the one in the spring that night you came? Would I hold you in my arms, and call you my lady now?"

"I lost my heart to Darach years before I came here." It seemed like a terrible answer, but it was honest. "I'm sorry, Camdyn."

"Aye, well." He rose and came over to her. "I'll collect the boon you yet owe me, my lady." He took hold of her hand, and raised it to his lips. "I ask you love my brother with all that fierce heart of yours. He's the best of men—and never tell him I said thus."

"I can do that." For a moment she thought he might kiss more than her knuckles, and then he tucked her arm through his and opened the door. "Are you coming back to the hall with me?"

"'Tis becoming my duty to escort there the ladies who save the clan," he told her. "Mayhap 'tis better. I've no patience with you wenches."

## Chapter Fourteen

Well-cloaked against the setting sun, Struan left Dun Deigh alone, riding down to the small graveyard outside the village. All of the revelations that had come from the MacRoss about Fyn had at last quieted the Carack clan. After seeing the ghastly things the hunter had cobbled together out of bone in the slope cave, the war master had returned to his stronghold and gathered the clan. Telling them the repulsive work Fyn had done in secret for centuries had left everyone appalled, as did the revelation that he had tortured and killed vassals from both clans.

"Laird Luthias agrees that we shallnae be held responsible for our demented brother's crimes against their vassals," Struan said, and saw many avert their gazes in shame. "I neednae tell you how fortunate 'tis for us that the truce remains yet intact. Nor shall we mourn Fyn, for he murdered Callum, and that I shall never forgive."

The one question no one dared ask yet lingered in Struan's thoughts: who had turned Fyn from a madman into a murderer?

He stopped a short distance outside the cemetery, tethering his horse before he approached the burial being performed. Revna stood by the grave as it was filled in by a pair of stocky villagers, her hair covered by a linen veil and her gown concealed under a dark tartan. She flinched each time the crier walking the narrow streets in the nearby village struck the bell he carried and called out the name of the dead. In her hands she held a small, ragged poppet that, suddenly leaning forward, she dropped into the grave. The men shoveling stopped their work and touched their brows, and she turned and walked toward Struan.

"What do you here, my lord?" she asked, her voice toneless.

"I wish to pay my respects to your sire." He looked past her at the villagers. "'Twas my brother murdered him."

Revna nodded, and went around him, walking toward a tiny cottage not far from the graveyard. He took a moment to stand before the grave and offer his silent apologies before he followed her. Someone had draped the cottage's threshold in nettles, which Struan knew the local mortals believed protected them against witchcraft. A small group of village men waited a short distance away, watching until he turned to regard them. Frustration and disappointment showed on their faces as they scattered.

*Vultures,* Struan thought, *eager to feast on the unprotected.*

After he knocked, the maid opened the door and stared at his boots. "My da cannae forgive you, my lord. He cannae even forgive your brother. He's dead and gone."

Struan grabbed the door before she could shut it in his face. "Nor can I make amends to the dead. I came to see you."

Revna went inside, removing her veil and the mourning tartan, and letting them drop on the oiled dirt floor.

To see where the young maid had lived before coming to Dun Deigh made Struan's jaw tighten. The clan provided better accommodations for livestock compared to the tiny, dingy, single room Revna had called home. No fire burned in the blackened hearth, and only a few moldy pears sat on the rough table. An ancient wooden bucket held cloudy water, obviously used time and again for washing. She had no bed, no furniture, and no candles or lantern; only one tiny window let in a little sunlight. On the floor the tartan he had given her lay in a bundle atop an ancient, moth-eaten woolen blanket. He knew she had used it as a pillow for her head, just as he knew after he left she would wash herself with the murky water, and perhaps even eat the spoiled pears.

"'Tis no' as nice as my room at the castle, I ken." Revna sounded disinterested. "Only 'tis how the poor live, my lord. My whole life I spent here, happy enough, I reckon."

"You neednae live in such squalor," Struan told her. "Gather your things. You shall return with me to Dun Deigh."

"So you may make better use of me, my lord?" She cocked her head. "You've plenty of wenches far prettier than me for that."

"You mistake your importance," he told her. "My steward cannae spare the time to train another to serve me."

"You're a clever one. The lies, they roll off your tongue so smooth." She began unlacing her bodice. "I'm yet a maiden, so you've the right according to the old ways. You neednae take me back to your castle for such. Fack me here, where none may see us."

Hearing that crude word come from her lips

struck him like a fist to the chest. "'Tis what you reckon I want?"

"I see how you look at me." With a few jerks she had pulled down her gown to bare her breasts. "Come, touch me. Put me on the floor. I shallnae stop you." When he didn't move she came to him, and took hold of his hand, pressing it over one small mound. She then slid her fingers over the bulge his erection made in his trews. "You're ever hard here when you're near me. 'Tis what a man puts inside a lass, aye? Do thus to me."

Her soft, cool skin entranced Struan. His cock still swelled in his smalls, stiff and ready to plumb the tender depths of her innocence. Like any man infatuated with a comely female he wanted to put his mouth on her, and tear away the shabby old gown so he could touch the rest of her. She wanted him, too, for her nipple pebbled under his palm. He longed to hear the sounds she would make when he came into her; to know if she would cry out his name as she found her pleasure and drenched his cock. In another moment he would have her on the dirt floor, and the thought did not repel him as much as what that would make of her.

It made him no different than the villagers who wished to slake their own lusts on her fragile body.

"No." He jerked up her bodice and pushed her back. "I didnae come here to use you thus."

"What more 'tis there?" She made a show of looking around herself. "I own naught but this cottage, which I must sell now to pay the crier and the grave diggers. Your groundskeeper came and collected all the traps and pelts my da left, for they belong to your clan. You may take back your tartan, I reckon. I'm never cold." Tears filled her eyes as she met his gaze. "So I'll give you my maidenhood, for 'tis why you came. Shall you pay me? The village *maister* said he would if I took him as my first."

Struan grabbed her, and gave her a hard shake. "You shallnae sell yourself to any man for coin. I forbid you. You shall come back to the stronghold, and do honest work in the kitchens, and live as my vassal. 'Tis a hard life, but an honorable one."

"I dinnae belong there," Revna told him, and when he pulled her into his arms she struggled for a moment before sagging against him. "Please, my lord. Please, let me go."

Holding her as if she belonged to him made no more sense than coming to fetch her himself. Yet he knew if he'd sent the steward Revna would have refused, and the dolt would have left her here to hoor herself. As poor and pitiful as she was, no one could take her pride from her.

"I cannae release you." The words tore from him. "I ken I should, only then I see you, forlorn and alone. You need my protection, and I...I need you safe."

She made a choking sound. "I'm naught to you. Naught to anyone."

"Would a laird come for you and drag you back to his stronghold if you werenae wanted and valued by him?" He stroked his hand over her narrow back. "I've come for you, lass. You're someone to me."

"I ken you want me," she whispered, hiding her face against his chest. "'Tis but fair I give myself to you."

"I'm in your debt now," he reminded her, his breath stirring her fine hair. "'Twas my hunter killed your sire. I cannae bring him back, but I may look after you in his place." He set her at arm's length. "Now take what you want from this hovel, and we shall go home."

All Revna took was his tartan, but she didn't wrap it around herself.

"You must never come back here alone," he told Revna as he lifted her onto his mount, and then swung up behind her and took the reins. "Or leave Dun Deigh without my permission. Promise me."

"Aye, my lord." She sounded exhausted now.

He kept his horse's pace slow so as not to jolt

Revna too much, and halfway along the road to Dun Deigh she slumped back against him, her head falling to one side. Under her right ear he noticed two small, overlapping purple bruises. They appeared to be the same size and shape as two fingertips, as if someone had tried to throttle her. Yet he saw no other marks on her neck.

Struan stopped a short distance from the stronghold and dismounted, catching Revna as she fell over into his arms. That woke her, and for a moment she clutched at him.

"Oh." She rubbed a hand over her face, looking like a sleepy child. "Forgive me, my lord. I've no' slept much since they found my da."

"Then you must take to your bed early tonight." He set her on her feet, and held her until she stood steady. "Rest well, for you've new duties. You're to prepare all my meals and bring them to me, and keep my water jug and basin filled with spring water. You must take my bed linens and garments to the laundress for washing, or to the seamstress when they're in need of repair. I shall teach you how I wish my boots cleaned."

"What say you?" Looking exasperated, she planted her little hands on her hips. "I'm no' a steward, my lord."

"No, you're my new chambermaid." Struan bent

his head to kiss her brow, and then swung up into the saddle. "Be a good lass now, and change into your work gown. Report to Cook and tell her of your new position. Then come to my chamber and prepare it for the night."

As he rode to the stables, the righteous pleasure he had enjoyed while rescuing the poor maid from her fate faded. He had taken her from one vastly unpleasant situation to place her in what might become yet another. Choosing Revna to serve his personal needs would cause resentment among the other maids, who had worked all their lives for the clan and doubtless hoped he'd favor them. His steward had already recommended a male vassal to serve as his varlet; he'd not take kindly to being ignored. Any member of the clan wishing to know more of what he did would plague Revna, and might even threaten her.

*Fack them. Ever I've asked for naught. I shall protect her, and keep her.*

By the time Struan had stabled and tended to his mount he knew what he had to do, and went to the sage's hall, where he found Reothadh in his work room studying some scrolls.

"My lord." The master sage stood and bowed. "How may I serve?"

He closed the door. "The elixir you made to bore

through stone works well. In a few days after the old tunnels have vented we shall go down and inspect them. Then I shall choose the miners I wish to work them. Do not ask why," he added as Reothadh opened his mouth. "I shall tell you more of my scheme once we ken the old shafts shallnae collapse."

The sage nodded. "Aye, my lord."

"'Tis one more thing," Struan said. "I've brought the trapper's daughter back from the village. He made no provisions for her, and, left there, the idiots who should protect her would have turned her to hooring. As I'm responsible for the death of her sire I'm taking her under my protection to serve as my personal chambermaid. She shall have the room adjoining my own."

Reothadh grimaced. "I dinnae ken if 'tis wise to show the lass such favor, my lord. She's an outsider, and, ah, different. 'Twill also cause the other vassals to revile Revna, and cast doubts on her chastity."

"Aye, which 'tis why you shall murmur into the right ears that in truth I've made her my bed wench. Say I'm too proud to openly name her as such." He folded his arms. "Also mention how angry I shall become should anyone bully Revna."

The master sage frowned. "I've never ken you to have a foul temper."

"Indeed." Struan smiled. "If anyone harms that wench, you shall make acquaintance."

From there he went to his chamber to undress, and found Revna snuffing out the braziers some fool had lit. He stood for a time to watch her graceful movements as she lit candles and placed them in the wall brackets, high enough that the heat of their flames would not plague him. Only when she finished at the back of the chamber did she turn and see him.

"Eventide, my lord." Revna bobbed, and smiled at him, her cheeks flushed. "I reckoned you wouldnae wish to roast in the heat of so many braziers burning."

Struan nodded, and gestured for her to continue. While she did he placed the apples he'd brought on the table, and took out his smallest knife.

"I've turned down the bed, my lord," she said as she came to him. "'Tis anything more I may do?"

"Aye." He cut a slice from the apple he'd been peeling and held it out to her. "Come and sit with me."

After the morning meal Charlotte walked out into the lists, where Darach stood with his back toward her while watching several men sparring. As soon as the clansmen saw her they grinned, but she shook her head and lifted a finger to her lips.

"Dinnae look at me, you daft eejits," her lover snapped. "Should the Carack attack on the morrow they'll no' be gazing about wondering what's what."

"Really." Charlotte slid her arms around him from behind. "So what's what, my knight?"

Darach went still, and then turned in her embrace and enveloped her in a hug.

"Lads, continue the matches and remember fight fair." He took hold of her hand and hustled her back inside, taking her into the garrison hall and then up to their chamber, where he drew her in before he bolted the door.

"I know that look," she said as she took a few steps back toward the bed. "When you were marked, your eye would turn more gold than red when you wanted me. But your eyes match now, and you just had me last night."

"Aye." He advanced on her. "And now, 'tis morning, and still I want you."

"That means someone else will have to take over training the men when you're not around—I'll guess Taveon will step up today, but soon you'll be sharing your command with someone else. Emery dropped some hints." She waited for him to scowl, which he didn't, and then smiled. "I never imagined you'd be okay with that."

"'Tis much work, and I'm not a selfish man. Then, too, I've a beautiful lady to coddle and comfort me." He picked her up and tossed her onto the bed. "As happens, I'm in dire need of such just now."

Charlotte propped her head with her hand as she watched him strip out of his clothes, her big eyes growing dark with desire. "I need to paint you like this."

"Now that I've a face to rival Camdyn's, you'd yet make sport of me?" He tickled her as he leaned over, and then quickly removed her gown, leaving her just in a thin shift. "If I look upon you naked, I shall spill on your thigh."

She tugged him down beside her, and rolled atop him. "Then I might just have to keep you here in bed with me all day." With her fingertips she traced the outlines of the birthing mark that no longer disfigured his face. "I never thought I'd see you again. Maybe that's why I can't stop looking at you. Waking up beside the spring and seeing you was the most beautiful moment in my life."

Darach hiked up her shift so he could come into her soft, wet quim, and once he had buried his full length in her he smiled. "You're the beauty, my lady.

I'm but yours—and more moments shall be ours, for we shall love forever."

~

MUCH LATER DARACH LEFT CHARLOTTE SLEEPING, and slipped out to the great hall. There he found Luthias standing in front of the portrait of Prince Ross, his expression thoughtful but his jaw tight.

"'Twas the only likeness painted of our sire during his lifetime," Darach reminded him as he came to stand at his side. "As much as you wish, you cannae burn the damned thing."

"For what you and your lady endured with that madman," Luthias said, "I'm yet tempted." He gestured for him to follow him to a table, where he poured them both a whiskey. "To Charlotte, who beneath all that beauty possesses the heart of a true warrior."

"To my beloved," Darach said simply, and touched his goblet rim to the laird's before swallowing the smoky spirit. He glanced up at the empty crystal casket over the great hearth. "When the Fire Sword vanished I imagined melting the blade in the forge when it returned. The thought makes me shudder now."

"Aye, I cannae tell you how often I've thought the

same." Luthias sat back in his chair. "Yet the sword brought to us our ladies, and saved the clan twice now." He took a long drink.

Darach sighed. "Taveon said you rode with the men who took the corpses back to the village, but you didnae name their killer."

"I left that duty to Struan Carack," Luthias admitted. "He came with his master sage to look upon everything Fyn had left behind in the cave, and 'twas he who at last deciphered the Fae symbols his brother had carved everywhere. NYF for the reverse of his name. For knife."

He recalled what the hunter had insisted was his name. "Prince Kaer ever referred to Fyn as such."

"Never shall I forget Struan's expression when he left the cave," the laird said. "'Twas why I accepted his apologies for the murders of our carpenter and blacksmith." He drained his cup and started to pour a second drink before thinking better of it. "I cannae drown my sorrows today. The Mag Raith should soon arrive."

Darach corked the jug for him. "You reckon this master Fyn claimed gave him orders, 'tis another Carack?"

"I dinnae ken, but 'tisnae a MacRoss." The laird's expression darkened. "From what the killer in Charlotte's time said of the bastart, he means to end both clans." His gaze shifted to the empty crystal crypt above the hearth. "I've set Camdyn to watching the sain in the forge. 'Twill be safe there."

"So shall we, Brother." Darach put his hand on his shoulder. "Stop blaming yourself for what you cannae ken."

"I should have taken better care of you and Charlotte." The laird gave him a sideways look. "If you ever leave the clan to travel through time again after your lady, on your return I shall have you flogged in the lists."

He chuckled. "No, my lord, you shallnae."

"Naked, in the lists. While your love and the entire clan watches." Luthias grinned fiercely. "And Emery, who I'd likely have to manacle to a target to keep from shielding you."

Darach held up his hands in surrender. "Ever shall Charlotte and I remain here at your side, my lord."

A short time later a tall, striking man with sea-green eyes came into the great hall, accompanied by a shorter, slender man with his long red hair in braids. Both had on new Pritani garments of a design that Darach had not seen anyone wear in centuries, and the red-haired man carried a pack marked with old healer's runes. From under their tunic sleeves golden ink glittered in the light from the lanterns, and they moved with the relaxed strides of men who knew they were among friends.

"Lord Domnall, Shaman Edane," Luthias called out, grinning as he went to meet them. "Welcome to Dun Lasair."

"Hey, is this why you wanted me to go to the village, which I didn't do?" Emery appeared beside her husband and grinned at the two visitors. "Hi, I'm Emery, his wife and before that the clan savior from the twenty-first century. You'd be two of the lost hunters captured and enslaved by time-hopping demons before you and your lovers escaped them, became immortal and took over a haunted castle?"

"The very same, my lady." Domnall bowed. "My wife Jenna was an architect in your future. Mayhap you should someday meet."

Edane grinned. "My Nellie as well, for she worked as a copper during Prohibition. Aye, and we've a Victorian governess, a World War Two resistance fighter, and a half-druid demoness with wings."

Emery laughed with delight. "I love medieval Scotland."

THAT NIGHT LUTHIAS PROMISED EMERY HE WOULD not be long before he left their chamber and went down to the forge. The door stood open, and when he looked inside he saw the armorer sitting at his work table, although he seemed lost in thought. As he went to join him, he saw a dagger in his hands. It had been polished to a finish so bright it reflected like a mirror, and looked exactly like the blade Charlotte had left in the future.

"I dinnae reckon the lady shall want that now." He watched Camdyn's fist tighten around the hilt. "'Tis a fine blade all the same."

"Aye, and she's to wed Darach, and stay by his side forever, while I remain here forging new blades and waiting for another desperate love scroll from Ailsa MacAnvoy." His eyes glittered with some savage emotion as he tossed the blade into his scrap bin. "How else may I serve, my lord?"

"Beginning on the morrow you're to train Muir to run the forge. He's eager to learn smithing, and possesses a strong arm and steady hand, so I expect 'twillnae take long. When he's ready to take over, I shall name you chieftain to serve as my second alongside Darach." Luthias nodded at his shocked stare. "The garrison, 'twill be commanded by you both."

Camdyn swallowed hard. "Why should you do such for me?"

Luthias remembered the long, silent look the armorer had given Charlotte when he had returned to the hall to hand her back over to Darach. He had appeared for a moment like a man seeing the wonders of Elphyne, and in the next like someone caste out of the Fae paradise. The armorer had finally lost his heart, or at least some of it, to a woman he could never have.

"You've given your all to the clan, and asked for naught in return," he finally said. "Taveon assures me 'tis no man better suited to command the garrison alongside Darach than you." He held out his arm. "Serve me well, Brother."

"Aye, my lord." Camdyn dragged a hand through his orange-streaked black hair before he clasped his forearm. "So I shall."

"Then, too, I came for the Fire Sword. After speaking with the Mag Raith, and his warning on leaving enchanted things unattended, I dinnae wish hide the blade here. 'Twould seem the threat to the clan, 'tis over, and yet I worry. We'll hang the blade in the great hall, and keep close watch." As Camdyn stared past him, he wondered if he had even heard what he'd said. "Never mind. I can return on the morrow."

"'Tis naught." The armorer took down a bundle of keys and went over to the large cabinet. "I took out the rest of the blades so I could check with a glance. I looked upon the Fire sword no' an hour past."

When he opened the doors he stepped back. "Och, fack."

Luthias walked over and looked inside, and then closed the doors of the empty cabinet. "'Twould seem 'tisnae yet over, Brother."

## THE END

· · · · ·

Another book awaits you in Immortal Highlander Clan MacRoss (Camdyn Book 3).

For a sneak peek, turn the page.

Sneak Peek

*Camdyn (Immortal Highlander Clan MacRoss Book 3)*

Excerpt

## CHAPTER ONE

August in Philadelphia meant a little less traffic to contend with, but Isabel Murray still preferred to bike the four miles to her job at the old auction house down by the river. Besides being great exercise, it gave her time to soak up the sun and improve her tan. Since summer had begun she'd used every excuse she could to be outdoors to bask in the light and heat. She'd always adored this season, as it seemed to peel away all the layers of weariness she endured while trudging through the long, dreary winters.

If there was a Heaven, Isabel hoped it would be an endless beach where the sun never set.

American flags still fluttered everywhere around the city; a few as remnants from last month's July Fourth celebrations. Most flew year-round, and nearly every business had a permanent show of some Americana. As the birthplace of the Declaration of Independence and the Constitution, and home to the Liberty Bell, Philly had always flaunted its perennial pride and patriotism.

Isabel certainly didn't mind. Like freedom she'd been born here, and while *The City that Loves you Back* might not have quite lived up to its marketing campaigns, CPS had kept her fed, sheltered and educated for eighteen years in foster care. Thanks to her own ingenuity—and quite a bit of good luck—she could now look after herself. That independence was all she had needed to make her life perfect.

*Almost,* Isabel thought as she avoided a couple of teenagers walking hand-in-hand. *I just have to meet someone nice, and then figure out how not to run away if they propose.*

Caleb, her ex, probably still hadn't forgiven her.

*I mean, did you have to scream like that?* he'd demanded, the last time they had crossed paths at the supermarket. *You scared the heck out of me.*

Isabel couldn't remember what she had mumbled

in response—probably some variation of *So did you*—before she had walked away from him, very fast. Okay, she had run again—and from then on she had shopped at another market, too.

Caleb had been a nice, steady boyfriend, always polite and punctual. Like her he never touched alcohol, and he seemed to really appreciate picnic and ice cream dates. That said, he had been a little too respectful, so finally she'd asked him if they were ever going to have sex. Isabel usually wasn't that pushy—she always preferred to let people do things at their own speed—but after three months of hand-holding and cheek and forehead kisses she had been wondering if he even liked girls.

Unfortunately it turned out that he wasn't gay.

To her horror Caleb had said that if she wanted to have sex with him she would have to first join his church and then marry him. He didn't see her jaw drop as he told her that he didn't believe in premarital intimacy or using any form of birth control. He'd assured her that while she'd have to quit her job to look after him and all the children they would be having, she could go on wearing trousers and shorts at home. She'd have to wear long skirts whenever she left the house, of course.

*Women should dress modestly in public once they're*

*married. You don't want to give other men the wrong ideas about you.*

As the shock of his demands set in, Isabel had even seen his version of her life flash before her eyes. Converting to his cult, being kept perpetually pregnant, attending brain-washing services multiple days a week, and tossing away her own dreams so she could work herself to death raising his spawn. In long skirts, no less.

Of course she had screamed and run away. Isabel still had nightmares.

Some food cart vendors had arrived to set up along the walkways in the park near the river, where they would provide hungry kids with ice cream, hot dogs and soft pretzels. Isabel sometimes wondered why the city's famous figure-eight pretzels weren't considered breakfast food; they were basically elongated, twisted bagels. As she passed a few early bird mothers herding their youngsters toward the playground, she grinned and waved. In a few weeks the kids would be heading back to school, but for now they could run around and play as much as they wanted. Growing up in foster care had cured her of ever wanting her own kids, but she liked watching them.

As for what she wanted in her love life, Isabel

wondered if she should take out a personal ad. She tried writing one in her head:

*Do not wish to marry, breed for, worship alongside, share my living space with or financially support my romantic partner. No interest in any alcohol-fueled activities, either. Prefer instead lots of time outdoors, thrilling nights filled with fun sex and soft pretzels for breakfast. You wear whatever you like, and I will, too. P.S., Bring Your Own Bike.*

After crossing the bridge from the park she slowed in front of a very old brick building that had been in business since the nineteenth century. After she parked her bike and locked it, she went in through the side door to the employee lounge, where she ducked into the ladies room, pulled her transformation kit out of her backpack and went to work.

A large wrap-around clip captured and rolled her coppery curls into a reasonably neat bun, which she secured with a few hair pins. She never sweated much when she biked, but she wiped herself down with a damp cloth anyway before applying her favorite ginger-peach body splash. A few pats of translucent powder and two swipes of rosy lipstick made her face business-presentable. She then unrolled and shook out her turquoise blazer, which covered her lavender tank top and made it look like a blouse front. After swapping out her bike shorts for pleated gray trousers, she toed off her sneakers and stepped into a pair of black flats.

*Presto,* Isabel thought as she checked herself in the mirror and added the finishing touch of two moonstone stud earrings. *I'm Ms. Murray, head auction clerk and front office manager for Downes Auction House.*

Before coming to work at Downes, Isabel had never dressed like this. YouTube videos, careful observation of other professional women, and haunting the right consignment shops had helped her acquire a decent wardrobe for her office persona. She knew she would never really fit in with everyone else, but she'd learned how to make them believe she did. Someday, when she started her own business, she could be as weird as she wanted.

As she walked towards the front office, Isabel heard a commotion and quickened her step. Darcie Blake, the newly-hired receptionist, came rushing toward her in a white and green polka-dotted dress that she must have stolen from the fifties. She stopped so fast she nearly fell, and grabbed Isabel's arms to brace herself as she teetered on three-inch emerald heels with little white bows.

"You're going to kill me, Ms. Murray," she said, her puppy dog eyes brimming with tears and misery.

Isabel reined in a sigh; Disaster Darcie regularly

lived up to her nickname. "Will it be justifiable homicide?"

"Could you tell Mrs. Downes that I tripped?" Darcie asked a few minutes later, anxiously hovering as Isabel worked under her desk. "She can't terminate me for having an accident, right?"

"It'll be fine." Drying everything under the desk that she'd found dripping from the receptionist's spilled mocha latte only required a towel and patience. "She didn't fire Jerry when he fell on top of that Civil War spool table last Christmas."

Lisa Talbot, the bookkeeper, made a scathing noise from her desk in the corner. "Yeah, but Mrs. D had me dock the repair cost from his checks for weeks, Ms. Murray."

"Please, Rainbow Dark," Isabel muttered. "Not today."

"I can't pay for a new computer," Darcie wailed, wringing her hands. "I have ten payments left on my wedding dress, and next week I have to make the deposit for the reception, the cake, and the flowers—"

"Let's see if there's any damage first before you start writing checks." Isabel came out from under the desk, and frowned at the clerk as she stood up. "Say, there's something stuck in your ear." She reached out and tucked a strand behind the other girl's ear, and produced the diamond solitaire ring she'd found on the floor by the tower. "You should wear this on your finger, you know."

Her little sleight of hand usually made someone laugh, but Darcie only choked back a sob.

"It's my engagement ring. It fell off, and that's why I dropped my coffee—oh, I told Josh I should have gotten it sized before I started wearing it." The receptionist jammed it onto her ring finger, and her bottom lip wobbled as she said, "I could pawn it to pay for a new computer, I suppose."

Isabel pulled Darcie's chair back over to her desk. "Try turning on the power first."

"My rent just went up, and we're trying to save for the honeymoon, too. Why am I such a klutz?" The other girl's hand shook as she sat down and pressed the power button. When the monitor lit up she made a squealing sound. "Oh, my gosh. You fixed it."

"I wiped down the wiring," she corrected. "Keep that towel there until the rug dries, okay?"

Darcie nodded so enthusiastically her glasses slid to the tip of her nose. "You're so amazing, Ms. Murray."

"As clumsy as you are, she has to be," Lisa put in.

Isabel glared over the receptionist's head at the bookkeeper, who cupped her hands into a heart and pretended to bite it.

"It's no problem." Isabel remembered how idiotic

she had been when she'd first started working at Downes, so forgiving the receptionist was paying it forward. "Just no more drinks at your desk, okay? Take them to the lounge on your break."

"Coffee is the only thing that keeps me alive until lunch time." The receptionist sat down and started tapping on the keyboard. "Looks like I only lost the page I was working on. Thank you so much. I could just hug you to pieces."

As a precaution Isabel took a few steps back—Darcie might literally do just that—but the receptionist seemed too mesmerized by her restored file to keep her threat. "Catch up on the sale reports. Lisa, please cover the phones for her until she does. I'll go see if Carlos and George have finished unloading the first truck."

Isabel went down the hall to the warehouse door, which opened out into the huge storage area behind the salerooms. At the very back of the building stretched a long, wide platform where trucks daily delivered fine antique furniture to be sold by the auction house.

*This is where I work.* Isabel would never get tired of those five words. *At one of the oldest and most respected auction houses in the country.*

The scent of wax and wood mixed with the sun-warmed breeze came in through the loading bay doors. As she passed straw-stuffed crates and mounds of cushioning wraps she caught glimpses of the polished wood, gleaming stained glass and burnished hardware they protected. Tomorrow at the weekly auction, these pieces would fill the salerooms and be sold to the highest bidder. Some would go for more money than she could earn in ten years, yet that fact never made her resentful.

Isabel knew exactly how lucky she was to have her job.

Three years ago she had fried chicken every day to survive. Foster care kids like her who didn't end up as addicts or prostitutes generally ended up in the food service industry, working two or three part-time jobs with minimum wages just to afford a miserable existence on society's fringes. Isabel wanted more for herself, so she'd started applying for better positions a few months before she turned eighteen. Most of the time she was turned down as unqualified sight unseen; the few interviews she got ended in less than five minutes.

"You haven't even got a high school diploma yet," one manager had said. She took in her thrift store blouse, hand-hemmed skirt and scuffed flats and sniffed. "Is this how you intend to dress for work, young lady? You look like you're on welfare."

"I wish I was." Isabel rose from her chair and held

out her hand. "Thank you. Next time I hope my clothes will be better."

Josephine Downes had looked like a snob, but she hadn't acted like one when Isabel had come to the auction house to interview for an entry-level clerk position.

"You have no experience in this industry." The thin, iron-haired woman lifted a hand to the single strand of pearls around her wrinkled throat. "What can you offer as an employee?"

"Me." Isabel looked into her shrewd dark eyes and on instinct spoke from her heart. "I learn fast and work hard. Please hire me, ma'am. You'll never regret it."

Mrs. Downes's expression turned skeptical. "If you wanted this position so badly, why didn't you at least shower before you came for the interview?"

Another girl might have cringed, but Isabel wasn't ashamed of how she smelled.

"I'm sorry. When we're done here I'm going back to my job frying chicken because I still have five hours to work on my shift." She reached into her backpack and pulled out the little visor she had to wear at the restaurant. "I do that thirty-seven hours a week, plus any overtime they offer me, so I don't smell it anymore. Don't get me wrong, I'm grateful for my job. They give me a free meal every shift I work. I'd go hungry toward the end of the month if they didn't."

"Then why would you leave it, dear girl?" Mrs. Downes prompted.

"I want to smell like this place—like you. I want to cook food I like for myself at home." She took in a deep breath. "I'm not stupid, it's just that no one will give me a chance. I'll do whatever you need me to. Please let me work here."

"Go back to your restaurant, Ms. Murray," the old lady said, and as Isabel's shoulders slumped, she added, "Before your shift ends, hand in your notice as well. I'll expect you to start in two weeks."

In three years since coming to work at Downes Isabel had never missed a day, and learned everything she could about the auction business. Promoted to head clerk last year, she now managed the front office and supervised Darcie and Lisa. She also lived in a small efficiency apartment in a decent neighborhood, owned a used but reliable car, and became a vegetarian.

Mrs. Downes had never regretted hiring her, either—Isabel had made sure of that.

As she approached the loading platform she greeted the appraisers who had come to look over the newly-arrived stock. Both men were seasoned experts in their field, as collectors, interior designers and museum buyers made up the bulk of the auction house's clientele. The top tier could and would pay a hundred thousand dollars for a pair of chairs without blinking.

Two of the three men responsible for unloading the deliveries stood on the edge of the platform looking into the nearly-empty truck. George, a former nightclub bouncer who no one ever messed with, scratched the back of his neck, while Carlos, his towering, skinny co-worker muttered softly in Spanish under his breath.

Meatball and Spaghetti looked worried, Isabel thought, which on the platform was never a good thing. "Any problems with the shipment?"

"Tommy called in sick," George told her, and nodded toward the interior of the delivery truck. "We got one of them huge cabinets in there, must weigh a ton. Can't use the forklift, though, 'cause it's middy-evil."

Isabel frowned and walked across the ramp into the truck to have a look at the last piece waiting to be unloaded. A foot taller than her, the ancient oak and iron armoire looked as if it might weigh half a ton. However, there was room on each side of the piece to tip it, and the carved bottom edges allowed her to see the space underneath it. The moment she put her hands on the wood a familiar jolt of excitement went all bouncy-ball in her chest.

*You've got a secret, don't you, you beautiful old thing?*

"If we get some heavy-duty sliders under it, we can turn and roll it sideways," she told George. "I'll help you."

The big man looked doubtful, but nodded and went to fetch the equipment they needed. A few minutes later Isabel was able to help them push the incredibly heavy piece across the ramp. The driver and the appraisers stopped to applaud them, but quickly fell silent as their employer walked onto the platform.

Isabel grinned, as she always did when she saw She-Who-Must-Be-Adored. "Morning, Mrs. Downes."

"Isabel, gentlemen. So this is why you weren't at your desk," the owner and general manager of the auction house said as she surveyed the piece and pretended not to see the men scattering. "Scottish, fourteenth century. Exquisite. It should fetch some very healthy bids tomorrow night. Why does the office smell of overpriced coffee? Darcie," she said before Isabel could answer.

"Just another little accident, Boss. No real harm done, but we should probably have the office rug cleaned." She grimaced. "I could kill her and make it look like an accident, but then we'd have to replace the carpeting."

Mrs. Downes pressed her lips together to hold back a laugh. "You're a wicked child."

"Maybe the Dark Ages are rubbing off on me." Isabel reached out to touch the blackened oak panel at the front of the ancient cabinet almost compulsively. She loved how heat and flame transformed things. "Do you think this was once in a fire?"

"That doesn't look like charring. Likely it was kept somewhere near a hearth—that was the only source of heat those poor devils had in those days. Wood smoke leaves that kind of residue over the decades." Her adorable boss walked around it. "Ah, yes, the back of the piece is much lighter in color."

She accompanied the older woman as she inspected the entire shipment, and took out the notepad she always carried to jot down some instructions for the pre-auction saleroom crew.

"Everything will need surface cleaning, except the armoire," Mrs. Downes told her. "I want that left untouched. The blackening adds some visual drama, and it may be snapped up by one of those set directors. We should put it in the front saleroom today. Tell Jerry to leave one of the doors ajar and drape a tartan over it."

Isabel nodded. "Did this really come all the way from Scotland?"

"I believe so, but assure the estate seller provided the proper provenance." The older woman pursed her lips. "If it were not so large I'd buy it myself. I've always had a soft spot for highlanders. They were quite heroic and independent—rather like you, my dear."

"I've definitely got the mop." Flicking her hand at her coppery curls, Isabel grimaced. "Murray is both a Scottish and an Irish surname. I could be either, or neither."

"You might even be both." Mrs. Downes touched her arm. "Be sure and find me after the auction tomorrow. I want to discuss a few things with you about your future."

*It doesn't include applying for unemployment, I hope.*

Isabel pushed aside the uneasy thought—if her boss wanted her gone, she would have given her a very genteel pink slip—and kept her smile in place until the older woman departed.

"My future is fine," she murmured to herself as she pocketed her notebook. "I'm going to save every penny I can while I learn everything you know about antiques and auctioning, and then when you retire and sell the business see if my bank will help me buy it. Why do we have to talk about that?"

Isabel returned to the front office, and checked in with Lisa, who had handled all of the incoming calls. Darcie seemed to be making some progress on her computer work, too, so she went in search of Jerry. She found the tall, lanky auctioneer arranging lot numbers atop the newly-delivered furniture in the largest of their salerooms.

"We've got a medieval Scottish armoire that just arrived." Isabel repeated Mrs. Downes' instructions for the display, and then asked out of curiosity, "Do you think there will be a lot of bidders for that piece?"

He nodded. "Not many of those on the market. I'm planning to open the bidding at fifty, but it should go for twice that."

A hundred thousand dollars for what amounted to a smoke-stained cabinet, Isabel thought, depressed now. She'd managed to save a little, but no way could she compete with bids that high to buy the armoire.

"You like it that much, huh?" Jerry asked. "That's how it starts, you know. You fall in love, and then the next thing you know you're a collector."

Isabel gave him a rueful smile. "I can't afford to collect anything, Jer, except maybe modern thrift store."

After apologizing several more times to Isabel that day, Darcie asked to clock out early to meet her fiancé at the jeweler's to have her ring resized. Silently reminding herself that the receptionist was young, Isabel gave her permission to bail on work. Lisa waited until the other woman left before she said anything.

"They don't make you a saint unless you're Catholic, you know." The bookkeeper brought over the ledger to have her sign off on the deposit amount. Behind her desk she looked dainty but professional; on her feet she resembled a little doll dressed up in business Goth.

"Pass," Isabel said. "I might become a Buddhist, though. Zen is very calming."

"If you let her, that girl will walk all over you," Lisa countered. "And she'll complain how her heels make her feet hurt while she does."

"Anger solves nothing." Isabel had other, very good reasons never to lose her temper. "Give her a break. She's just a kid."

"Disaster Darcie's three years older than you. Once she gets married I bet she'll hand in her notice, too." She made a scathing sound. "All she dreams about is getting pregnant and being a stay-at-home mom."

"Watch it, Rainbow Dark," she warned. "Not all of us want to breed."

Lisa rolled her eyes. "How should I know? You're my only straight friend, and sometimes I think you're gayer than I am."

During her job interview Lisa had aggressively volunteered that she was a lesbian and an LGBTQ activist, and shoved a flyer for the city's annual gay pride parade at her, as if she meant to shock Isabel. She'd been the one startled when Isabel had offered to carpool with her to the volunteer meetings she was already attending for the event.

"Just let me know if Darcie ever ditches Josh. She and my ex would be a match made in heaven. Literally." She signed off on the deposit slip, and them sighed. "Maybe I should try dating women. Or atheists. Or celibates. No, not celibates. I like sex too much."

"Get a dog," Lisa, who had had her heart broken by her cheating ex-girlfriend, suggested. "They're always happy to see you, they won't cheat on you, and they love you no matter what you look like."

"I'm allergic, unfortunately." Isabel reached into the bank bag, tugged the little spray of magical silk flowers from her sleeve, and handed the bunch to Lisa. "And you should start dating again, so you can get these from someone magical."

"You're such a dork." The bookkeeper's lips twitched, but she handed the faux bouquet back to her. "Save these for the kids. You're going to the home this weekend, right?" When Isabel nodded she said, "I've got a box of clothes my kid sister has outgrown. They're all like new. I'll bring it in tomorrow."

"Oh, thanks. You're a doll, Lisa." She ducked to avoid the other woman's swat.

On her way out of the office later, Isabel switched off the lights and locked the door, and then hesitated. She knew from waving good-bye to them that Meatball and Spaghetti had already gone home. Jerry and the appraisers always left at five, and Mrs. Downes never stayed past six.

*I'll just take another quick look.*

Jerry had moved the medieval armoire into the center of the saleroom's back wall, and set up two angled spots that illuminated it as soon as Isabel turned on the lighting. A red, black and gold tartan now lay draped over the top of one of the half-open doors, which had beautiful golden wood on the inside panel.

Isabel gripped the straps of her backpack as she approached the blackened front of the piece, but she knew that wouldn't prevent her from touching it. Something about beautiful old things like this made her fingers twitch. More often than not they held secrets: writing scribbled somewhere inside, buttons and buckles that had fallen into a seam, or even a folded paper wedged in a crack.

"One quick peek," she promised herself as she took off and rolled up her jacket to stuff it inside her backpack. "Then I'll go home to my thrift store decor and dream of collecting IKEA."

Isabel tugged down the tartan before opening both doors. The iron hinges made a rusty, grating sound as the doors revealed an inside space large enough to hold two of her. The left side of the interior appeared to be the inside panel of the outside wood, but the right side appeared to be much thicker—as if several panels had been nailed together to the inside. Her hand moved over the glass-smooth surface of the oak, and then she made a fist and tapped her knuckles against it.

A hollow sound indicated a gap behind the oak panel.

"I knew it." Isabel stuck her head inside as she looked for a seam or latch that would open the hidden compartment, but her body blocked the light from the overhead spot. After shifting back and forth, she stepped inside the armoire, and then closed the left-side door so that the light would be focused on the suspicious panel. "I'm already breaking all the rules here, Scotty, so why don't you give it up and show me the magic?"

The problem, she saw, was the tightness of the seams. The panel had probably gotten stuck in the closed position. After examining a series of oddly-interlocking slats at the top of the inside of the armoire, she moved the right-hand door a few inches and saw them shift.

"I don't give up so easily," Isabel muttered, taking out her phone and switching on the light before she reached for the edge of the open panel. With a quick jerk she pulled it shut, watching the slats as she did, and then lost her balance and fell sideways.

The armoire shuddered, and then several things she couldn't see made popping sounds. Isabel froze, terrified she had damaged the valuable antique, and then tried to push the doors open again. Neither of them moved.

"Say, wait a minute." She shifted back and aimed her phone light on the inside of the door panels, which now appeared like a single seamless wall of golden oak. On closer examination she saw more of the interlocking slats. "You're not an armoire. You're a medieval burglar trap."

Gently poking and prying at the slats didn't loosen them, and Isabel was afraid to do more than that. Mrs. Downes would absolutely fire her for damaging such a valuable artifact; the auction house didn't own any of the pieces they sold. Given that the cabinet had been made as some kind of elaborate trap meant it was even more rare than her boss had realized; it might even be one of a kind.

Isabel's heart pounded in her chest, and her lungs had grown so tight she had to struggle to inhale. As she grew dizzier she realized it wasn't panic or claustrophobia but the stuffy interior that was making it hard to breathe. The seams of the armoire fit together so well they must have sealed off the inside, just as gaskets did on a refrigerator.

*If I don't get out of this thing, I'm going to suffocate.*

• • • • •

Buy *Camdyn (Immortal Highlander Clan MacRoss Book 3)*

# Glossary

Here are some brief definitions to help you navigate the medieval world of the Clan MacRoss series.

Almany - present day Germany
arnae - are not
arse - ass
bampot - a foolish, unpleasant, or obnoxious person
bannocks - a flat, unsweetened cake made with oatmeal or barley flour and typically unleavened
barrowman - one who fills barrows, baskets, or small wagons with excavated material
bastart - bastard
Beira - the mother to all gods and goddesses in the Celtic mythology of Scotland; also known as Beira, Queen of Winter
Belerion - Land's End, present day Cornwall

GLOSSARY

bespell – to cast a spell on, enchant
blackdamp - choking or suffocating gas, typically carbon dioxide, found in mines
blaeberry - European blueberry
bluetongue - insect-borne, viral disease
boak - Scottish slang for vomit
borecrystal – a Fae crystal that when heated melts through anything
broadhead - arrowhead used for war or hunting
broch - hollow-walled stone round house
by-blow - an illegitimate child
Cairngorm - mountain in the eastern Highlands of Scotland
chebs - Scottish slang for "breasts"
clootie - traditional pudding of flour, bread crumbs, dried fruit, suet, sugar, spices and milk, wrapped in cloth and boiled
coldfire – a glass sphere filled with a Fae crystal that produces heatless blue light
Cornovii - ancient tribes of present day Cornwall
cossetted - to give a lot of attention to making someone comfortable and protecting them from anything unpleasant
CPR - cardiopulmonary resuscitation
crabbit - cantankerous
cranachan - a Scottish dessert made with whipped cream, whiskey, oatmeal, honey, and raspberries

crannog - artificial island used as a dwelling
croft - small rented farm
da - dad
darenae - dare not
dinnae - don't
dreamstone – a Fae crystal that acts like a strong sedative when consumed
eejit - Scottish slang for "idiot"
Éire - Gaelic name for Ireland
Elphyne – the otherworld kingdom of the Fae
epistola de Re recta - "a letter about the right thing" is an early alchemical writing by the Persian polymath Avicenna or Ibn Sina
Érieann galloglass - elite Norse-Gaelic mercenary warriors from Ireland
fack - fuck
fae – a race of powerful humanoid immortals who wield magic and live in Elphyne
feverfew - a bushy aromatic Eurasian plant of the daisy family, used in herbal medicine to treat fever and headaches
firesteel - fire striker
Flanders - a medieval principality now divided between Belgium, France, and the Netherlands
footslog - walk a long distance, wearily or with effort
Francian - French

gallóglach - foreign mercenaries principally from Norse Gaelic clans of Ireland

Gerard de Sabloneta - aka Gerard of Cremona was an Italian translator of scientific books from Arabic into Latin

gibbeting cage - human-shaped cage used for public execution

gob - beak or mouth

gowk - Scottish slang for "simpleton"

habeas corpus - a writ requiring a person under arrest to be brought before a judge or into court

hackit - ugly, very unattractive

hadnae - hadn't

halfling – a term used for the offspring of Fae and mortals

hasnae - hasn't

heartstone – a Fae crystal that positively influences emotions; used to make love charms

hoor - whore

hurrier - someone who drags baskets or small wagons of excavated material from where it's dug up to the surface

icestone -- a Fae crystal that contains the elemental power of ice; very dangerous

icewine – a Fae alcoholic beverage which Beira, Queen of Winter, drinks

Insii Catt - earliest name for Shetland, meaning

Island of the Cat or Cait tribe
jagoff - a stupid, irritating or contemptible person
jawn - a thing, place, person, or event that doesn't have a specific name
jetton - counter or token
jobby - Scottish slang for "shit"
justiciar - medieval title for judge or minister
keepe - the strongest or central tower of a castle
laboratorium - laboratory
laird - lord
leine - long shirt
lists - area enclosed for combat or contests
mam - mom
manroot - penis
màthair - mother
maynae - may not
melia - tree fae
minced – Scottish slang for drunk
neednae - need not
nighean - daughter
nightstone – a Fae crystal that negatively influences emotions; used to make hatred charms
och - expression of surprise, disapproval, regret
otherworlder – a being belonging to a species from another world or order
perry - an alcoholic drink made from fermented pears

## GLOSSARY

philosophorum – a retreat on the Isle of Skye where sages go to rest and relax

pished - Scottish slang for drunk

poppet - doll

priss - a prissy person

Pritani - Britons (one of the people of southern Britain before or during Roman times)

privy - toilet

quern - a stone hand mill for grinding

randy - sexually aroused or excited

ret - soak in water to soften

rood - a measure of land equal to a quarter of an acre

ropewalk - long narrow building or lane for making rope

sain - a protective charm; saining is blessing, protecting, or consecrating

scuddy - naked

scullery - a small back room off the kitchen where the dishes or laundry are washed

scutch - dress fibers by beating them

selkie - a mythical creature that resembles a seal in the water but assumes human form on land

sevenday – literally seven days

Sluath - soul-devouring demons who ride storms in search of helpless mortals

swipe - have sex with

tadger - slang for penis

tight-bawed - tight-balled
tirl - rotate, turn, or twirl
'tis - it is
'tisnae - it isn't
trews - trousers
Tu gràdh mo bheatha - you're the love of my life
'twas - it was
'twasnae - it wasn't
'twere - it were
'twill - it will
'twillnae - it will not
'twould - it would
'twouldnae - it would not
varlet - an attendant or servant
wanderling – a half-Fae, half-mortal female child which Queen Beira gave birth to while she was wandering around Scotland
werenae - were not
wimple - cloth headdress covering head, neck and side of face
witchmark – a superstitious name for a birthmark by those who believe it indicates an evil or cursed nature
wont - a routine behavior or habit
wright - a maker or builder
wulver - wolf-like humanoid creature

Pronunciation Guide

A selection of the more challenging words in the Immortal Highlander, Clan MacRoss series.

Ailsa: AYL-sah
Aklen: AK-len
Aleen: uh-LEEN
Ameron: AM-er-ahn
Athdara: ahth-DEER-ah
Auley: AW-lee
Beagan: **bee-ah-GAHN**
Beira: BY-rah or BARE-uh
Belerion: bel-AYR-ee-ahn
Ben Cruachan: **BEHN KROO-a-kahn**
Bethanne: behth-AYN
Brida**: BREE-duh**

## PRONUNCIATION GUIDE

broch: BRAHK
Brynna: BREN-ah
Cadha: **KAHD-uh**
Cailean: KAH-len
Cairngorm: KAYRN-gorm
Callen: KAY-len
Callum: KAH-luhm
Camdyn: KAM-din
Carack: KER-rick
Caytir: KAH-tcheer
Cerys: **KAYR-ess**
Cinead: **shin-AYD**
Cornovii: kore-NOH-vee-eye
cranachan: KRAH-nah-ken
Danyel: DAHN-yell
Darach: der-RACK
Domnall: **DOM-nahl**
Dugal: **DOO-gahl**
Duine: DOO-in
Dun Cluaran: **DUHN KLOO-ah-rahn**
Dun Deigh: **DUHN DAY**
Dun Lasair: **DUHN LAH-sah**
Edane: **eh-DAYN**
Emery: EM-er-ree also goes by Mery
Ensley: **EHNS-lee**
Érieann galloglass: AY-run GAL-oh-glass

Erlach: **ER-lahk**
Fae: **FAY**
Fuachd: FYOO-itched
Fyn: FIN
Gallóglach: **guh-LOW-gluhk**
Geamhradh: gee-AR-rud
Gildie: **GEEL-dee**
Insii Catt: EEN-see CAYT
Jamie: **JAY-mee**
Kaer: KEE-ayr
Keithen: KEE-thun
Kendric: KEN-drik
Kerrich: **KEYR-itch**
Kyal: KY-el
Lachlan McDonnel: LOCK-lin mik-DAH-nuhl
Laith: **LAYTH**
Lamond: luh-MAHND
Leathan: LAY-hahn
Liath: LY-eth
Loch Ness: **LAHK NEHS**
Losgadh: **LAHS-gah**
Lusk: LUHSK
Luthias: loo-THY-uhs
MacAnvoy: MAK-an-voi
MacRoss: muhk-RAHSS
Maeva: **MAY-vah**

PRONUNCIATION GUIDE

Maeve: **MAYV**
Macdui: mak-DOO-wee
MacEntosh: MAK-in-tosh
Mag Raith: MAG RAYTH
Magda: MAG-duh
maister: MAY-ster
Mairi: MAH-ree
Mathe: **MAH-tee**
melia: MELL-yah
Mery: MAIR-ee
Morag: **MOR-uhg**
Muir: MEER
nighean: NEE-uhn
Nyf: **NYF**
Parlan: **PAR-luhn**
Ramsay: RAHM-see
Reothadh: REE-oh-thahd
Revna: **REHV-nah**
Ross: RAHSS
Seona: **SHAW-nah**
Sgur: SGOO
Shayleen Damhair
Sluath: SLEW-ahth
Sradag: **sir-REH-dehg**
Struan: STROO-ahn
Tamhas: **TAHM-hahs**

Taveon: TAH-vee-ohn
Tavish: TUH-vish
Tolmach: TOHL-muhk
Tu gràdh mo bheatha: oo rah muh veh-ah
Wal: WAHL

# Dedication

*For Mr. H.*

# Copyright

Copyright © 2022 Hazel Hunter

This is a work of fiction. Names, characters, places, and incidents are products of the author's imagination or are used fictitiously and are not to be construed as real. Any resemblance to actual events, locales, organizations, or persons, living or dead, is coincidental.

All rights reserved. No part of this book may be used or reproduced in any manner, stored in or introduced into a retrieval system, or transmitted, in any form, or by any means (electronic, mechanical, photocopying, recording, or otherwise), without the prior written consent of the copyright owner.

The scanning, uploading, and distribution of this book via the Internet or via any other means without the permission of the copyright owner is illegal. Please purchase only authorized electronic editions, and do not participate in or encourage electronic piracy of copyrighted materials. Your support of the author's rights is appreciated.

Made in United States
Orlando, FL
19 June 2023

34318859R00202